W9-DIM-664

THE BROKEN COVENANT

THE BROKEN COVENANT

Carroll Hofeling Morris

Deseret Book
Salt Lake City, Utah

Printed in the United States of America

Library of Congress Cataloging in Publication Data

Morris, Carroll Hofeling.
The broken covenant.

I. Title.
PS3563.087398B7 1985 813'.54 85-1491
ISBN 0-87747-656-X

First printing March 1985

For my grandmother, Winiferd Harris,
whose love of beauty and constant search
for knowledge has been my inspiration

I doubt that they [the saints] ever had it in mind to become saints. If that were the case, they would have become perfectionists.

Viktor E. Frankl,
Man's Search for Meaning

PART ONE

One

In the spring of the year that Kathy Montgomery turned thirty-eight, she committed a sin—a major sin, not to be compared with the less serious sins that decorated her daily life. It was not something she could sometimes indulge in fondly, like overeating; nor was it something she could refer to as if it were an old friend, saying, with a rueful shake of her glossy black curls, "Oh, I always do that!" It was too dreadful, too secret, too awful in its repercussions.

If she had considered what the repercussions of such an action might be, she would have rejected it as unthinkable. If she had called it by its real name instead of the less-condemning aliases given it by the world, she would have turned from it, horrified. But she had never considered it dispassionately, which made her all the more vulnerable; it was a sin of passion.

The committing of the sin was itself the unmasking, the ripping away of all the sparkling, gauzy disguise that had made it seem desirable, and then it seemed too ugly to be looked at straight on. But she had to look at it, even though the effort seemed more than she could bear, and when she gave it its true name, she began to understand her guilt: she, Kathy Adams Montgomery, had committed adultery after attending the weekly rehearsal of a well-known Midwestern choral group.

She hadn't meant to, she would have told you then, and truly she seemed to be in a state of shock as she groped in the darkness gathering together her things. She didn't speak to the man or look at him as they drove back to the university lot where her car was parked. She didn't even hear what he was saying to her, which was ironic. He was saying the very words she had been longing to hear ever since she had read her first Gothic novel, *Nine Coaches Waiting*. The fervent, poetic declaration of love was exactly what she had always wanted her husband, Robert, to say, although she would have discounted it if he had.

She finally did look at him as he pulled up beside her car. What she saw startled her, it was in such opposition to her own feelings of horror and disgust. His face reflected warmth and tenderness, expectancy, happiness. His countenance changed when he saw the look in her eyes, but she scrambled out of his car and into her own before he had a chance to say anything more than "Kathy!" He was standing in the lot looking after her in bewilderment as she drove away.

It was after midnight when she pulled up to the garage of the house on Ridgeway Road. Like most of the homes on this fashionable street in the prosperous northern Iowa city of Lemburg, the two-story Tudor was large, surrounded by a spacious yard, part of which was well lit despite the hour. Robert had left the outside light on as he always did for those occasions when she was out after he went to bed. She unlocked the door and went inside, turning out the light after her. She hung up her jacket and put her purse on the kitchen desk where she always kept it, then went into the living room and put her folder in the music cabinet by the baby grand. It would have been understandable, given her frame of mind, if she had just thrown them in a heap on the floor, but her neatness was the result of strict discipline developed over the years, and it allowed no variation, not even now.

She stood motionless in the hallway for a moment, then walked up the stairs, turning out the hall light when she reached the top. She was moving automatically, conscious neither of what she was doing at the moment nor of what she would have to do in the future. Her mind was numb; her heart (that registrar of truth) was filled with pain. She felt as if she were in a nightmare from which she couldn't wake. If only she could open her eyes and find herself in the big bed, her back warm against Robert's chest!

She wished desperately for the moment of decision to be before her again, but she wasn't sure which moment it was. And even if it were before her again, would anything change between her and Jay Enders, the man she had just left? She had the uneasy suspicion that it would be like the instant replays of sports events: "The Moment of Triumph," "The Moment of Despair," played again and again, in stop motion, in slow motion, from different camera angles, but always the same in the end.

A sudden thought struck her, and she laughed, a harsh, constricted sound. It was exactly like the time she had eaten that piece of cheesecake! She ducked into the children's bathroom and grabbed a towel. Holding it over her mouth, she continued to laugh, a laugh that now had an edge of hysteria. She shut the door and sat on the stool, rocking and laughing in the dark.

Just like the piece of cheesecake she had left out on the counter the first day of her latest diet. She had been so confident of her power to resist! And for some hours she had resisted, actually giving it a mocking smile whenever she glanced at it. She never remembered taking the first bites; it was as if she had been sleepwalking, only to awake and find herself, plate in hand, eating the last crumbs furtively, quickly, lest she be seen by Robert and the kids.

"It was so tempting, so tempting!" she gasped, not sure if she was referring to the cheesecake or to the warmth of Jay's embrace. She smothered a hiccup and tried to stop laughing, but the ludicrousness of the comparison set her off again. "The last bite gone so fast and then . . ." And then the spark of momentary satisfaction smothered by self-loathing and guilt. She didn't need to rely on remembered feeling in this regard. The laughter stopped but still she rocked, towel pressed to her lips. Towels could muffle sobs as well.

Sometime later she turned on the light and ran the tub full of water, as hot as she could stand. Slowly she sank into it and lay there steaming, sweat beading along her hairline and trickling down the line of her jaw. She was aware of only two things: the tremendous heat and the sense of betrayal. This wasn't the way it turned out in the books.

Robert always told me I shouldn't be reading that stuff, she thought, wondering for the first time how much the romantic novels she enjoyed influenced her thinking. That was a part of her personality her husband had never understood. "I can't believe you read those things," he would say. "How can you have *Man's Search for Meaning, The Bridge of San Luis Rey,* your scriptures, and a couple of 'the 3-G's' on your night table all at the same time?"

"The 3-G's" was Robert's phrase, and she had grudgingly admitted it was quite clever. It stood for "The Glory and the Garbage Genre," the designation he gave to all books with a foreboding castle and a beautiful, long-haired heroine—with or without accompanying hero—on the cover.

The name she gave them was only slightly less uncomplimentary. "They're my Mental Flops," she would counter, and as an escape device, they filled their function well. They demanded no intellectual involvement, only a "willing suspension of disbelief." In return, they served up romance, adventure, "noble" suffering, the righting of all wrongs, and a happy ending, all well spiced. *And I usually end up rooting for the fornicating couple,* she thought, frowning. "But I love reading them," she murmured to herself, thinking of the times she had read two or three a week. They were the adult version of the fairy tales she had loved as a child.

But what about the happy ending? Tears mingled with the drops of sweat and collected on her chin until she wiped them away. This wasn't a happy ending; and it most certainly wasn't a happy beginning, in spite of what Jay thought. She knew he was expecting their relationship to continue. She had seen it in his face, and she hadn't been able to look at him again, seeing that.

Nor could she look at herself. As she dried her flaming

skin, she avoided the mirrors, which suddenly seemed to be everywhere in the small bathroom. *What am I afraid I'll see?* she asked herself, forcing her eyes upward to meet their reflection in the fogged glass. She was almost disappointed to see that nothing had changed.

The wiry, wild bush of her hair around her face was nothing new; the scarlet in her cheeks, though heightened by the heat, wasn't a surprise. Nothing was different about her wide mouth (the kind that smiles easily, though it was not smiling now) or the hated nose ("It's cute," her mother used to say. "I like pug noses." "It's not cute and it's not pug. With this nose I could stand in for Bob Hope!"). Under arched brows her eyes were dark and bottomless. They looked inutterably sad, but sadness was an expression she met often in the mirror. She saw only herself.

She turned off the light and tiptoed down the hall to the master bedroom, dumped her clothes in the hamper, and walked to the bureau, where she faced the first of the nasty decisions that were before her: whether to put on a pair of temple garments.

Having broken sacred covenants, she knew she was no longer worthy to wear them. But to her shame, that was less of a consideration than the questions Robert would surely ask if she didn't. She hastily pulled a pair from the drawer. Moments later, she eased into bed, and as she did so, Robert turned in his sleep and reached out. He put his arm around her waist and snuggled up to her.

"How did things go?" he asked sleepily.

Her voice was unsteady as she replied, "We had a good rehearsal."

"How late is it?" he murmured.

"No later than usual," she managed.

He made a noise, and the weight of the arm around her increased. He had fallen back asleep. But for Kathy, there was no such release. A seething mixture of duplicity, shame, and disgust kept her half-awake until the weak light of a spring dawn began to show through the trees outside the bedroom window. Then, as lights were being turned on in the milking parlors of the farms surrounding Lemburg, she finally slept.

It could only have been a little over an hour later, as the traffic on the freeway picked up and the newspaper carriers began making their deliveries, that Kathy Montgomery's alarm clock rang. She moved heavily to one side and turned it off, wondering vaguely why she felt so awful. For although she had not been asleep long, her mind had still had enough time to blanket memory of the fact that was so repugnant. But awful or not, another day was facing her, and it was time to get up. With a sigh, she rolled out of bed, pulled on jeans and a sweatshirt, quickly washed her face, and brought some order to her curls.

"Susan, time to get up," she called as she passed her daughter's door. "Brad, time to get up." She didn't open Grant's door or call to him—at seven he still had quite a few years of sleeping in before he had to get up for seminary. Having heard answering groans, she hurried down to the kitchen and began making lunches for all three.

Bologna for Brad, mustard, salad dressing, no lettuce. Bologna for Grant, no mustard, lots of salad dressing, lettuce. Apple and cheese slices for Susan. She moved quickly and mechanically, but she had that unsettling feeling a bad dream leaves in its wake as it passes into the night. She looked out the large kitchen window into the familiar confines of her backyard and sighed again.

This morning, the usual sense of accomplishment that the house had always given her was missing. Its absence added to her feeling of unrest because it was, in the deepest sense, her house. She had planned and decorated it; it complimented her in every way. It was a well-crafted setting in which she normally shone.

The city, too, was her city. She loved shopping in the boutiques housed in the old brick storefronts along the banks of the White River, and in the modern city center, which was complete with pedestrian zone, fountains, and even a sidewalk cafe. Beyond the city itself, she was happy in her community. She was actively involved in the PTA and in a neighborhood book club, and she was busy with her cooking classes. But most important to her, aside from her family and the Church, was her membership in the Parker-Jeffry Chorale.

Open to townspeople as well as to students, the chorale rehearsed in Old Church, a lovely brick building on the National Register of Historic Buildings. With high arches and stained glass windows, Old Church had marvelous acoustics and a solemnly grand interior that seemed to inspire the chorale members to greater beauty of song. Kathy loved singing there, and sometimes she wished that the new building that housed the Lemburg Ward weren't quite so functional.

From home to community to chorale, Kathy's thoughts skimmed over the surface of her subconscious like a stone skipping on water. From the chorale, they went on to Jay Enders, who was also a member. There her thoughts lost their impetus and sank below the surface, coming in contact with something that intensified the unpleasant feelings of the morning.

Frowning, Kathy sought for an explanation. She thought she could remember snatches of a bad dream . . . something about her and Jay. And then it came down with a crash almost physical, so that she grabbed onto the counter for support. It was not a dream.

The night before, she had wished for it to be a dream; this morning, some process dedicated to self-protection had almost succeeded in transforming it into a dream. But it wasn't. She felt panic rising and searched the room as if looking for somewhere to hide. At that moment, her eighteen-year-old son noisily came down the stairs, asking her whether she had seen his "seminary stuff."

"You ask the same question every morning, Brad," she said in an aggravated tone.

He grinned. "Yeah, but you keep giving a different answer, so I've got to keep on asking!"

"I think I remember seeing your books on the desk in the family room," she said, a weak smile wavering.

"Right," he said. As he left the kitchen, Susan came

down, singing a song that had questionable lyrics.

"Susan, are you listening to what you're singing?" Kathy asked sharply.

"Be cool, Mom. They're just words. I only sing them because I like the melody." She went to the cupboard and got down the granola that she always had for breakfast.

"Granola for breakfast, apples and cheese for lunch, junk food at McDonald's after school, and a bite or two of whatever we're having for supper. How do you live on that?"

"Not again," said Susan, a hint of disgust in her voice. "Listen, Mom, I'm okay. I'm healthy, right? And I'm just where I want to be." She made a pirouette, showing off lean legs and a trim waist. She was wearing a lilac pullover that brought out the pink in her cheeks and the blue of her eyes. At sixteen, she looked so lovely, fresh, and innocent that Kathy couldn't resist giving her a hug.

"I'm sorry I started off the day like that," Kathy apologized. "I didn't get much sleep last night." She touched Susan's fine light brown hair, then drew a breath and returned her attention to the eggs and sausage she had been frying.

"What's that smell? Is somebody burning toast again?" Robert came into the room, his nose wrinkled up as he sniffed the air.

Kathy swore under her breath as she rushed for the toaster.

"It must be those late hours you kept last night," her husband said. "How late was it when you finally got home?"

"No later than usual," she replied, hoping her face didn't look as hot as it felt. "I took a long bath after coming home. I hope I didn't wake you."

"You did, but I must have gone right back to sleep. I don't remember much about it." He took orange juice from the fridge and poured it into the glasses, then sat down and picked up the morning paper, which Brad had brought in. For once Kathy was grateful that he always read the paper at breakfast, grateful that his thin face with its sharp eyes and too-large nose was not turned her way. She served him and Brad, then stood leaning against the counter, drinking her juice.

It was still early, before six-thirty, but she and Robert had decided when Brad had first started seminary that they would eat breakfast with him before he left in the morning. It had been hard to get used to at first, but now it was just the way things were. And Kathy always felt good, knowing she had sent Brad and Susan off with a good breakfast. She smiled. *Yes, granola and milk is a good breakfast,* she admitted to herself.

Her thoughts were interrupted by the sound of a car coming up the driveway.

"Oh, they're here already!" shrieked Susan, bolting the rest of her granola. Brad grabbed some more sausages and put them between two pieces of toast. Kathy caught a glimpse of him as he ran out the door, one sleeve of his jacket on, books and lunch under the other arm, the sausage sandwich between his teeth. Then the room was quiet.

Kathy looked at Robert, who was still reading the paper, eating his breakfast absently. He wouldn't leave for work until almost seven-thirty; by then Grant would be up, wanting his breakfast and all her attention until the bus picked him up at eight-thirty. Could she make it till then? *I'll scream if I don't find something to do,* she thought, and she fought back the impulse to tear her hair, slam cupboard doors, and throw pans at the wall. More frightening still was the need to rip the paper out of Robert's hands and say, "Look at me! Something terrible's happened! I'm not the same person who's been putting your breakfast in front of you for the past nineteen years!"

She pulled out her bread mixer and put all the ingredients for bread into it. *Clever machine,* she thought. *You can do it all, all by yourself.* She turned the mixer on and left it to knead while she unloaded the dishwasher. By the time she had loaded the dirty dishes from breakfast, the bread was ready to be made into loaves. She greased the pans and formed the loaves, all exactly the same size, and put them on the stove top, covering them with a towel. She turned reluctantly to the table, but Robert was not there; he was back upstairs getting ready for work.

"Robert, would you tell Grant it's time to get up," she called. Then she smiled grimly. It was a day like any other day. It could be any day in a month of days, in a year of days, for all that their routine had changed. But she knew it was different, that she was different and that their lives could never be the same again. *Only they don't know it yet,* she thought, shaking her head.

Robert strode quickly down the stairs, briefcase in hand. "I'm going to leave a little early today—I've got a lot to do." He came around the table to give her the usual good-bye kiss—he never left the house without kissing her first—but the kiss was a habit done without much thought, which may have accounted for the fact that on this day he didn't notice how stiff she was, how she drew back from the touch of his lips against hers.

"See you about six tonight," he said and was gone. It was seven-fifteen.

"Hi, Mom," she heard a sleepy voice say, and she turned to her seven-year-old, holding open her arms. He was warm from sleep, cuddly, comforting. She sat down and drew him onto her lap.

"Have a good sleep?" she asked.

"Yeah." It was a distorted sound, coming as it did from around his left thumb. He was very much the baby of the family, although he was already in first grade.

"Ready for breakfast?"

"Yeah."

She pulled out the plate of food she had put in the oven to keep warm for him. While he was eating, she went down to put in a load of wash. "Hurry up," she told him as she returned with an armload of folded clothes. He dawdled when he ate, and she was anxious to get him ready and out the door. By the time she had made one more trip, he had eaten all he was likely to eat, so she sent him upstairs to get ready for school. Then she stacked the last of the dirty dishes into the dishwasher and turned it on rinse and hold.

There was still far too much time before he would leave for school. She groaned and began pounding the table with her fist, then caught herself. *Not yet. Not until he's gone.* She went upstairs to see how he was doing.

He was still in the bathroom.

"Did you brush your teeth?" she asked him, smoothing down his dark hair.

"Of course I did," he replied indignantly and blew a peppermint testimonial at her, his mouth open so that she could see his teeth. They were still mostly baby teeth. At seven he had lost only the bottom two.

"Is there time for a story today?" he asked. She looked at her watch.

"Yes," she said, sighing.

"What's the matter, Mommy?" he asked, putting his arm around her neck, serious and sweet.

She felt the tears sting but held them back. "I don't feel very good about things this morning," she said.

"Just don't put yourself down so critically," he said earnestly.

She couldn't help laughing. She didn't know where he had picked up that phrase. Maybe she had said it once, or Robert, or perhaps a Sunday School teacher. But Grant had remembered it and trotted it out whenever he felt she was being too hard on herself.

She ruffled the hair she had just smoothed and said, "Come on, let's go read that story!"

Today it was *Harold and the Purple Crayon.* Harold drawing a spaceship with his purple crayon and flying out into space in it. Harold drawing a planet so his ship would have something to land on.

Grant giggled and squirmed with enjoyment as she read, chattering about what he would like to draw if he had a crayon like Harold's. She let him talk, hardly listening to what he was saying, until finally it was time for him to go. She helped him with his jacket and backpack and handed him his lunch, then stood at the door watching him skip down the road to the bus stop where other kids were already standing.

She closed the door and waited for the scream to roll up and burst out, but nothing came. It was an incredible letdown. She waited a little longer, then went slowly downstairs, took out the wash, and put it into the dryer. She put in a second wash, climbed upstairs and straightened the beds, stuffed the dirty clothes and towels down the chute, cleaned the bathroom sinks, and polished the mirrors. On she continued, dusting, vacuuming, and fluffing, and all the while she was redrawing her life with Harold's purple crayon, drawing new choices, future possibilities.

She drew herself coming home right after the rehearsal, sleeping soundly next to Robert. She drew a farewell scene with Jay, wherein she said, "Yes, I do love you, but I have a husband and a family. And they come first." The follow-up to that scene was a life of dedicated service, made possible by the secret knowledge that she was passionately loved. (She had enough humor left to laugh at this one; she knew exactly which page she could find it on.) She drew herself not married to Robert anymore, following Jay into a new life. She noticed the children weren't in this picture. She drew herself living two lives at once, one with Robert, one with Jay, attempting a balancing act without a safety net. But even as she drew, she knew that they were all impossible because there was something else that belonged in any drawing containing Robert: the Church. But didn't the Church belong in any drawing containing Kathy Montgomery? She drew her temple recommend, then drew thick black lines through it. And burst into tears.

This time she did not hold back. Great, ugly, wracking sobs shook her. She cried with the abandoned, physical intensity that leaves one exhausted and wretched. When she had cried until she could literally cry no more, she became aware of a dull, throbbing pain in her head. She made her way unsteadily to the bathroom to search for something to stop the throbbing. As she was about to take two extra-strength tablets, she happened to glance at the mirror. Her face was puffy and colorless; her eyes, bloodshot and rimmed with red; her mouth, loose.

Suddenly the shrill ringing of the doorbell split the silence. *Who can that possibly be?* she asked herself in panic, but she had a strange, certain knowledge that Jay was at the door. *I can't let him see me like this!* she thought wildly, and she moved to the far corner of the bathroom, cowering there, anticipating yet dreading each sharp trill of the bell.

Go away! she screamed silently. But the ringing continued. *He knows I'm here—my car's still sitting in the driveway. Why didn't I put it away last night?*

Then a startling thought came to her: If he wanted to see her, why not let him? It was his fault that she looked like this. It was his fault she had stayed awake all night and then cried until she was sick. She strode from the bathroom and almost ran down the hall, jerking the front door open with all her strength. It was a good scene, and she was going to play it to the hilt. But the moment she saw his pleasant face fill with concern, she slumped.

"Kathy! What's happened?" he exclaimed, coming into the entryway and closing the door behind him. He reached out his hand to touch her, but she jerked away from him.

"You of all people ought to know the answer to that question!" she retorted.

He didn't answer immediately; he first took her by the arm, led her to the couch, and pulled up a chair, sitting down across from her. "I had a feeling you'd be upset after the way you left last night, but I had no idea I'd find you like this!"

"How did you think I'd feel!" Kathy exclaimed. "I have a husband, I have a family, and I *thought* I had a friend."

"We've been more than friends for a long time, you know that."

"Is that so?"

"Come off it, Kathy! Who have you been turning to when you needed someone to talk to, when you've been excited or upset about something? You haven't talked to your husband about it, that's for sure. You waited to tell me!"

"That was a mistake, I see that now. I should have tried to talk to Robert more. I should have tried to make him understand!"

"You see? That's the whole point. You don't have to try

to make me understand. We're on the same wavelength; you've said that often enough."

She turned away from him, and her voice caught as she said, "I know. It just seemed so . . ." She couldn't finish the sentence, so he finished it for her.

"So natural. Like we belonged together. We do belong together."

She made a gesture of denial.

"Kathy, you and I have had something going for months, only there wasn't any physical part, beyond a quick hug or kiss. We've just added a new dimension!"

"You make it sound so innocent!"

"But it is," he said, smiling and reaching for her hand. She drew it away, and he leaned back abruptly in his chair, but neither his expression nor the calm, certain tone of his voice changed as he added, "We love each other."

"It's a sin!" she cried, ignoring what he had said. "I've committed . . . I've done something I can't even bring myself to say aloud! I feel dirty, ashamed! Don't you?"

He let out a long sigh and rubbed his chin thoughtfully. He seemed to be in the process of making a crucial decision, and all his attention was turned inward. Kathy noticed his withdrawal and felt it safe to let her gaze rest on him. She could scarcely contain the swell of longing she felt as she really looked at him for the first time since answering the door.

Why did it have to turn out this way? She knew the texture of his wavy, light-brown hair, the feel of his sharply angled cheek and his full, down-turned lips. She knew what could be read in his gold-flecked hazel eyes, knew exactly where her shoulder fit when his arm was around her. And she knew that to experience his nearness again would be to trade pain for pain. *And now I know which is the harder to bear,* she thought sadly.

He shifted in his chair and looked up at her, catching her eyes full of unmasked emotion. "Kathy," he said tenderly, "I'm really sorry about what happened last night. I guess that's one subject we have different ideas about, although I must admit I'm a bit confused about yours. You didn't say anything about it being a sin, you didn't call a halt . . ."

Tears were now spilling over and rolling unheeded down her cheeks as he continued, "If I had understood before how you felt about this, things would be different today. But to tell the truth, I don't feel that we've done anything wrong. I love you, and I'm willing to make a commitment to you. I thought you knew that."

"Commitment! What are you talking about!"

"This is not quite the setting I had imagined proposing in, but I want you to marry me," he answered, smiling gently.

"What are you talking about?" she almost screamed. "I'm married to Robert! I can't leave him. I can't leave my children!"

The tender expression in Jay's eyes turned hard. "You're playing games, Kathy. Without actually leaving Robert, you came to me with things a wife is supposed to share with her husband; but as long as there was nothing physical between us, you felt safe. Didn't you realize what you were doing? How far things had actually gone? Nothing has changed since last night, Kathy, nothing except that now you can see how far away from your husband you've really moved, and you're scared to death!" He gripped her shoulders. "Be honest with yourself! I love you, and I know you love me!"

When she didn't answer, his grip softened. "I'm serious, Kathy," he said, trying to catch her eyes. "Will you think about it?"

She shook her head, her eyes closed so that they wouldn't have to meet his. "I can't," she whispered. "Robert and I were married in the temple. I can't just . . . forget all that."

"But you did last night," he reminded her softly.

She held up her hands as if to ward away something threatening. "Oh, please. Go away! I don't want to hear any more!" Covering her face with her hands, she repeated over and over again, "Go away, go away!"

He listened to her muffled entreaty for a moment, then

touched her cheek lightly. "Will you think about what I asked you?"

"It isn't even a possibility, Jay!" she said, raising her anguished eyes to his. "Don't you understand? No, how could you? This whole affair"—she said it as if it meant 'this whole business,' then realized with a rush of blood that it had another, more pertinent meaning—"means something different to you than it does to me."

"You'd better explain that!" he demanded.

"To me it's a mistake, a terrible mistake. And it's put me in a terrible position. I have to make things right with Robert, and I have to make things right with the Church! To do that, I have to say good-bye to you. I can't ever see you again, Jay, ever!"

He held back his anger and took her hands. "There is another option, Kathy. Don't forget that. You're not bound to Robert forever!"

"That's just it. I am." She withdrew her hands from his and said sadly, "I . . . Jay, there's no way I can explain it to you. Just believe me. I'm bound to Robert in a way you can never understand."

"Then what was the meaning of all this?" he demanded, his eyes dark. "The weeks of waiting for Tuesday, just so we could see each other? The hours we've spent talking and laughing together? You owe me an explanation!"

"I can't give you one! I can't even explain it to myself!"

"I don't accept that!" He looked at his watch with an irritated twist of the wrist. "I have to go now," he said curtly, "but this isn't the end of the conversation!"

"It has to be!" she cried, but he was already on his way to the door, and if he heard, he didn't give any sign of it. She continued to sit on the couch, her eyes dry, staring straight ahead. The hours passed, but she was unaware of their passing until she heard the door open and Grant come in. He brought the smell of fresh air with him.

"Hey, Mom!" he called. "I'm starved! Have you got something good to eat?"

Only then did she remember the bread she'd left on the

stove counter hours before. She rushed into the kitchen. The loaves were sunken in the middle, dough hanging over the sides. She began to laugh and cry together, but the crying won out.

"Mommy!" Grant pulled at her sweatshirt. "What's the matter!"

"It's nothing, sweetie," she said, wiping her tears with the back of her hand. "I just have a very, very bad cold, and I need to go to bed, okay?" She was pulling dough from the pans as she talked, throwing it into the garbage. "Look, there are tater tots and fish sticks in the freezer. You guys have that for supper."

"Oh, good!" he said with enthusiasm.

Thank heaven he's so easy to please, she thought gratefully. "And when Brad and Susan come home, you can tell them I've gone to bed and that I don't want anyone to bother me, okay?"

He nodded. "Can I watch cartoons?" he asked hopefully.

"Yes, as long as you don't turn them up too loud." She gave him a squeeze and went up to bed.

Sleep came and went. Now and then she would hear voices from below, sometimes from the television, sometimes from her own children. Once in a while, she heard angry sounds and thought she should really get up to see what was going on, but she couldn't wake up enough to do it. She was asleep when Robert came home and looked in on her. She hadn't moved when he came to bed late that night.

Two

The next days had a nightmarish quality about them. By pleading a cold, Kathy excused her pale, red-eyed appearance and easy irritability. She went about her normal tasks—cooking, cleaning, driving kids here and there, and teaching—though every moment was intolerable. Deception did not come easy to her, and it seemed as if everything she did was a deception since it prolonged the illusion that all was well in the Montgomery household. She half-expected Robert to accuse her every time he looked at her or talked to her, but he didn't seem to notice her distress. Surprisingly, she found she wanted him to say something; she could barely conceal her anger at his seeming indifference. *As long as the house is clean and food is on the table and he has ironed shirts in the closet, it never occurs to him that anything might be wrong!* she inwardly raged.

The kids were no different, except for Grant. Brad and Susan were so caught up in their own school, Church, and social activities that they scarcely had time to notice the adults in their lives. Grant, however, was home with his mother after everyone else had left and before everyone had returned, and he knew that something was wrong. She did everything she normally did, but she cried while doing it. He began watching her, and often she would look up to see his dark eyes on her; and the solemn expression on his face would cause her to cry out, "Oh, Grant!" Then he would hug her and give her a pat on the back, which would only make her feel like crying more.

She dreaded Thursday, knowing she would have to stand before a dozen women and explain the intricacies of cooking crepes, but that turned out to be surprisingly easy. Preparing for her class and actually teaching it gave her a wonderful break from her inner turmoil, since her mind had to focus on something totally different.

Nights were the hardest. Ever since their marriage, she and Robert had made it a point to go to bed at the same time whenever possible. Often, when he had work to do, he would lie down beside her for a few hours of sleep and then get up in the middle of the night to work. They had a queen-sized bed, but they slept in a huddle that would almost have fit a twin bed. It was contact that had always been important to both of them.

Now she couldn't bear lying next to Robert. It was as though she feared he could somehow divine from the touch of her skin what had happened. So she went to bed early, at nine o'clock sometimes, long before he would watch the news (he never retired without first watching the news). And contrary to her usual feelings, she was glad when he said he had a meeting Friday evening and didn't anticipate being home until late.

This unusual behavior is what finally caught his attention and led him to inquire, "Are you mad at me about something?"

"No," she said, not turning to look at him.

"Come on," he said, taking her by the arm. "Something's up. What is it?"

She managed a smile. "Nothing's wrong, honestly. I'm just not with it today."

"Or last night either," he said. At this moment she was sure he would press her until the truth came out.

Not yet! she thought, horrified. "It's just this darn cold. I can't seem to shake it. My head's plugged up and my muscles ache."

"Here." He turned her around and began to massage her shoulder muscles. "Listen, you haven't been yourself since the rehearsal," he said. "Did something happen between you and Jay?" He felt her stiffen, but he continued to massage the knotted muscles. "I know you and Jay are good friends. You know I don't understand it and I don't like it; we've talked about that often enough before. But his friendship is important to you, and . . . I guess I'd be sorry for you if something happened to ruin it."

It took all her control to keep from running from the room, but she only sniffled into her tissue and repeated, "It's just this cold." Her back was still turned to him, so she didn't see the speculative look he gave her as he continued to rub her back comfortingly.

"Well, you make sure you get enough rest. Take it easy for a while." He paused, then added, "You could cancel your cooking classes."

She turned quickly. "No, I'm all right, really. I can keep things going. I'm not going to cancel my classes!"

"Okay," he shrugged. "It was just a suggestion."

"Oh, really?" her voice challenged him. "You've hated those cooking classes ever since I started teaching them. You wish something would happen to make me quit. Well, I'm not quitting!"

He held up his hand. "Right, right. I understand. You think you're proving something by teaching those classes. I'm not sure what, but I don't want to fight about it now."

Kathy stared at him as he turned to leave the room, wondering why he was walking away from an argument he had always pursued. Then her heart stopped as he paused and looked first at the bulletin board and then back at her with a quizzical expression. She realized that during the week he must have noticed first one, then two, and finally three notices on the board. They all said the same thing: Call Jay. The last was underlined and followed by an exclamation point.

It was only when Susan asked her if she could spend Sunday at a friend's that Kathy realized she had another decision to make: whether or not to go to church.

I can't go, I can't! she thought, feeling things close in on her. *They'll all know, just by looking at me! Even if I do go, what will I do when the sacrament is passed? I can't even think of taking it, not after what's happened! And if I don't, I'll have to explain to Robert why I didn't. He'll invite me into his office "for a little talk," and then it will all come out in the open.*

She retreated to her bedroom and drew the blinds. Lying in the half-dark, she realized that she was just about out of time. She couldn't go on pretending that nothing was wrong, but she was too ashamed and too frightened to confront Robert or to do the things that would come after. Suddenly the things she had complained about so often—her unexciting life; Robert's steady, unromantic presence; the daily grind of being wife, mother, teacher, and church worker—seemed safe and solid. *How could I have jeopardized all that?* she anguished.

But the pressing need was to figure out how to avoid the approaching Sunday. *I'll visit mother,* she finally decided. *I'll drive down to Bancroft tomorrow.* That meant she would have to tell Robert tonight, before he left for his meeting. She got up and went down to the kitchen, where she prepared a green salad and thawed some spaghetti sauce in the microwave. She was conscious as she did it that she was counting on the effect a good meal always had on Robert, hoping he would more readily agree to her plan.

After supper (*had he enjoyed the meal?*—she couldn't tell), she followed him up to the bedroom and sat on the edge of the bed, watching him get ready for a meeting. They exchanged a few words about the weather, what the lawnmower repair bill might be ("We absolutely have to get it in before the repair shop gets too full!"), and the miles Brad was putting on the car when he went out on dates. Kathy's heart raced and her ears were burning. *Now! I have to say it now!* she ordered herself.

"I'm going to drive down to Mother's tomorrow," she forced the words out, her voice sounding flat and queer.

He looked at her in surprise. "Any special reason?"

"It's been a while since I've been down. Anyway, the weather's been so mild, I thought it might be a nice drive."

"Are you planning to take the kids with you?"

"No." She saw his look and added quickly, "Grant can probably stay at Tamara's, and Susan and Brad can take care of themselves. I told Susan she could spend Sunday afternoon at the James's."

"What about me?" he asked with a petulant turn to his mouth.

Kathy looked at him steadily. He had meant it to be a joke, but she knew that he was really serious. "I'm quite sure you can get along without me for a couple of days," she replied dryly. "There're some casseroles in the freezer, and the house is clean."

His eyes probed her reflection in the closet mirror. Without turning he asked, "Did you forget that Davis is coming in from New York tomorrow? We're supposed to take him out to dinner tomorrow night, if you remember."

"I remember. But I thought you could keep him entertained without me." She straightened the cream-colored, hand-woven bedspread to avoid looking at him.

"Humph" was his comment, and he began to comb his thin sandy hair. Kathy watched him as he began the ritual she knew so well. He had a side part, and he kept the top hair long so he could brush it over the increasingly balding center of his head. He also kept the sides somewhat long so they covered the tops of his slightly protruding ears. He combed with quick, even motions, and though his hair hadn't looked out of place before he'd begun, he combed and smoothed and combed some more.

Kathy sighed. Compared to Jay, he certainly wasn't handsome, but he was impressive. When he spoke, the force of his personality caused one to overlook the curiously colorless eyes, the nearly bulbous nose upon which his horn-rimmed glasses sat, and the straight humorless mouth beneath it. No one ever thought of him as weak, although his body was far too thin for his six-foot-two-inches, and his suits always hung loosely on him, as if on a hanger.

He cleaned his glasses, looked at his reflection in the mirror one last time, then turned to her. "I wish you had talked to me about this before," he said, irritation plain in his voice. "In fact, I think you and I are due for a good, long talk. Things have been strange this week, and I don't just mean because of your cold. What's the matter with you?"

"Nothing I want to talk about at the moment," she said studying her nails. "I need to get away for a while, that's all. I'll probably cancel my Tuesday classes, just in case I decide to stay into next week."

"Cancel your classes? You cling to those like a magnet!" He looked at her sharply. "First you spring this little trip of yours on me, and then you say you might stay into next week! Slow down a minute, okay? I have nothing against a weekend trip to your mother's, but this is pushing it too far."

Her own strength surprised her as she said, "Well, I've made up my mind—I'm going! But I may not stay that long; I don't know yet," she ended on a conciliatory note.

"You're going to cancel your classes," Robert stated softly, more to himself than to Kathy. He half-turned, then looked off out the window, forehead knit in serious thought.

Kathy immediately regretted her words—canceling her classes was a clear signal to Robert that something really was wrong. They had been a source of major contention ever since she had first come up with the idea. He had been against her starting a home business, thinking that she had enough to do without adding that kind of responsibility.

"But Robert," she had pleaded, "It's not really a business—it's only a class or two and just for fun. I know I can do it! The sisters at Relief Society always tell me my cooking classes are as good as anything they've ever seen!"

"But why?" he had asked.

"I want to have something of my very own. Something that I do."

"As if you don't already do plenty! You're my wife. You're a mother. You're busy enough. Forget it," he had said brusquely. It didn't bother him that his reply didn't bear any relationship to her stated need, that it was the stock answer of a man who is satisfied with his life and doesn't want any changes.

"There's another reason why I want to do it," she had continued, her voice cool.

"What's that?"

"I need some money of my own."

"Money of your own? Don't I give you enough?" His gesture included the spacious, antique-filled living room and the large expanse of green outside the window.

"I know it sounds . . . ridiculous, but I have to provide an accounting of every penny I spend! Can you imagine how it feels to be granted a certain amount each month for household expenses and to have to ask for more if I want to buy something special or something just for me? Or a surprise for you! Can you imagine how it feels to sit across the desk from you like a disobedient child while you lecture me about the necessity of holding to a budget you made without consulting me?"

"I do consult you!"

"Hah!" Her anger forced her out of her chair, and she began to pace.

"I do. We have family council every month, and we decide together how we're going to handle things."

"No," she said flatly, leaning slightly over the desk. "I sit there"—she pointed at the chair she had just vacated—"and you *tell* me how things are going to be handled. That's not the same, and you know it!"

"You didn't object to it when we were first married."

"Maybe not, but I have since then. Only you don't listen to what I say. You have never listened to me, not really."

"I'm listening now," he said, clearly angry. The line of his lips was tightly compressed; his eyes, icy.

She spoke slowly; the words she had drawn together to form a statement of policy were painful to her. But she had no doubt as to what she wanted to say: she had been planning this speech for months.

"I think there is no form of dependency worse than financial dependency. Over the years of our marriage, I have come to understand that the one with the purse strings is the one who calls the shots. I don't want to be totally dependent on you anymore, for all that I love you."

"You must not love me, or you'd trust me to take care of our finances. To take care of you," he added.

She smiled ruefully. "I do love you, you know. But

we've been married long enough for me to know that we have a totally different attitude about money and that you are convinced your viewpoint is right."

"But it is. If we handled the money the way you want to, we'd be in a real mess. You can't even add!"

"I've never had to add!" she countered, furious that her voice was unsteady and that tears were gathering in her eyes. Robert hated it when she cried. Nothing she said was credible if she started crying; in his eyes it would merely be the ranting of an "emotional woman." She took a deep breath and, speaking slowly, went on, "I've never had total responsibility for any money at all. That's why I want to make a little of my own so I can spend it however I want to, accounting only to myself."

"What would you spend it on?"

"Oh, I don't know. Maybe I'd buy tickets to the opera when the Met goes to Minneapolis in the spring."

"You're still mad because I thought spending that much money on opera tickets was ridiculous."

"No. I don't think I'm mad any longer. I'm just determined to have some money of my own to spend. The way you do. After all, you have enough electronic gadgets in your office to buy six months' worth of opera tickets!"

"So you're going ahead with this ridiculous project?" he asked, leaning back in his chair. "You'll spend more money than you'll make, most likely. But when you need me to bail you out, just come and ask."

Her eyes were as cold and steady as his when she replied, "I won't need you to bail me out."

And she hadn't needed any help from him, financial or otherwise. The classes were a success right from the start. She was doing something she loved to do, something she was very, very good at. Even he had to admit that, however reluctantly. And he was surprised and not a little pleased to see that she ran her small business with a high degree of professionalism, never canceling unless absolutely necessary.

Until now.

He walked up to where Kathy was sitting on the bed and

stopped directly in front of her, waving his finger at her in exactly the gesture he used when reprimanding the children. "We are going to talk about this, and we are going to talk about it now. I have a right to know what's going on!"

Kathy drew back from him, almost frightened of his commanding presence. Even though she knew that she'd made the choice to stay with her husband when she'd sent Jay away and that she would have to tell him eventually, she couldn't tell him now, not with him standing over her like that.

She reached out and touched his hand. "Please don't do that. I'm not seven years old."

"You're avoiding the issue," he accused, but his hand dropped.

"You're right, of course," Kathy murmured. "There is something we have to talk about, but I can't do it now. Maybe when I get back."

"This does have something to do with Jay, doesn't it," he stated in an odd tone.

"I told you, I can't talk about it now! I've got to get out of here; I've got to have some space. Can't you just let it be!" she shouted.

And to her surprise, he could. He turned and walked out without saying another word. They both knew he could have pushed the issue then, could have insisted upon her telling him what she was holding back, but perhaps he wasn't ready to talk about it yet, either.

Three

The morning was bright and clear as Kathy pulled out of the driveway and headed south. The winter snows had at last yielded to the warm persuasion of the sun, revealing fields of winter wheat that stretched on either side of the freeway. Clumps of trees had a delicate wash of green that spoke of leaves half-unfolded, and the air had a damp, sweet smell.

She drove with the window down, enjoying the warm, soft breeze. Just getting out of the city was a relief, and she had always liked driving, so she gladly put everything out of her mind and focused on the road and the traffic ahead. It was one of the first nice weekends of spring, and people were on the road. She gassed up after she left the freeway, stopping at a country station, where she got a smile, a bit of rambling conversation along with her gas, and a can of Diet Pepsi—"to keep me awake. I still have quite a ways to go."

She loved the well-kept farms, patchwork fields, and windbreaks that lined Iowa 61. It was typical midsection U.S.A., and Bancroft was a cliché of corn-country towns. It had a main street consisting of a drug store, a couple of small markets, a steepled church, a five-and-dime, a co-op, and an International Harvester dealership, plus the inevitable gas stations and beer joints. The small brick school she had attended was on a side street, the playing field behind. There were a city hall in the brickwork of the 1930s and a city park with pavilion and playground. And street after tree-lined street of wood-framed houses, some with porches, gingerbread, and stained glass; others in a more sober style. Most were white.

The house she had grown up in was one of the former. Though it didn't have as much gingerbread as some, it had a wide, screened-in porch on the south and east sides and leaded glass in the front door and windows. There was an air of spaciousness and graciousness about the house still known as "The Judge's."

How I love it, Kathy thought as she drove up before the home. Then she saw her mother bending over the tulip bed, a short, white-haired woman in a pink, flowered housedress and a patterned apron—it was orange and brown and clashed with the dress but somehow was just right. "Oh Mother," she whispered, "will you be glad I've come after I tell you why?"

Her mother straightened up and turned at the sound of the car, and Kathy opened the door, calling out, "Hey, need some help?"

"Kathy! You're here already!" Clarice Adams reached up to hug her daughter, then stood back and asked, "You're not still driving too fast, are you?"

Kathy flushed. "A bit," she admitted with a grin.

"That's going to get you into trouble some day. You wait and see. Well, come on, let's get your bags. I've got peach cobbler in the oven, and it's probably just about done."

The smell of the cobbler filled the air, warm and rich. "Umm. Smells good!" Kathy said as she walked into the house. "But it's not Weight Watchers, I can tell. And there's cream to go on it, too, I bet."

"You're right. Here, wash up if you'd like, and then we'll have that cobbler while it's nice and warm."

Half an hour later they were sitting at the table, nibbling the remains of the cobbler, too full to eat any more, but savoring the candied bits of brown sugar sauce. Kathy felt her mother's eyes on her and asked, "What is it? Do I have something on my face?" She wiped her mouth with her napkin.

"You don't look well, Kathy," said her mother. "You've

got circles under your eyes, and you've put on a little weight."

"Don't say that after you've plied me with calories," Kathy joked, but her mother didn't laugh. Kathy nodded. "I know I've got a pound or two to lose. But what with my classes, I eat more than I need to. Besides, it's my reaction to stress. I've always wished I were one of those people who stop eating when they have difficulties."

Kathy's mother was listening attentively, and her eyebrows had drawn together in a worried frown. "You didn't bring Robert with you, or the children. You've come because there's trouble."

Kathy traced the design of the orange-and-white tablecloth. Then she sighed and looked up. "You've always been pretty perceptive. Yes, I've got troubles, but is it all right if we wait till tomorrow to talk about them? It was a long drive and I'm bushed. I'd like to get a good night's sleep first."

"Which you may get, but I certainly won't, given the circumstances. You're here because you have troubles, but you don't want to tell me what those troubles are. The nights are still long, and I've always had an active imagination!"

"You're right, that was a stupid suggestion," said Kathy with resignation. "I shouldn't have expected you to put it on the shelf till tomorrow. But it's not pleasant, and I don't know if you'll like me very much when I get done telling you."

The older woman patted her arm. "Oh, come now. It can't be all that bad," she encouraged.

"Wait till you hear what I have to say." There was a pause which Clarice didn't interrupt, and Kathy looked down at her hands and began rubbing them. She had had the nervous habit since childhood. In fact, there was much of the little girl that could still be seen in her—Kathy's cheeks were full and smooth, and though she looked tired, there was still some of the high natural color the cheeks had always had, color that only emphasized the pale, lovely skin. Her snub nose hadn't changed, nor had her hair, which was still thick, dark, and curly, framing her face with tendrils no matter how severely it was pinned or pulled or straightened.

"You know I've been singing with the Parker-Jeffry Chorale for a couple of years," Kathy began. "I've gotten to know the others in the group pretty well in that time. I've told you about some of them before. Maybe I've even mentioned Jay, Jay Enders. Have I?" she asked.

"The name doesn't sound familiar, not right off" was the reply. "Perhaps if you tell me a little more about him . . ."

"Ah, what should I say?" Kathy raised her hands and then dropped them in her lap. "He's a little older than I am, forty-one. He's a tenor and a good singer, of course, or he wouldn't be in the chorale. He works for an ad agency in Lemburg. I can see why; he's clever with words. He's a great conversationalist and lots of fun to be around."

"Is he married?"

"No, he's divorced. He and his wife had a rather hard time of it from what he's told me. I don't think he trusts women very much. Actually, I think the reason we got along so well to begin with was the fact that I'm married. That made him feel safe," Kathy said with a grimace.

"Any children?"

"No."

"He isn't a Church member, is he?"

"No. But he's a solid person, nonetheless. You know, just because he's not a Church member doesn't mean he's suspect. He's kind and thoughtful and—"

"You have told me about him," Clarice interrupted. "I just forgot the name."

"Really? What do you remember about him?"

"Nothing specific, but I remember being worried as I listened to you talk about him then. There was something in your voice, and I hear it again now."

"Oh." Kathy went back to tracing. *Am I so transparent,* she wondered.

"Have you let yourself indulge in romantic notions concerning this Jay? Are you thinking you're in love with him?"

"Indulging in romantic notions! That's a good way to put it."

"Well?"

Kathy could feel Clarice's gaze but couldn't bring herself to meet it. "Not at first," she began hesitantly. "He was fun to talk to, and when a bunch of us would go out to eat after rehearsal, I'd always find myself talking to him more than to anyone else. So after a while, we began sitting at a table all by ourselves, and after that . . . we didn't go with the rest—"

"That's dangerous, young lady! Surely you know that!"

Kathy laughed shortly. "Oh, I know."

"Then you'll stop meeting with him . . ."

"Mother, that's not the problem. It's gone beyond that."

Clarice turned away, one crabbled hand clutching her apron front. "I'm not sure what you mean, and I'm not sure I want to know what you mean."

Kathy felt unbearably hot, though one of the kitchen windows was open to the cool evening air. She pulled her sweater off, but still she felt smothered. She got herself a glass of water and put another before her mother. They both drank, avoiding each other's eyes. Then Clarice put her empty glass to one side and said, "Now, suppose you be specific about what you're trying to tell me." Her expression was full of resolve.

Kathy opened her mouth, hesitated, closed it again.

"Is it so hard to say?" asked her mother.

She nodded.

"I want to hear it, however hard it may be. I want to know what we're dealing with."

Her strength was intimidating. Kathy rose and walked to the open window, drawing in the damp, somewhat raw night air.

"I spent part of a night with him," she said finally.

"Doing what?" The words were matter of fact, but Clarice's voice was taut with unreleased emotion.

"Why are you acting so obtuse!" shouted Kathy. "You know what I mean. You're not that naive!"

"No. But I want you to say it."

"I can't—it sounds so crude! Whatever there was of tenderness and affection is taken away, and all that's left is . . . lust." She finished on a whisper and leaned her head against the window frame.

"And how long has this been going on?"

Kathy whirled around. Clarice had a thoughtful look on her face that reminded Kathy of her father. In fact, this whole conversation reminded Kathy of the way she had seen her father deal with her brothers—aggravatingly judicial. She had wanted her mother to cry with her, to scream with her or even at her, but this firm questioning caught her totally off balance. "It hasn't been 'going on' as you put it!" she exclaimed, her face contorted. "It happened only once, and I'm not even sure how it did happen!"

Clarice was unmoved. "You're sounding like a teenager, Kathy. And if I may use the expression of the day, I don't buy it. You're a married woman. You understand sexual response, your own and that of a man." There was only a faint hesitation as Clarice spoke unaccustomed words. Then she added, "I'm sorry, but you can't plead ignorance."

Kathy could hardly believe what her mother was saying. That Clarice had even said the word *sexual* out loud was in itself surprising, but more unexpected still was the flat rejection of her blamelessness.

"Mother," she began, but Clarice was implacable.

"I was afraid something like this might happen when I heard you talk about this man before. I even warned you."

Kathy's head jerked up, and her eyes flashed. "Warned me? When?"

"Then. I don't remember exactly what I said, but I tried to get you to see that you were sounding like a fifteen-year-old with a crush."

"I don't remember any such thing!"

"Oh, let's not argue about that. That's unimportant now. The important thing is, have you told Robert?"

"No. That's why I had to come. I don't want to tell him yet, but he knows something's up. If I had stayed home another day, I would have had to tell him."

"So you thought you'd try out your story by telling me first."

Kathy swore, but her mother didn't flinch. "I wish I hadn't come! You just don't understand!"

"Don't I? Let me put it in a less offensive way. You needed to tell me first as a way of getting things sorted out. Saying it aloud to someone else makes clearer what you will want to say and what you will want to leave out."

"If you think that's any less offensive, you're wrong." Kathy pushed out her chair and began picking up the dishes and forks.

"Come now. Every good lawyer does the same. As we ought to know," Clarice said, smiling faintly. "How many nights did your father stay up in that study, trying out words and effects before presenting a case? He always said that even an innocent man needed to have his case presented with a certain flair, that the facts could be dull and flat . . . and damning." She paused. "And remember how he always followed that up by saying, 'Of course, there's no such creature as an innocent man, strictly speaking.'"

Kathy looked at her mother gravely. "You seem to have picked up a lot from Dad. So did my brothers. Somehow I feel like it all went over my head."

"Oh, that's understandable. You were far younger than your brothers, and the only girl in a household of men. You were coddled and protected, by your brothers and your father. I think to Harvey you were the only innocent."

"But I wasn't."

"I know that! And so did he. But he was so strict with himself. He always looked at things straight on, and he was deadly earnest in everything he did. You were the one bit of romance he allowed in his life—no wonder he fed you on fairy tales and dreams."

"I suppose that's what it was with Jay," she said after a while. "A dream, a fairy tale. The old minnesingers who sang to their true loves and kept their distance were right. Jay and I should have kept on singing."

"Kathy, how do you really feel about this Jay? Do you think of him as your 'true love'?"

"If I weren't already married I would say he's perfect for me," said Kathy slowly. "We think the same, we like doing the same things, we have such a good time when we're together."

"What about church? You don't think the same about that."

"No. But I'm happy when I'm with him. And it's been such a long time since I've been happy, it didn't seem important." She heard her own words and thought, *Can I really be saying that?*

"And what about Robert? Have you forgotten about him? Obviously, he didn't seem important anymore, either."

Kathy was about to deny it, but she remembered Jay's accusation, *You forgot about him last night,* and she knew it was true. "In a way I have. We don't see each other as individuals anymore. He's just the person I talk to about what's on the calendar, what the kids' teachers said at conferences, and what needs to be repaired. To him, I'm nothing but the cook and maid and live-in baby sitter. I might as well be a paid housekeeper."

"How long have you been married? Nineteen years?"

"Yes."

"What you're describing sounds like many marriages of nineteen years. Most long-term relationships eventually approach the point where both partners take each other for granted. It's hard to avoid."

"I suppose so. But it's so . . . dehumanizing!"

"It can be. But it can also be the starting point for a richer relationship if both partners are willing to make some changes and to rediscover things they like about each other."

Kathy looked at her mother curiously. "Did you read that out of a book, or are you talking from experience?"

Clarice Adams smiled and flushed slightly.

"Mother! You're talking about yourself and Dad, aren't you?"

She nodded. "We'd been married about nineteen years when things between us reached a low point. That was when I packed my bags and almost left your father."

"What?" Kathy's jaw dropped in surprise. "I never knew that!"

"Probably because you were too young to know what was going on at the time. You were only six. And later on, it didn't seem necessary to tell you."

"Will you tell me about it now?"

Clarice looked at her daughter. "It seems to be a night for confessions," she said. "I never thought I'd be telling you this—we haven't confided in each other much."

"I know," Kathy said softly, taking her mother's hand. "We always seemed to be on opposite sides of the fence."

"I suppose we would be now as well, if your father were still with us. You'd be in the study with him, and I'd be getting things ready for Sunday dinner."

Kathy looked at the blue-veined hand. It was true. But she knew that interview would have proceeded much differently. Her father would never have wanted to hear the truth, not from his Kathy. Clarice had taken over his role and played it better than he himself would have played it.

"Am I right?" asked Clarice.

Kathy smiled ruefully. "I don't know why it always turned out that way, though."

"You were his girl, it's that simple. And that's part of what led to our confrontation. I saw the love I needed from him going to you, the tenderness, the laughter. He didn't have much of those qualities, not enough for both of us." She sighed. "I don't mean to say it was all his fault. Those early years were very hard; maybe as they went by I lost more than my youth.

"You know, I heard a joke in Relief Society the other day. It seems someone was interviewing a good sister who had been married for many years. The interviewer asked 'In all those years, did you ever think of divorce?' 'No,' the sister answered, 'but I did think of murder!'"

Kathy snorted humorlessly.

"All the sisters laughed except me. I remembered too well how it felt to be trapped, but there is a way out, even if people in the Church don't talk about it. There is another choice besides sticking it out in a miserable marriage, and there are cases in which it is the best and perhaps the only course of action for those involved."

"You felt like that? But you didn't leave. What made you change your mind?"

"Oh, a mixture of things. For one, I was afraid the leap might be from the frying pan to the fire. What would I do with five children and no place to go and no way to earn a living? Then one night I looked at him across the table, and for a moment I could see something of the young Harvey Adams I'd fallen in love with. I realized I had enough love for him left to want to try again."

"So you simply went on with things the way they were?"

"No. I learned to fight. I stood up for the things I needed, though sometimes I was frightened. There was no such thing as 'assertiveness training' in those days, you know. And your father didn't want to change. He felt he had a divine right to manage his family as he saw fit. That's not to say he wasn't a good man or was purposefully hurtful. He didn't realize that his way of talking and taking charge made me feel like a nothing. He thought I was exaggerating when I told him how I felt."

"Then what happened?"

"Well, I guess you could say I threw a temper tantrum!"

"You what?"

"It seemed to be the only way I could impress upon your father that I wasn't happy. As far as he was concerned, I couldn't be unhappy. He paid the bills, loved his children, and was faithful to me and his priesthood covenants. But the absence of negative things didn't make up for what was lacking—respect for me as a human being. I needed kindness, thoughtfulness, and tenderness. But as I've said, you were the one romance he allowed himself. I used to be jealous, but I think that's long gone."

Kathy's eyes filled with tears. "I never knew . . . Didn't it ever get better, Mother?"

"Oh, we managed to find a few compromises that smoothed things out a bit, though Harvey's way of looking at the world didn't change right away."

"But you stayed with him."

"Yes. It was the right choice. Although he could never bring himself to say flowery things, or even to bring flowers home, he did learn to be more sensitive to my needs. So after a while things did get better. We still had our ups and downs, but that's only normal—and when things weren't going too well, I learned to hang on until the cycle brought us close again. And . . ."

Kathy's curiosity was piqued by the pause. "And . . . ?" she prompted.

"And I discovered the joys of beating the bed with a broom!"

"What? Not when he was in it, I hope!"

Clarice's eyes sparkled mischievously. "Sometimes, you know, I imagined he was."

"Was it really like that, Mom?" asked Kathy, suddenly subdued. "Funny, but I don't remember those things. It almost seems like you're talking about another person when you talk about Dad this way."

"I'm not surprised. You saw only what your love for him allowed you to see. And if he were here, we'd get another side of the story as well." Clarice paused. "It's also true that by the time you were old enough to begin noticing such things, he had mellowed. He was different after the boys all left home, and he changed even more after you married. I think his habit of always asking questions finally caught up with him."

Clarice's face had grown soft with remembering. *She loved him, she really loved him, in spite of the difficulties,* Kathy thought.

"Wait here," said her mother, pushing herself out of the chair. "I want to show you something I've not shown anyone else."

Kathy followed her progress until she was out of sight. The thickened body, the puffy ankles, the difficulty in walking brought a catch to her throat.

"Here, look at this," Clarice said, returning with a jeweler's box in her hands.

"What is it?" asked Kathy curiously.

"A gift from your father, from the old Scrooge himself."

Kathy opened the box and gasped. On the satin lay a simple ruby and diamond pendant framed by ruby and diamond earrings. The stones were small, but the workmanship was fine, and the effect, rich but understated.

"I can't believe it! Why, these are beautiful! Did they cost as much as I think they did?"

"Probably not. The years of habit aren't easily overcome."

"Still, the fact that he bought them at all surprises me. He was always so conservative with money!"

"He was to the end. But when he gave me these, he said it didn't make any sense at our age to have money sitting in the bank."

"When did he give them to you?"

"On our anniversary the year he died. You know, your father was quite famous for his summations and later for his instructions to the jury—sometimes law students from Des Moines would sit in when he heard a case—but he was literally speechless when it came to expressing the tender feelings I know he had." She touched the pendant lovingly, then continued, "I think toward the end, he wanted to put those feelings into words, but he found he had waited too long. It was easier to buy these."

Kathy touched the stones appreciatively. "Oh, Mom, thank you for showing them to me!"

Her mother wiped her eyes on a corner of the orange and brown apron and came back to the issue at hand. "We're kind of far afield from where we started, aren't we?"

"I wish we could forget why I came! After hearing what you went through to keep your marriage to Dad going, I feel even more ashamed."

"That's not why I told you about it."

"I know."

"Kathy, are you so involved with this man that you are thinking of leaving Robert?"

"He wants me to. At least that's what he says. I don't know if he's really considered it seriously. I hadn't considered it at all before he, uh, asked me to marry him the morning after." Kathy flushed.

"Really?" Her mother was the calm inquisitor again.

"You're tough to get around, aren't you. I guess I did think about it. When I was mad at Robert, I imagined what it would be like with Jay, but I never seriously contemplated divorce; it was, well, a daydream, I guess."

"Are you considering it now?"

"Mom, the thought scares me to death! I'm afraid of all I'd have to give up!"

"But you said you were happy when you were with him," reminded Clarice. "Is that kind of happiness worth the price you would have to pay?"

"I don't know!" Kathy cried. "I guess I don't know how to differentiate between happiness and excitement, or between love and passion. And maybe contentment is just a degree north of boredom. I'm so confused!"

In the ensuing silence the grandfather clock in the living room struck midnight. "Maybe the hour has something to do with it," said Clarice.

"Maybe so," agreed Kathy, looking at her mother. The grey, sorrowful face seemed to bear no resemblance to the rosy, cheerful one she had seen bent over the tulips earlier that day. She was swept with regret. "I'm so sorry I brought you into this. At this time of life, you should be gathering laurel leaves instead of hemlock."

Clarice supressed a smile. "Don't get histrionic!" she said. "There's nothing about age that exempts anyone from sorrow. And I understand sorrow, Kathy. I know that it's heavy and dark, but it isn't too heavy or too dark for the light of Christ. I have my joy in Christ, and I can always count on that."

"I wish you had been able to count on me."

"Oh, my dear. We have let each other down at the most inopportune times, I know. But at this moment we're together. You came to me, and I didn't close my ears to what you were saying. That's a good start."

Kathy threw her arms around her mother and cried into her shoulder. Clarice patted her back and murmured over and over again, "It's all right. Don't cry. It'll be all right."

Four

The next morning Kathy woke to the twittering of birds outside her window. The sun was shining again, and its rays fell across her bed, adding to the warmth and contentment she felt. She could hear her mother moving around in the kitchen, opening and closing cupboards, turning on the faucet. Clarice was fixing breakfast, as she had done for decades, to the accompaniment of a religious music station. Lying in bed and listening to the familiar sounds, Kathy felt much like a little girl again—to be home in her own room, her mother within calling distance. Savoring that feeling, Kathy snuggled back down under the covers and closed her eyes again.

The opening of her bedroom door woke her from a light doze, and she sat up. Clarice entered the room with a tray in her hands, which she brought over and set down on the bed next to Kathy.

"Hey," Kathy said with a sudden sense of shame. "I should be bringing breakfast to you!"

"You were still asleep when I got up, so I thought I might as well fix you a little something. In any case I needed to fix my own breakfast. Brother Johnson will be picking me up for church in a few minutes."

"Oh." Kathy looked down at the tray. Clarice had picked a daffodil and put it in a vase on her tray and had folded a napkin festively. There was a boiled egg, toast, juice, and milk.

"I didn't wake you when I got up," her mother continued. "I didn't imagine you'd be wanting to go with me."

"No, Mom. I don't want to go."

"Will you be all right here alone?"

"Yes, of course. I need some time to think. I have to make some decisions."

"Well, eat your breakfast while the egg is still warm," Clarice encouraged her. "Oh, that must be Brother Johnson now," she said, as a car drove up. She leaned over the bed and gave Kathy a quick kiss. As she left the room she called, "There's a roast with potatoes and carrots in the oven, so you don't need to worry about getting lunch. I've set the temperature low so you don't have to check on it; it'll be done about the time I get home."

She left as quickly as she could get her portly body to move. Kathy heard a man's cheerful greeting and her mother's lively reply. A car door shut, then another. The engine started, and then the car moved off into the distance. In her mind's eye Kathy could see the road they would be driving. She knew every curve and could guess just how long it would take before they reached the parking lot in Hillsdale, where the nearest branch was. She could see the meetinghouse as well, a small brick building in a residential area. It did not hold many happy memories for her, that building. There had never been another girl her own age in all the years she had attended the branch, and none of the girls who had been there ever became a close friend. It had been a lonely time, made bearable by her brothers' willingness to include her in some of their Church outings. However, since the age difference was significant, even those excursions didn't fill her need for companionship.

There was one very special memory connected with that building, however: her first spiritual experience, the first time she had really felt the burning in the bosom. She had been reading the *Pearl of Great Price* before sacrament meeting when the phenomenon she had heard described but had never experienced came upon her. She had read on, overwhelmed by the beauty of the moment, scarcely moving, scarcely breathing, for fear any motion would drive it away.

It did fade after a time, but Kathy learned to her delight that it was not a one-time occurrence. After that she could rarely read the scriptures without the sweetly painful opening up of her heart. She began to count on its occurrence during sacrament meetings, and when she went to the "Y" she felt it often during devotionals. But the most memorable experiences with the Spirit took place on the Salt Lake Temple grounds and while she participated in the endowment sessions in the temple itself.

That feeling of having been cleansed, lifted up and out of the world, was unspeakably precious to her. Often the Spirit was so strong in the chapel before a session that tears would start flowing then and never entirely stop until she sat physically exhausted but spiritually full of strength in the Celestial Room.

The years she had spent as a Spiritual Living leader in the Lemburg Ward were also rich. She had spent many late hours sitting before a pile of books and copies of the *Ensign*—priceless hours in dialogue with the Lord. She had also felt promptings with respect to the welfare of her family, even with respect to the running of her cooking classes. The Spirit had never entirely left her; for many years she had always felt a small, warm "pilot light" within, every day, every hour of the day.

She sighed, a drawn-out, shuddering sigh. *I'm a long way from that now,* she thought bitterly, and the sheer loneliness of it seemed to swallow her up. She lay back and tried to recapture the more pleasant feelings of the morning. The sun was still shining, its light falling in different patterns now, but the birds had stopped singing; and all was quiet in the way that small towns are quiet on Sunday mornings, the stillness punctuated by the sound of a car passing and then fading away, by a voice calling, a dog barking, or the church bells ringing. And by the ticking of the clock in the living room.

Beside her on the bed lay the breakfast tray, still untouched. Kathy drank some of the juice and ate a few bites of buttered toast. *So nice of Mom to bring me breakfast, just like she used to when I was sick or when it was my birthday,* she thought, recapturing a moment of childhood. It felt good to be a child again and to let her mother do things for her. But she knew that couldn't last—she would have to go home, where it was her job to be the mother, to be the safekeeper-of-the-children. And she would have to go to church again soon, unless she had in mind to stop going altogether. Again a sense of loss swept over her.

She tried to formulate some concrete plans. If she wasn't going to abandon the Church and her family entirely, she would need to do some unpleasant things. She would finally have to talk to Robert. *There's no way to avoid that,* she thought. *But I hope I never have to talk to the kids about it. I hope they never find out!* There was one more person she would have to tell, the bishop. But how could she force her lips to form the words? In spite of her mother's insistence, she had never really spoken them last night. In an interview with the bishop, though, she wouldn't be able to skirt the issue. She would have to say the words, shameful and ugly, "I have committed adultery. What do I do now?"

With a wry smile she realized she was doing exactly what her mother had accused her of doing. She was trying to find a way to say it without making her actions seem so awful, without making herself seem so guilty. She felt rather that she had been more the victim of fate, of circumstance. After all, she did love Robert, she told herself, and she loved her children. She also knew that she had borne a true testimony not so very long ago when she had said that she loved the Lord and believed in the gospel. Given that, how could she be guilty of the "malice aforethought" that would put things in such a different light?

So she contented herself with this line of reasoning, giving up for the moment the belief that one always has a choice. It was much easier to believe in a great passion overriding the decision-making center just at the most opportune time.

Tense and restless and in need of physical movement, she got up, dressed, and went out onto the porch. *How little things have changed,* she thought, looking down the street toward the park. She began walking in that direction, noticing a new fence here, a different color of paint there, a new split-level sandwiched between two dignified, three-storied old-timers. But essentially it looked the same as it had that fall day her father had driven her to the airport in Des Moines and sent her off as a freshman to BYU. The same, except for the lack of snow, as it had looked when she came home for Christmas a few months later to tell her parents she was in love.

"Oh, Dad, he's so wonderful! He's, well, he's quite a bit older than I am—he's a graduate student working on an MBA. That's a Master's of Business Administration," she had explained with a smile, proud of her knowledge. "And he's a returned missionary . . . No, he's not what I'd call handsome, exactly, but he's got a nice face. He's tall and thin, kind of like a beanpole, to tell the truth. Mom, Dad, he's so neat; I'd marry him in a minute if he asked me."

I wanted him to propose to me, Kathy said to herself, conjuring up memories of the tumultuous, uncertain longing of youth. *I remember thinking I would die if he didn't!*

She had seen him first at a dance held in the Helaman Halls cafeteria that fall of 1963. The place had been crowded with students standing in groups, talking and looking. A few couples were dancing, but most were not. They were searching, eyes catching someone's glance, then moving on. She had felt awkward, embarrassed, and left out. Not knowing anyone well, she had stood at the edge of a group of girls who she knew came from her dorm, hoping to look like part of them. They were talking animatedly, making their visual forays from the safety of numbers. Her smile was uncomfortable, and she hated her own unsureness.

Then she saw him standing by the main door to the cafeteria, alone. He was taller than most of the other students and very thin. His aloofness caught Kathy's attention immediately. He was gazing impassively at the moving crowd, showing no embarrassing need to be part of it. *Maybe that's because he's older,* she thought. His hair (*was it dark blond or light brown?*) had already started to recede somewhat, and his face had a stern expression that made him seem light years removed from the freshman boys she had seen at registration.

I'd like to be like that, she thought. Her own uncertainty was painful, and she considered leaving, but she couldn't bear to accept her failure to attract. So she stayed another forty-five minutes, moving now and then to a new position, purposefully, as if looking for a friend. When she looked back to where she had seen the tall, self-contained young man, he was no longer there.

After that, she saw him often as he got his mail or stood in line in the cafeteria or passed sacrament at church (they belonged to the 17th ward). If they were near enough to each other to warrant a greeting, she would say "Hi," and he would reply pleasantly, though he never initiated a conversation. Then he was assigned to be home teacher to a group of girls in her dorm, including herself.

It was at that point that Kathy really got to know him. She found that he was indeed self-contained and quiet, a soft-spoken person who rarely laughed aloud. But she soon learned that a certain twist of his narrow lips was a half-smile and that many of his dry, seemingly serious statements were an attempt at humor. She tried to read his eyes for hints as to his feelings, which was only marginally successful; he had a way of "hiding behind his glasses," as she mentioned once to her roommate. He reminded her a little of her father.

The resemblance seemed strongest when he gave the lessons. How well he knew the scriptures, how strict he was in his interpretation, how adamant in defense of them against the attempts at testing that some of the girls indulged in. She herself had thought it might be fun to sleep in one Sunday, to miss church and spend the day puttering around. But the one day she did that, he called her up and made it clear that he expected more from her.

His manner of speaking had irritated her, but at the

same time, it had excited her and made her feel proud. He had noticed her absence—he was concerned about her! She could hardly believe that a returned missionary, a graduate student, would pay attention to a mere freshman.

Still, it wasn't until after Christmas vacation that he asked her out on a real date. With an unbelievable surge of joy, she understood that he had a date in mind, not just a group activity with the "family." They went to a basketball game, and here Kathy saw an unexpectedly lively part of his personality. He was completely involved in the game. Whenever the team made a mistake, she caught explosive bursts of sound that could have been muttered curses (although she assured herself they weren't). He jumped up, yelled encouragement and instructions whenever a drive was on, clapped vigorously, and at times berated the players and coach.

Afterward, she thought he would be somewhat embarrassed at having been so vocal, but he only made a self-deprecating comment and took her by the hand as they walked out into the cold air. Maybe the fact that she had seen him so unreserved at the game had loosened him up a bit, because he seemed more open, smiled more, carried more of the conversation than usual. Kathy was enthralled. She found he was not as grim as she had feared, only highly reserved, very serious, and dedicated to the proposition of perfection.

And he was looking for a wife.

He let her know very soon what that meant. The expectations he held for his future wife were as high as those he held for himself: She should consider her home to be the center of her life; the care of her husband and children, her primary task. She should be willing to have as many children as the Lord would send; she should therefore not have any ambitions for outside employment and only pursue those outside activities that in no way interfered with the running of the home. Her testimony should be strong, and she should be willing to support her husband as a priesthood holder and as head of the household.

Kathy was not overwhelmed by his outline of necessary

qualifications; unable to distinguish between principles of the gospel and the authoritarian, provincial culture sometimes transmitted along with those principles, she considered them to be necessary to a good Mormon home. In any case, such had been the organization of her own family, and she had always assumed that she in turn would be the wife and mother in the same sort of family when the time came. Harboring secret hopes, she began sitting in on courses in child development during spring semester.

The proposal, when it came, filled every romantic expectation she had ever nurtured. In fact, the whole courtship preceding it was like a dream. He sent her flowers, took her to fine restaurants and to concerts (once they heard Eileen Farrell sing in the Tabernacle). There were little cards, unexpected gifts, and telephone calls just to say the words that always surprised her—"I love you." The night of the proposal, he gave her a corsage and took her to dinner at the Hotel Utah. They lingered over their meal, then walked through Temple Square, savoring the peaceful atmosphere within the walls. He proposed to her as they paused under a light, putting a half carat of flashing diamond on her finger.

Only years later did she realize that his romantic behavior had had a practical foundation. If he were courting, he would act like a young man courting ought to act! "I did it right, didn't I?" he asked once, with obvious satisfaction.

Yes, he had done it right. She accepted that March evening, and they began making plans as they strolled around the temple grounds. They were married there three months later, after he had graduated with honors from the MBA program.

It had happened so fast; for all intents and purposes, she had moved directly from her parents' home to Robert's home, from the protection and guidance of her father to the protection and guidance of her husband. Kathy sighed ruefully. During that one semester before she had started dating Robert, she had hardly had a chance to see what it would be like to be on her own. Would things have been different if she had had a chance to find out what she wanted from life, or who she really was?

I've been asking a lot of useless questions lately, she said to herself. *'What if?' is an absolutely useless question. The real question is 'What now?'* It gave her plenty to think about on her way back to the house. It was almost one; her mother would be home from church soon.

The way Kathy and her mother spend the remaining hours of Sunday was almost too natural, too much like any other visit to Bancroft. They ate lunch together, then took a Sunday-afternoon nap. After that, they strolled down to the park, taking the same route Kathy had walked earlier in the day. Then they ate a light supper, and now they were sitting in the living room watching TV. Not one word about the reason for Kathy's visit had been exchanged.

Kathy tried to get interested in the plot of the *CBS Sunday Night Movie,* but it seemed inane. She got up and went to the kitchen for a drink of water, came back for a few minutes, stood up to open a window, and sat down again. The slick mystery movie had all the requisite turns of plot, but it was only make-believe, and the trials of the hero and heroine seemed superficial. Kathy had real problems that were far more pressing. She got up and went for another drink of water.

"Kathy, you've gone to the kitchen for a drink of water five times in the last ten minutes!" observed her mother.

"That's probably exaggerated," laughed Kathy, embarrassed. "But I'll admit to three times in the last fifteen minutes!"

"Is there anything I can do for you?"

"I don't know. It just seems so stupid to sit here calmly watching TV while the whole world's been turned upside down!"

Clarice, in her elderly, flat-footed gait, walked to the set and turned it off. "I suppose you're right," she admitted. "But I didn't really want to talk about it anymore at the moment." Her lower lip betrayed emotion. "It took all the strength I could muster to be calm and reasonable last night. I'm not sure I have any left. If we start talking now, I won't be able to hold onto my feelings." Already her eyes were huge with unshed tears.

"Mother—" began Kathy.

"It's true we haven't been very close all these years. I've regretted that, and so last night I tried to be the understanding mother. But so help me, I don't understand, I really don't! I'm only glad your father didn't have to be in on this. It would have broken his heart to know his 'Princess' was involved in something so ugly, so unspeakable!"

"Mom, please!"

"And how are you going to explain it to the children, tell me that!"

"The children? Why, I'm not going to tell them at all!"

"So you really think you can keep it from them? I don't think so, not for a minute! Especially Brad and Sue. They'll eventually add up what's in front of them and they'll know. You can bet on it!"

"But I don't want them to know! I don't want anyone to know!" The thought of the deed done under cover of darknesss being brought out into the light was terrifying.

Then a new thought brought her upright. "Mom, what will the bishop do? Will they announce anything in church?"

Clarice pulled a handkerchief from her pocket and wiped her eyes. Struggling to regain her composure, she replaced the handkerchief and then looked at her daughter. "I don't understand the workings of the Church very well in such cases. Perhaps everything can be taken care of privately between you and the bishop."

"Perhaps!"

"Kathy, you're aware that there may be a bishop's court, aren't you?"

Kathy groaned.

"That, of course, would be confidential, but things have a way of getting around, even when you're very careful. I think you can count on some people finding out, but how many find out in the end depends pretty much on who you tell in the beginning." She paused, then said, "I really don't think you can keep it from Brad or Sue."

"I feel so sorry for them," Kathy cried.

"So do I. It's a bad age for them. Teenagers take things so hard. And they have enough problems coming to grips with their own . . . sexuality," she finished quickly.

"What will they think of me when they find out? They'll hate me, just like you hate me!"

Clarice touched Kathy's tear-stained cheeks. "I don't hate you, Kathy. I imagine your children will be terribly disillusioned, though. And then angry. It may take a long time, but in the end I think they'll be able to look at you again and be glad you're their mother. The way I'm glad you're my daughter."

"Are you really?" She reached out to Clarice, and they clasped hands tightly. "I wonder if Robert will ever be able to say he's glad I'm his wife. He's not going to take it very well."

"That's an understatement if ever I've heard one!"

Kathy's grip tightened. "Mom, I'm scared."

"Yes, I know," said Clarice. "But I'm glad you are. I'd be much more worried if you were feeling rebellious and brash."

"But what if I can't hold out?"

Clarice looked at the dark head and spoke sharply, "Don't even think such thoughts! Don't even think of giving up before you've taken the first step! Kathy, listen to me! I love you, you're my daughter. You can come to me whenever you need to, do you understand? Or I'll get a bus ticket and come to Lemburg!"

"Oh, thank you, Mom," Kathy managed.

They hugged each other tightly, and then Clarice patted her daughter on the back. "Now, why don't you take a nice hot bath and get a good night's sleep? That way you can leave bright and early in the morning."

"How did you know I wanted to leave tomorrow?"

"That was easy. You've made up your mind to take the

bull by the horns, as it were, and if I know you, right now is already too late. It's 'all or nothing,' 'now or never,' with you!"

"You know me pretty well, don't you," said Kathy, grinning. Then she added regretfully, "It's not been much of a visit, has it?"

"No. But there'll be other visits."

"You're a remarkable woman, do you know that?"

A flush of pleasure brightened Clarice's face. "Thank you. I accept the compliment. Now take your bath!" she said, her smile belying the brusqueness of the command. Then she turned the TV back on, but she couldn't really see anything that was on the screen. The unexpected expression of admiration had brought too many tears to her eyes.

PART TWO

Five

Robert Montgomery was distracted. His face, normally so unreadable, had an expression of mingled disbelief and pain, as if he had just heard the worst and was asking himself over and over again, "But how did it happen, how?" And indeed, that very thought, half-formed, was throbbing within like the beating of a second heart. Still he went about accomplishing his duties with the same dry, professional manner that had brought him to the office he now occupied, that of chief financial officer of Industrial Investments, a large Midwestern corporation. He was dependable, that was for sure; and he had never let family concerns interfere with his effectiveness at work—being effective and successful was a matter of principle.

That he had become so successful was no surprise to anyone who had known him as a weedy, sober-faced child. On the contrary, they would have been surprised to learn that he hadn't. His future success was an accepted fact in Beaver, Utah, the town closest to his parents' ranch.

"I never need to tell him anything twice," marveled his first-grade teacher. "He always knows the answers when I call on him in class" was the report from his Sunday School teacher. "He's going to he the youngest boy in our Scout troop to ever get an Eagle!" exulted the Scoutmaster. And whenever he walked into the feed store, the men assembled there would eye him sharply, repeating predictably the words they had said so often, "You watch that boy—he's a sharp one!"

Then another Levi-clad rancher would usually respond with "James is a lucky fellow. He couldn't hire someone to do all the work that boy of his does."

"Hire someone!" a third would laugh. "He'd have to hire three hands and an accountant besides!"

And it was almost true. Small towns like their legends, and one of the favorites is "Small-Town Boy Makes Good." So they told stories about him, speculated about his future, and basked in the knowledge that even Beaver could produce an important man or two.

His father appreciated the unusual blessing he had had in his firstborn son, Robert. The boy had always been a willing helper, wanting to tag along even before his hair had darkened from baby white to dusty blond. He loved being out in the high mountain ranges, loved being around the animals, and, most especially, loved working alongside his father.

James Montgomery had not been surprised by the first-grade teacher's comment; he had already recognized that quality in his son, and he exploited it while delighting in it. He taught Robert all the workings of the ranch, explaining things in great detail, forgetting that he was addressing a boy. But Robert watched, absorbed, and performed. He grew more capable year by year, something which caused his cousins much grief. "Why can't you be like Robert?" became a refrain they dreaded and hated.

Even so, James's brothers were surprised when James began to bring Robert to their planning meetings. Since the brothers had inherited adjoining ranchland, they had joined together to expedite their work and increase their profits. Robert showed an unexpected grasp of the business aspect of running ranches, partly due to the hours spent with his father on the range and at his desk, and partly due to his native ability. In spite of his youth, his father and uncles gave serious consideration to his suggestions, especially after his predictions in several instances very nearly matched the eventual outcome.

Then, in the spring that Robert turned eighteen, his

father died. The first rain had come early and hard that March, and James had chanced to be in one of the arroyos of the bony southern Utah country when the run-off had filled the gulleys with dirty, raging flood waters. No one ever knew exactly what had happened, and no explanation they could think of made the facts any more understandable. Everyone shook his head, saying, "James was too smart to get caught like that!" But he had. His pickup was located at the bottom of a gulch after the water had abated, and a day later his body was found further down. Thus Robert became the head of his father's household.

Despite the shock, he seemed to have no difficulty taking over that position. The day of the funeral, he returned home and went directly to his father's desk, and from that day on he took the seat at the head of the table. He even advised his younger brothers and sisters in the same tone of voice that his father had used. At that, they rebelled; but their mother said sharply, "You listen to what your brother tells you!" She firmly believed that a man belonged at the head of the table and at the head of the household.

During the months of adjustment following his father's death, Robert cultivated two annoying habits. First, he learned to hold his head so that light would reflect off his glasses and make his eyes unreadable—that way no one could tell what he was thinking. Second, he learned to wait, unreadable behind his glasses, until the silence grew so uncomfortable that the other person would be compelled to talk. At such times, they usually said more than they had intended, giving him the advantage of knowing what they had in mind. He himself never revealed what he was thinking until he was sure his plans would succeed.

This new way of maintaining the upper hand had disappointing results on his siblings. They needed to be handled in a much more straightforward manner. Most of the time, they just laughed at him and said, "Look! Robert's doing it again!" They needed to be handled in a much more straightforward manner. But with adults he found it extremely effective. If he had not been so well liked or if he had not been so solid and dependable, the adults he dealt with in this manner would have turned away from him, angry at such manipulation. As it was, this odd behavior simply became part of the legend, the legend of Robert Montgomery (no one ever thought of calling him Bob.)

His family always assumed that Robert would go to Southern Utah State College at Cedar City after his graduation from high school and that after two years of undergraduate work there, he would go on a mission. He was determined to hold to these plans. In a meeting with his uncles, he laid out a plan whereby his father's ranch could be worked in his absence. He had given consideration to how many cattle he would run and on which ranges, how much hay he and the hired hand could stack themselves (with the help of his little brothers, of course), how much hay would need to be bought, and what the additional feed costs would be. He had already spoken to a young family man who would be willing to move into the little house that had been his grandparents' home and would help the hired man who had been with them for fifteen years. He didn't notice, or chose not to notice, that now and again one of his uncles would clear his throat and that surreptitious winks were making the rounds.

"Robert," said his Uncle Mark, "we can divide up the work among us—Alma, John, and me. There's a good deal we do as a group anyway, and it wouldn't make much more work if we took over James's ranch while you're gone. Especially since you've already spoken to a new man about helping out."

"No. Thank you, anyway," he added stiffly, hearing how abruptly he had spoken.

Thus, in the fall of 1957, satisfied that all had been settled, and with the agreement and blessing of his mother, Robert left as planned for SUSC. He studied more than he actually needed to and, overprepared, had little difficulty getting *A*s and little sympathy for those whose learning came more tediously. On weekends he drove his blue-and-white '51 Ford back to Beaver and to the concerns of the family and the ranch. The first summer he spent on the ranch, but at the beginning of the second summer he got his call to the Eastern States mission.

Two months later he said his good-byes, awkwardly thanking his uncles for agreeing to incorporate his father's ranch into their own holdings during his absence. At his farewell, he shook the hands of the members, nodding as they told him how proud they were that he had managed two years at SUSC and now was leaving for a mission "in spite of everything." He was puzzled, frankly at a loss as to what they were suggesting. He had never questioned whether he would fulfill a mission; he was only doing the inevitable. He was a Mormon—he had been raised on the doctrine of progression. Of course, he would go to college and on a mission!

The two years he spent in New England were happy years for Robert, marred only by the fact that he didn't have as many baptisms as he would have liked. But he was successful at making contacts; his quiet, laid-back manner, his habit of listening, and his unshakable confidence in the rightness of what he was doing made him the perfect messenger of the gospel to the people of the area. Other missionaries plucked the fruit of his labors, sometimes years later, baptizing contacts who had never forgotten "Elder Montgomery" and his message. He came home a bit taller—which made him look even thinner—permeated with a grand feeling that his life was fitting into place exactly. The next phase was to attend BYU with the dual objectives of getting a degree and getting a wife.

The former proved to be far simpler than the latter. He hadn't associated much with girls, and his inability to make small talk and his probing gaze made light flirtation or easy interaction impossible. He hated the way some of the fellows in the dorm took a different girl out every weekend—sometimes working in a date or two during the week as well—trying them out as if they were shoes. He hated the way they discussed their dates over the sinks in the morning. *The way they talk about the merits of various girls is worse than the way old Parkins calls out the virtues of a cow at auction!* he thought disgustedly. When he felt discouraged, he reminded himself that everything in life had a certain order and that when the time was right, the right girl would be there.

The summer after he graduated with a Bachelors in Economics, he enlisted the help of a lawyer and, with his uncles' consent, had the necessary papers drawn up to make the incorporation of all the Montgomery ranches a legal as well as a family matter. "It will give us all tremendous tax advantages," Robert said.

It would also assure the continued smooth running of the ranch, which was important because he had decided to go back to BYU for an MBA and for another, last try at finding a girl, although he would have been offended if anyone had suggested that as a possible motive. He also had the feeling that he would not be coming back to the ranch. His years away from it had opened up his eyes to a wealth of other possibilities in the realm of business, of high finance and power. He liked the idea of someday having ultimate control over something far-reaching and important.

Although he proceeded slowly after he met Kathy Adams, he never doubted whether it was the right time or she was the right girl. She was pretty, with unruly, black, naturally curly hair; snapping dark eyes; and a fresh, unpredictable, frolicsome manner that delighted him while making him feel somewhat stodgy. He liked the way she smiled and the way she threw back her head when she laughed, although he thought it a little unladylike. She was like a young kitten, sure that she was pretty, loved, and that the world was a good place to be. She reminded him of his Aunt Emma.

He had been quite surprised at the relief he felt when he learned that she also had a testimony of the gospel. It was an indication that there was more behind his choice of her than the practical fitting of a new part into the plan. He was drawn to her with a need that was frighteningly physical. To find a wife, to marry her and to have children, that was one thing. To need her presence, to hunger for her quick, impish smile was something quite different. He tried to banish this sign of weakness but wasn't entirely successful. During their courtship he became more open, more impulsive, and certainly more romantically inclined than he had ever been before or after.

He had found his girl. She wanted a good Mormon home and was willing to let him take his place at the head of it. That he ran this new family unit like a corporation was not really surprising; he had been successful at management by objective since he was thirteen years old.

But now he sat at his polished desk, plagued by an unsettling feeling that something was facing him for which he was not prepared. Only rarely had he ever gone to a business meeting uncertain that he would be in control, directing the progress of events. He had that fear now. Kathy had called him from her mother's to let him know she was on her way home and wanted to have a private talk with him that evening.

Kathy had already prepared the supper by the time Robert got home. Although the family ate the meal together and Robert helped Kathy clean the kitchen, they put off speaking about what hovered between them. Neither one wanted to begin until all the children were in bed. Because it was Monday night, they had a short family home evening lesson, then Robert and Kathy played some games with Grant until it was time for him to go to sleep. Brad and Susan both had homework that kept them busy until late. Kathy finally demanded at ten that they go to bed, reminding them of the early hours they had to keep. Then she puttered in the kitchen, and Robert busied himself in the family room until all was quiet.

Finally, as Robert came into the kitchen, Kathy realized that there was nothing more to do, no more evasion tactics that would be successful.

"I've put some logs on the hearth," Robert said. "It's crisp tonight, so I thought we might as well enjoy one last fire."

"Nice," Kathy murmured. At least he had not invited her into his study. She couldn't have stood that. In the family room by the fire was a good place, she thought, irrationally concluding that being warm and comfortable would make what she had to say somehow less devastating.

"Well?" he questioned as they sat contemplating the fire.

The light from the fireplace was bright and glinted off his glasses in an oddly disturbing way. *I'm not going to get any help from him,* Kathy thought. *It's going to be my show entirely.* She felt a sudden rush of panic.

"I really don't want to have this talk," she began in a choked voice. Then in a surge of resolution she blurted out, "I've gotten more involved with Jay than I should be, and I've got to talk to the bishop about it!"

At first Robert didn't speak or move, and in the silence Kathy could almost hear her nerves hum. *Speak! Yell! Scream!* she commanded inwardly.

"I think you've got to talk to me about it first," he finally said. His voice was detached except for a slight overtone of emotion. She stared at him, bewildered. She had been prepared for anything except this. There he was, asking her calmly to tell him about it. *Maybe he doesn't care,* she thought, and the pain she felt told her how important it was that he did care. *Or maybe he had already guessed what I had to tell him.*

A conversation that had taken place in his study some months ago came to mind and confirmed her conclusion.

She had been angry that day and, in a voice filled with bitterness had confronted him. "Why can't I have lunch with Jay if I want to? What's so bad about that? We're friends! If I wanted to have lunch with Myra or Ronnie, you wouldn't object!"

"It's not quite the same," he had replied evenly.

"Oh, but it is," she had retorted.

"Kathy, the Church has made it clear that it is better not

to go alone to places with a member of the opposite sex. They have a reason for taking that stand."

"They just think the worst of people!"

"Well, obviously the worst has happened, even between two Church members, or they wouldn't even mention it, much less instruct brothers and sisters not to drive to meetings with one another unless there's a third person in the car as well."

"Do you really think I'm going to have an affair with Jay?" she had asked scornfully.

He had moved uneasily in his chair. "Kathy, I have to admit that I don't understand your relationship with Jay. I feel very uncomfortable about it." He had paused before looking away from her and, in a rare moment of unguarded emotion, had added, "I feel left out. You share things with him that you don't share with me."

It could have been the beginning of a more personal conversation than they had had in months, but Kathy had ignored the plaintive tone in his voice. "I would share them with you if you were interested! What do you read besides the *Wall Street Journal* and your business publications? When I want to talk to you about something I've been reading, you listen politely for about two minutes and then you start sneaking glances at an article on the stock market! That doesn't do much for me wanting to share anything with you!"

It was as if he hadn't revealed himself at all. In a doubly frosty tone he had stated, "Listen, you restrict your meeting with Jay to rehearsals!"

She had risen out of her chair then, dark eyes glittering with hostility. "Is that a proclamation? Are you telling me what I can and can't do?"

"As your husband I have the obligation and the right to counsel you in this matter."

If she had been less concerned with her indignation and with the need to break out of his restrictive control, Kathy might have recognized that his coldness was merely a defense against emotion he was unable to express. As it was, his flat statement had goaded her to fury. "Robert Montgomery! We've been married in the temple. We have three children. I go to church every Sunday. I teach in Relief Society. Does that sound like the description of a person who runs off with another man?"

"You forget that I have sat in high council courts. It happens to people you might think the least likely, sometimes." She hadn't noticed the sorrow edging his voice.

"Well, it's not going to happen to me, and I resent the fact that you have so little trust in me!" she had shouted, running from the room.

"I wish I had listened to you then," she whispered, more to herself than to Robert. A log slipped and sent sparks flying. One landed on the carpet, and Kathy deftly brushed it onto the hearth, then set the fire screen in place. *Odd that Robert forgot to do this,* she thought.

"When did it happen?" asked Robert in a constricted voice.

"After last week's rehearsal," she replied, trying to be calm and factual.

"That was the only time?"

She bridled. "What do you think I am? Of course it was! I'm not capable of that kind of deceit!"

He was obviously referring to the conversation she had just remembered when he said, "Not so long ago, you didn't think you were capable of doing what you did."

There was nothing she could say to that, so she remained silent until he asked again, "Then it happened only once?"

"Yes! For heaven's sake, yes!"

"Did you plan to sleep with him?" There was only the faintest pause before the word *sleep.*

She felt her face grow hot. "No! No, no, no!" she exclaimed and instinctively moved farther away from the fire.

He drew a heavy breath. "Oh, Kathy."

She began to cry. "I'm so sorry! I never meant for it to go so far!"

"Have you thought about what you want to do?"

"What do you mean?" she sniffled, searching for a Kleenex.

"Beyond talking to the bishop, have you made any plans?"

She looked at him warily. "What kind of . . . plans are you talking about?"

"Do you intend to stay or leave?" He might have been asking whether they were going to have chops or spaghetti for supper.

"Where would I go?" she asked, suddenly childish. "This is my home."

"By getting involved with Jay you broke allegiance with me and the children. You no longer have an assured place in this house."

She gasped with shock. Fear sent prickles up her spine, and she felt faint. How could he turn her out, just like that? She peered at him across the dimly lit room, which was illuminated only by a small milk-glass lamp and the glowing logs, but he was a shadowy figure in the wing-back chair. She couldn't see his knuckles white with tension, had no way of knowing that he was holding himself above a flash flood of emotions by pretending this was only a business meeting, a particularly unpleasant business meeting.

"But Robert," she said in an anguished whisper, "I can't just walk out on the children! I can't just leave!"

"You did that when you went to your mother's. And that's really what you did Tuesday night. You left us then."

"Do I have to go?" she asked so softly that he had to ask her to repeat it. "Do I have to go? Do you want me to go?"

He was silent.

"Don't you love me anymore?" she asked stupidly.

She had wanted some reaction from him since the beginning of the conversation, but now the raw emotion in his voice startled and frightened her.

"Are you joking! The question is, do you still love me? The answer seems to be no."

The doubts that had tortured her for months vanished.

"Oh, I do, I do," she cried, coming to kneel before him. "That's why I'm telling you all this now! I don't want to throw away my marriage and my family!"

"You should have thought about that a week ago," he said, bare hostility vibrating from him. He roughly stood up and walked away, leaving her kneeling before the empty chair. She leaned against the upholstered arm, tears coming freely.

"I wasn't thinking about anything then," she sobbed. "I wasn't thinking at all."

"If you decide to stay," he said, the emphasis on *if,* "it will have to be on my terms."

At that, her hackles rose. "What's so new and different about that? Everything has always been on your terms!"

He ignored her comment. "First and most important, you must promise never to see Jay again."

"But I can't promise that! Every time I go to rehearsal, I'll see him whether I want to or not!"

"You will simply quit going. I've never liked you driving alone at night anyway."

"Please, Robert! It means so much to me!"

"More than your marriage?"

"No," she whispered.

"And there are to be no telephone calls, either."

"I've already put a stop to that. He's called several times since then, and I've refused to talk to him. Don't you see? I don't want a relationship with Jay! I want to be your wife, I want to be with my children!"

Suddenly he was before her, his hands gripping her shoulders like a vise. "Then why, in God's name, didn't you think about us and what you were doing to us before!" The stern lines of his face were melting in the heat of emotion, and the suffering visible there shocked Kathy with its intensity. She shook her head, unable to speak. He pushed her rudely away and with his back to her said, "And you will talk to the bishop."

"I've already said I would."

"You will do everything he tells you to do."

"What do you want me to do, sign something in blood? If I didn't intend to, why would I go in the first place?"

"I don't want you talking to any of your friends about this, either."

"I'm not likely to broadcast what's happened! But what concern is it of yours, anyway! Don't want your reputation hurt, I suppose. Don't want anyone to know that all isn't well in Zion."

His voice was cutting. "I don't want the children to learn about this unless they have to, and I certainly don't want them to hear about it over the back fence."

"Oh. Of course." She felt totally defeated. The fire was down, and the room was gloomy and growing chilly.

"There's no point in talking anymore tonight," he stated, banking the coals.

"I'll sleep down here," she said.

He was quick to reply, "You will sleep in our bed as always. The kids will know something is very wrong if either one of us begins sleeping here."

"Another condition," she murmured as she walked up the stairs. She put on her nightgown quickly and climbed into bed, staying as close to the edge as possible. She closed her eyes and barely breathed as he turned down the covers on his side. Then he got in, as carefully as she had, and they lay in silence, not touching.

Six

Robert lay awake, tense and uncomfortably immobile long after Kathy's breathing had slowed to the deep, even cadence of sleep. He could have changed position, but he was afraid any motion at all would release the urgent need to strike back. He wasn't sure what would happen if he inadvertently touched her. Would he explode into a flurry of blows or would he imprison her in his arms and weep?

The weight of pain that had settled on him was crushing. It would have seemed so to any man, but to one who made a virtue out of denying and repressing emotion, it was enormous. The anger in itself wasn't so unbearable, and the sorrow only a bit worse, but the sudden release of years of doubt and fear threatened to swamp him.

Fear, doubt, and fear of doubt—they were a powerful combination of physical as well as mental anguish. He felt them almost as a mocking presence, could imagine them whispering, "You thought you had banished us to a place of no return. But we have only gone to a place where we could gain strength!"

He had first felt the specter of doubt when he had asked his father a question about the Church and had learned that his father would entertain no questions that began "Why?" No matter what the circumstances, James Montgomery, descendant of Mormon converts who had crossed the ocean and then the plains, never questioned why. He saved his energy for doing—for going on a mission when already a married man with small children, for working on the stake ranch when he was behind in his own work, for giving the last of his family's reserve when the building fund needed extra support.

Robert's mother was the same. Faye Henderson Montgomery, a frail woman whose thin, pale skin hardly seemed an adequate covering for her skeletal frame, could do and did do more in a day than her more robust sisters in Blue Mountain Stake. She knew her duty and she did it—efficiently, quickly, determinedly. The frame ranch house was always spotless, and the vegetable garden was a reproach to less industrious sisters. She was one of those persons for whom order is a need. Brigham Young would never have needed to preach on orderliness and finding things in the dark, had all of the Saints' homes looked like Faye's.

Robert's uncles had envied his father because of the kind of woman he had for a wife. Robert knew this because he had heard them talking together as they leaned against the corral one summer evening.

"I could probably do the same if I had a wife like yours, James . . ." His Uncle John was speaking.

"She's an exemplary woman," agreed Mark.

"Did you see the quilts she took to the Nevilles after the fire? Made up three in a week! Had a little help, of course, but they wouldn't have got done but for Faye," James said proudly.

"And all the donations you give, like supporting the Sprague boy on his mission. Wish I could do the same," sighed John.

"Well, why can't you?"

"Aw, it's Emmie, to tell the truth. She has, well, she has needs, you see. Faye is happy wearing the same dresses year after year and leaving the outside of the house unpainted. But Emmie, she just couldn't do without a couple of new dresses this year."

"And there's the new Packard Bell," reminded Alma with a sly grin.

John blushed. "She loves music, you know. Just has to have it."

"Opera!" groaned Alma, leaning over the fence as if sick.

Robert wanted to come to his aunt's defense, but he was afraid of what his father would say if he were caught listening. So he didn't move from his protected corner of the tack shed.

"Oh, it's not as if Faye doesn't like nice things. She just knows what's important and what isn't." James had puffed up like a rooster.

"Gave you a nice family, too," said Alma. His face was pained. He and his wife had only one child, a pale, puny boy who hated the ranch.

"Yup. In spite of all her troubles. Doctor told us we shouldn't have any more after the third boy came, but Faye, she just knew the Lord had more up there just waitin' to come to us. And she was right. Seven fine children! We outdid the whole bunch of you, all put together! Shouldn't have given up with three, John!" he joked.

"Wasn't my idea. But Emmie had her troubles, too. Remember that time after Marion? She almost died. Then we found out Marion had, well, you know Marion's problems. After that Emmie never did want any more kids. Never did have any visions of someone waiting, like Faye. She's a good woman, but she's not like your Faye!"

Don't say it like that! Robert had wanted to cry out.

It was true, Aunt Emma was not like his mother, but he treasured her difference. Tall, thin, and dark, she had flashing eyes and a quick temper ("There's got to be some Spanish somewhere in your genealogy," his Uncle John would joke) but also a rich, warm laugh, and when she hugged him, she was soft. That always puzzled Robert; she wasn't much fuller of figure than his mother, yet she had a way of cushioning him in her arms. Best of all, she wasn't desperately serious, furiously clean, or determinedly saintly. And she never used the phrase upon which he had been weaned: "That's not too much to ask from someone whose ancestors crossed the plains."

He had heard it almost daily, it seemed. It kept him

working on glorious fall Saturdays when his eyes kept turning to the hills and his thoughts to his horse. It shamed him when his parents were told by neighbors that he had been one of a group who had tipped over the inevitable outhouse. It kept him dressed in jeans and plain shirts when all his schoolmates were wearing a more expensive plaid. It made life simple: there were not many choices for someone whose ancestors had crossed the plains!

It became a chant, and like any often repeated phrase, it could induce a certain state of mind, a readiness to conform and to obey. Over the years, its power became such that it was not necessary to say the whole phrase. Just the first part had the desired effect: "That's not too much to ask . . ."

And it applied to spiritual matters as well. It was not too much to ask of pioneer descendants that they believe without question. Their ancestors had recognized the truth, had been baptized despite opposition, had lived through the dark days of the martyrdom, and had followed Brigham Young to the Salt Lake Valley in search of Zion. One didn't just ignore their suffering, one accepted it and their belief as part of one's inheritance. Rather like a young Jew shouldering his Jewishness, one shouldered one's Mormonness.

His father need not have responded to his youthful intellectual explorations the way he did, however. It wasn't necessary to remind Robert of his duty to believe—Robert wanted to believe. He longed for things spiritual, hungered for truth, had an everpresent desire to see eye to eye. The questions he asked were not challenges; his belief would not have been shaken by honest examination, or by admitted doubt. Lack of intellectual explanation for the mysteries of God and admission of human fallibility among the Saints would not have troubled him. But his father's refusal to even discuss such questions began to undermine his certainty. He began to ask himself another *why: Why doesn't Dad want to talk to me about such things?*

He began to fear that perhaps the gospel, which was so sweet to his soul, was spun sugar, fluff that would melt in the summer sun. Then it was that he grabbed onto the hated phrase and held tightly. He would ask no more questions. He would look neither to the left nor to the right. He would keep on going, straight down the marked path, no matter what came into view. It was not too much to ask . . .

His Aunt Emma was the one who had noticed the new, grim set to his mouth and the absence of the spark that had livened his oddly colorless eyes.

"What's the matter, youngster?" she had asked one day, patting the cushion beside her in invitation. Her own three children, younger than Robert, were out swimming in the stock pond; she was glad of the company. "You look pretty humorless these days," she added.

"There doesn't seem to be much use for humor at our place," he replied.

"There might not be much use for it, but there's a terrible need for it," she replied, smiling.

She had been sitting in the middle of what his mother would have termed a mess, knitting and listening to Beethoven's Seventh, looking very bohemian for a rancher's wife in a shocking pink blouse and flowered skirt. Her hair was in an exotic pile on her head. She either didn't notice or didn't care that a pile of dishes was heaped in the sink, that papers were stacked on the table by the couch, and that the counter was filled with pans of milk, which at home would have been mounds of butter and jars of buttermilk by now. But flowers decorated the windows, and a delicious smell came from the oven, and there was Aunt Emma, unhurried, content and smiling.

"I wish I could be like you," he said, turning away to hide an unmanly quiver in his chin. "You seem to be so happy all the time. You like what you're doing. You know how to have fun!"

"James and Faye have managed to squeeze all the juice out of living, haven't they?" she commiserated. "That's too bad. They'll get through life all right, but they won't enjoy the trip."

He forgot about trying to be grown up. At fourteen he was unusually mature, but at that moment he wished he were little enough to fit on her lap again. He leaned against her shoulder and said in a cracking voice, "They don't even seem happy about the gospel. They make it so hard and cold."

"Listen, Robert," said Emma, "some people believe in suffering. I don't myself, but your parents do. They're good people, don't misunderstand me, dear. The very best. But they believe in looking for trials and troubles as God's proof that he loves them. Sounds kind of dumb, doesn't it?" She smiled down at him. "Why, I've even heard them say that if you don't have troubles, you should ask God to send you some. Fools!" Her voice was suddenly full of bitterness, and Robert wondered if she weren't also talking about her husband, Uncle John. "All a body has to do is stop looking for imagined troubles, and the real ones will step right up to introduce themselves." She arose from the couch and turned to face him.

"How do you do, Ma'am? Strife between Husband and Wife come to pay a visit!" She bowed low, her hand sweeping to the ground, so that Robert could almost visualize a plumed hat.

"And I have brought with me Difficulty in Learning. He is the special guest of your third child, Marion. And to complete the trio, Arthritis. He's your special visitor, Ma'm. He's ugly, I know, but you'll get to know him well and perhaps someday accept him as a permanent member of the family."

Robert couldn't keep his eyes from focusing on her hands, the large knuckles already showing signs of her illness. He smiled weakly.

"Sorry if I wasn't very funny," she said, tousling his hair as she took her seat again. "I meant it to be. Don't pay any attention to me—I get carried away once in a while. It's the old affliction, you know. I was pretty stagestruck when I was young." She sat back down beside him and took up her knitting.

"Aunt Emma?"

"What is it, dear?"

"If I don't look for any imaginary problems and I don't have any real ones, at least not any real big ones, is it all right for me to be happy?"

She was fierce in her reply. "Yes, it's all right to be happy, even if you have problems, big ones! There's always something to be happy about. I can find something to smile over every day. Robert, I don't know that my life's turned out the way I wanted it to, but I'm satisfied with what I have. I'm grateful to the Lord for each new day, and I try to enjoy every minute."

After such a long speech she patted his arm and suggested a hot roll with butter and honey, thinking that she might have said too much. Besides, her nose told her they were just about done. He was on his third roll when he asked her another question that had been bothering him.

"Aunt Emma, what do you do about things like the Mountain Meadows massacre and the negro and the priesthood and stuff like that?"

"Nothing," she said, buttering a roll for herself. "They don't have much to do with the things I hang onto."

"You mean you just forget about them?"

She smoothed the jet-black hair that was beginning to grey dramatically. She spoke slowly. "I guess you might say that. There're lots of things in the history of the Church that we don't know too much about. Some pretend they didn't even happen, and some Mormons get highly upset at the suggestion that Church leaders can be less than perfect, that some mistakes were made. It seems kind of beside the point to me. Not that I go in for white-washing, mind you, but fussing about those things makes a person forget what a testimony is. It's knowing Joseph Smith was a prophet and that the Book of Mormon is scripture.

"And here's another example for you. Investigators or even members who try to prove Joseph Smith was a prophet by studying history are going about it all wrong. They need to read the Book of Mormon. If they do that, and they're humble, they'll get a witness that it's scripture. Then they'll know Joseph was a prophet, and no matter what they hear or read in the future, they'll never question that."

"I know he is—I'll never question it," said Robert proudly.

"You just use that as your foundation, hon. Stand right on that knowledge and don't forget that the gospel is really pretty simple: 'God so loved the world, that he gave his only begotten Son, that whosoever believeth in him should not perish, but have everlasting life.'"

"But there're so many things you have to do to get into the celestial kingdom! That doesn't seem simple to me!"

"No," she sighed. "I know what you mean. We have a problem with that, your Uncle John and I. He's like your mom and dad. They're all so concerned with doing good works, they forget about grace. I do my best to keep the commandments and do what is asked of me, but truthfully, I can't bring myself to worry about it all that much! Because actually there's only one thing that matters: love!"

"What!" He was shocked.

"Now I'm really going to be in trouble!" she said, near laughter. "You know, I'm considered the resident heretic in our ward. You'd better not go around telling your mom and dad everything or I'll be drawn and quartered!

"Listen, dear boy. I love the Lord, I love the scriptures, and I love having the Spirit with me. I always try to do whatever the Spirit prompts me to do. That makes me happy, and my love for the Lord grows even more. In fact, I feel a whole lot of love for everyone and everything around me. And that's the best I can do. Love the Lord and my neighbor, and try to obey the Spirit. I only hope the good Lord will think that's enough. I sure won't get to heaven on my merits as a housekeeper!"

"I think it's enough!" he cried, hugging her. But his heart hurt. *Oh, Dad,* he cried inwardly, *Why couldn't you have told me that!*

He tried to remember the part about love in the days and months after that, but the orientation of his parents was too strong an influence. The sober mask became habitual. Once, when he caught himself saying "It's not too much . . ." to his little brother, Abe, who was struggling with a bale of hay, he stopped in shocked surprise. He almost reached over to help him get the bale to the manger, but the momentary feeling of compassion faded. Instead of giving his brother a hand, he drove home the lesson he had been taught over the years. Then he went back to his own chores, feeling angry for being soft, and justified himself in leaving the boy to deal with the frustrating task alone.

A decision had been made, though he didn't know it. But his Aunt Emma did, noting with sadness that he didn't come to visit as much any more.

The phrase became his own, then. He began to say it to himself when assailed by moments of doubt, worry, or exhaustion. It was his support when his father died, making it possible for him to undertake the heavy responsibility of running the ranch. Many of the things that others thought were easy for him were actually accomplished only because of it. Each repetition made a link, and the links formed a chain, and the chains built a fence. And behind the fence, he hid away the emotions and thoughts that made him feel uncomfortable or vulnerable or that he felt slowed down his progress. He didn't realize that he had put tolerance, warmth, patience, and humor behind it as well. Like his parents, he didn't really believe that "Men are, that they might have joy." If someone had asked him whether he were happy, he would have rejected the question as unproductive.

But the fence, which had held up so many years, was buckling; and in the darkness, stiff and fatigued, he struggled to shore it up against the heavy, oppressive burden of the word, *why*.

Seven

Kathy woke in the morning stiff from having slept in the same position for so long. She turned and saw Robert standing in front of the window, looking out into the grey dawn. The eastern sky was lighter than usual at this time of the morning; the days were getting longer.

She wanted to say something to him, but "Good morning" seemed a little ridiculous, so she said nothing. She got up, called the older kids, then came back to dress.

"If you're not going back to bed, I'll make it," she said.

He didn't turn. "Go ahead. I can't sleep anyway."

She stood looking at him for a moment, then went down to get the kids' lunches. They could make their sandwiches themselves, of course, but it was something she wanted to do for them. When Brad and Sue were younger, she had insisted that they make their own lunches, saying that they should learn to take care of such things. Now, she chose to make them herself, a loving service for her teenagers, who would not be at home much longer.

In accordance with Robert's instructions, she tried to go through the morning routine as usual. She made little comments, joked with Sue and asked Brad when he was bringing his girlfriend over.

"Which girlfriend," he asked, counting them on his left hand. But Sue was looking at her quizzically. *Perhaps I'm overdoing it,* Kathy thought. It was clear to her that her mother was right—they would find out. *Oh, Lord, give me some time,* she prayed.

After everyone had gone, Kathy made two phone calls. First she called the secretary of the Parker-Jeffry Chorale to tell her that because of family considerations she would not be able to continue singing with the group. She felt as if she had deliberately cut off a finger. Singing filled an inner space in a way that nothing else could, but she could not continue singing with the group under the circumstances.

The next call was more unpleasant—to Bishop Mangus at his place of work.

"Bishop Mangus, this is Sister Montgomery. I'm sorry to bother you at work, but I need to talk to you."

"Is it something you can talk about over the phone?" he inquired.

"No. What I really called for is an appointment."

"Well, I'll be in the building on Thursday after Mutual, if you'd like to come in then."

"I'm sorry to have to ask you to come in at a separate time, but I'd much rather not come when other people will be there. And I need to talk to you sooner. It's quite important."

"Can you come to my office tonight?"

"Oh!" *Tonight! So soon!* she thought, and then she caught hold of herself and replied, "Yes. Yes, thank you. What time should I . . . ?"

"Come around 7:30."

"I'll be there," she said and hung up the receiver.

I've got a few more days, maybe even a week before the kids will have to be told, she thought. *But please, let things get all worked out without having to tell them!*

However, that very afternoon, her daughter said something to make her realize again that she would have to tell them. She had been working in the kitchen when she suddenly noticed the scraps of paper on the bulletin board with "Call Jay" on them; she had forgotten to take the messages down. She quickly removed the papers from the corkboard and was in the process of throwing them away when she heard Sue's voice, "Have you called him back, Mom? He called at least a dozen times before you left for Grandma's."

"No. I never got around to it."

"But don't you think you ought to? It's rude not to return a call. Besides, it might be important!"

"Not any more," Kathy said flatly.

"He loves you, doesn't he?"

Kathy felt the room lurch, and her eyes flew to her daughter's face. But there was no trace of the knowing and disgust she had expected to find there.

"What makes you say that? We're friends, but nothing more."

"Oh, just the way he looked at you the other night after the concert. I wish someone would look at me that way sometime. Someone that handsome, too. With my luck, the boy with the most pimples will be the one hanging around!"

Kathy laughed too loudly, relieved beyond belief. "Oh, my dear! Don't be in a rush. It will happen one day, and by the time you're old enough to take it seriously, all the boys you know will be long out of the pimple stage!"

"Do you like Eric Lucas?" asked Sue, looking carefully at the pencil she was turning with her fingers.

"Yes, he seems to be a nice boy."

"A nice boy," mimicked Sue.

"What's wrong with being a nice boy, for heaven's sake?"

"Oh, I don't know. It's just that romance is supposed to be exciting, but all Eric can think of doing is going to school baseball games and McDonald's afterward. Or to a movie or a Church dance." Her voice quickened. "Mom, do you remember that musical we went to at the university last year, *The Fantasticks?*"

"I remember there was a song or two I didn't approve of!"

"I'm not talking about those songs. But there was this one song the girl sings about wanting romance . . . You remember the words—something about not being evil but a little wordly wise, the kind of girl designed to be kissed upon the eyes. That's what I want, something exciting and romantic."

"Susan, that's dangerous." Kathy was facing her daughter, speaking earnestly. Something of her own longings were being voiced by this child, and it disturbed her greatly.

"Dangerous? What do you mean?"

"The excitement, the romantic evenings, the sort of things you see on TV or in the movies isn't real."

"You mean nobody ever has that kind of romance?"

"No. That's not quite what I mean. I'm not so far away from those feelings as you might imagine," Kathy said, picking her words carefully. "I know what you're talking about. But the notion of being swept away with emotion or carried off by Prince Charming, the idea that the whole world changes in an instant just because someone has looked at you a certain way, that's not love, Susan."

Susan gave a small sigh. "It might not be love, but it sure must be nice."

"For that one moment, but not for the long run." Kathy's voice was bitter. She wondered what Susan would think when she found out that her own mother had succumbed to the very longings she herself was feeling.

Susan's next question caught her by surprise. "But don't you feel that way about Daddy?"

"I suppose I did, a long time ago when we were first married. But that part doesn't seem to stay. Something more practical, more steady holds people together after the first flush."

"Ugh. That sounds cold and boring and, uh, old." Susan blushed as she said the last word.

"Old and with all the fires burned out, huh?" Suddenly, Kathy wanted to tell her daughter that she was still capable of falling in love with all the fervor of a first romance and was just about to say something when the shock of realization prevented her from speaking.

She was proud, *proud* of what had been between herself and Jay! At least up to that last night and, she realized with horror, maybe even including it. It was confirmation that she was still attractive and desirable. The words she had been saying to Susan were coming from her head, not her heart.

"Mom?" Susan's hand was on Kathy's shoulder, her face questioning. "Hey, I'm sorry if that sounded rude. Don't take it so personally."

"Don't worry about it," Kathy said, recovering. She straightened up and looked gravely at Susan.

"Promise me something. If Eric asks you out to another Church dance, go with him. Enjoy a simple relationship, friend to friend. Don't think McDonald's hamburgers are silly. Actually, they're quite nice!"

"Mom! I thought you hated McDonald's! And don't worry. I'm not going to do anything stupid. I really do like Eric—he's not so bad, even if he is a bit dull."

And she began telling Kathy what they had done after school together. Kathy listened absently, finding it impossible to focus on what was being said. The coming appointment at the bishop's office filled her consciousness, the way a throbbing wound blocks out awareness of any other part of the body.

For the rest of the afternoon and early evening time passed quickly, too quickly, yet at the same time, too slowly. She was relieved when the clock finally read seven and she had to get ready to leave. She put on her sweater and walked into the family room for a last-minute check on the kids.

"Hey, where are you going?" asked Grant, grabbing onto his mother's sweater.

"I'm just going over to the chapel for a few minutes. I have to talk to the bishop."

"Bet he'll ask you to be den mother or something," joked Brad. "Maybe even Relief Society president!"

"No, I doubt it," returned Kathy evenly. "Grant, you be sure to hop into bed at eight-thirty, okay?"

"I'll make sure he goes to bed on time," offered Robert, coming into the room. He walked out into the garage with her. "Are you sure you don't want me to go with you?" he asked in a low voice. It was the first time he had spoken to her that day.

"Thank you, but I'd rather go alone."

"If you're not up to driving home afterward, call me."

"I will," she said. Then she laughed slightly. "At least you're still worried about me. After last night, I was afraid you hated me."

Something moved in his eyes. "I don't hate you, Kathy."

"But you don't love me anymore."

He turned away. She waited a moment longer, and when he didn't say anything, she got into the car and drove out of the garage.

The light was on in the bishop's office when she drove up to the chapel. She parked the car and climbed out. "Here goes," she said grimly, but the fear she had been able to handle during the day crashed over her. *Why am I doing this?* she cried silently. *I don't have to put myself through this!*

No, came the inner answer. *You don't have to walk through the door if you're willing to give up the solemn warmth of sacrament meeting; if you're willing to give up your family; if you can convince yourself that what you have done is no sin. You can turn around right now if you can live with things the way they are.* She nearly ran into the building and up the hall, pausing before the door of the bishop's office to catch her breath. She resolutely knocked.

Bishop Mangus called out, "Come in." As she opened the door, she saw him coming around the desk to greet her. He shook her hand firmly, then invited her in again. Barely taller than herself, the bishop had a David O. McKay-ish mane that made him seem taller, an effect amplified by his erect carriage. He moved gracefully, purposefully, carrying his mature years well. His full cheeks were still youthful, and there were only a few fine lines around his eyes. His face was open and readable; and his love and concern for her now were obvious.

"Sit here," he said, indicating a chair drawn up comfortably to the side of the desk. She was grateful he hadn't asked her to sit in front of the desk. She knew a desk could be used as a symbol of power and authority and that the single chair placed before it offered precious little support. She had learned that in the "interviews" Robert had had with her from time to time.

"Your phone call sounded urgent," he began, after they had taken their seats. "What can I do for you?"

Kathy lowered her eyes. "This is hard," she whispered. "I don't . . . I . . ." She stopped, clearing her throat before trying again. "I've done something awful." Her voice trailed away.

He leaned toward her and smiled gentle encouragement. "Kathy, before you go on, let me tell you that as your bishop, I will keep confidential anything you say. And remember that as your bishop and friend, I'll do everything I can to help you with your present difficulties."

"You'll think I'm terrible," she said, as if she were a child seeking reassurance.

"I'll think you're human," he said quietly. "Tell me when you're ready to," he added, leaning back in his chair.

She couldn't look at him and speak at the same time, Kathy found. Her eyes dropped again. "I've gotten involved . . . with another man," she said, so softly he had to strain to listen.

"Sister Montgomery, I'm not sure I heard you correctly. I'm sorry to have to ask you, but would you please repeat what you said?"

She raised her head and spoke clearly. "I've gotten involved with someone."

The mixture of love and compassion that radiated from him was painful in its intensity, but it didn't prevent him from being blunt. "Will you be specific about the nature of your involvement?"

"I've been with another man," she said, still seeking for less bald words.

The bishop restated the sentence in just the words Kathy had been seeking to avoid: "You mean you've had sexual intercourse with someone other than your husband."

"Yes," she whispered, rummaging in her purse for a tissue. He took one from the box on his desk and handed it to her automatically. The thought came that he must do that quite often.

"Kathy, I am going to have to ask you some questions.

Some of them you might not like to answer, but I need more information so that I can get a clear picture of what has happened."

She nodded in reply.

"How often have you repeated this action?" was his first question.

I might have known, she thought. *It's the first thing both Mom and Robert asked.* "It happened only once," she said aloud.

"How long ago was that?"

"A week ago, exactly. Last Tuesday night."

"Have you spoken to your husband about it? Does he know why you are here this evening?"

"Yes. I told him last night."

"Have you seen this man since the night in question?"

"No. I mean, yes. Just once. He came to the house the morning after. I told him we had nothing to say to each other. I haven't seen him or spoken to him since."

"Will you tell me who he is and how you met him?"

"His name is Jay Enders. He lives in Cedardale. He's also a member of the Parker-Jeffry Chorale—that's how I got to know him."

"Is he a Church member?"

"No."

"Is he married?"

"No. He was, but he's been divorced for quite a few years. He and his wife never had any children."

"Hmmm. So you would see him when you went to rehearsals?"

"Yes. And then, we'd go out to eat afterward."

"Alone?"

"No, not at first. But then we did start going by ourselves."

"That was at night, I assume."

"Yes. Practice was usually over about 9:30. By the time we'd get to a restaurant and order, it would be about ten."

"And after the meal?"

"We'd stay and talk for a while, then I'd drive home myself."

"What time would that usually be?"

"Eleven or so."

"So you would go to a restaurant, just the two of you, late at night. Was it a well-lighted or an intimate place?"

Kathy felt some surprise at the question and had to think before she could answer it accurately.

"I think at first we went to places like Pancake House or other busy, well-lighted places. But . . . I guess that changed after a while." She paused, amazed that the nature of their meetings had altered so subtly that she hadn't been alerted to the change. "I didn't notice it—I didn't even think about it until now," she continued.

"Who suggested the more intimate places," he queried, leaning forward slightly.

Kathy looked at him, at a loss for words. "I don't really know," she said finally. But her thoughts flew back to the week before. She herself had suggested they go to the small soup-and-sandwich shop on University Avenue, where the seating included booths softly lit by antique tulip wall lamps.

"I did, last week," she found herself saying. "But before that, I honestly don't remember."

"At the conclusion of these evenings, was there any physical contact?"

Kathy didn't answer for a moment. She was beginning to see the picture that was developing as she answered his questions. It was clear and sharp; there was no impressionistic blurring of the edges. She didn't like it. "Yes," she said, though she had to force herself to say it. She tried to lessen the damning quality of her admission by adding, "You know, some people are touchers. I could name members of our ward who are. They hold your hand a long time after shaking it in welcome. Or hold onto your arm or give you a hug or kiss. Jay is like that. He just likes to make contact, I guess."

But even as she spoke, she knew she was not saying all that could be said. She was putting all the blame on Jay, neglecting to mention how she had wanted him to touch her, had waited for the brush of his hand against hers, attracted by the very smell of him, a mixture of fresh, lime-ish aftershave and something musky and masculine that was simply Jay.

"What was the nature of the contact?"

Kathy tried to focus on what he was asking. "He'd put his arm around my shoulder or take my arm as we were going to the car. Sometimes he'd kiss my cheek."

He seemed to read behind her words, and Kathy shifted position uncomfortably. *Why did everything sound so different now?* She felt like crying out, "It wasn't what you think!" but the strength of her need to protest confirmed that the picture taking shape was accurate. She only hoped that as they kept talking, perspective and shading would be added to the stark outline now visible.

"Tell me what you talked about when you were together."

"Everything," she said simply. "Politics, current events, books we had both read, philosophy. It was so easy to talk to him."

"Did you talk to him about your family or the Church?"

"Yes . . ." Kathy hesitated. "I guess I talked to him quite a bit about Robert."

"What about Robert?"

Again she ducked her head. "I guess I talked to him about all the things that were bothering me."

"And had you talked to Robert about those same things?"

"A million times," she said bitterly. "But it didn't change anything."

Bishop Mangus had the odd habit of tugging at his nose when he was thinking; now he hooked the first finger of his left hand over his nose and made that curious gesture. "Kathy, if your daughter came home from a date and recounted to you what you have just recounted to me, how would it seem to you?"

Kathy closed her eyes and imagined Susan sitting on a kitchen stool, eyes animated, telling her about "this neat, romantic restaurant we went to, kind of dark, but not too dark. There was soft music playing and hardly anybody was there but us. We had something to eat, but mostly we just talked and talked. Mother, I've never talked so much with someone in my life! We just seem to know what each other is thinking and feeling, and (she would blush slightly here) as we left the restaurant, well, he gave me a little kiss. Just a little one, Mom, but I can tell he likes me, he really likes me!"

Her voice was shaky as she said, "I would think that it was terribly intimate."

"And how long have you been meeting with Jay in this intimate fashion?"

"Five months, I'd say."

"Five months!" His voice was incredulous. "Did Robert know about this?"

"Well, not all about it, but I did tell him we were getting a bite to eat after rehearsals."

"And did he go along with it?" he asked, eyebrows raised.

Shame inundated her. "I didn't tell him we were not going with the group anymore," she said.

"But he was aware of the fact that there was some sort of relationship between you and this man?"

"Yes. Robert knew he was my friend. I introduced him to Jay after a concert about a year ago. Once we all went out together after a concert; Brad and Susan were there as well. And sometimes, not often, Jay would call me at home, and we would talk for a while on the phone. I always told Robert about those calls."

"Did he ever express concern about this relationship?"

"Yes. He didn't like the idea of me having a man for a friend. He told me that I should come home directly after rehearsals."

"In spite of the fact that you hadn't told him about the private meetings, he was worried?"

"Yes."

"And what did you say to that?"

Kathy's voice dropped almost out of hearing range. "I told him I could take care of myself and that he was silly to worry about something so harmless."

Bishop Mangus's voice was heavy. "Kathy, would you say that you had been warned about the danger of the course you were pursuing?"

She nodded reluctantly.

"Didn't you have any doubts yourself?"

"I remember thinking Jay was on my mind too much, while Robert wasn't on it at all."

"Did you ever consider putting an end to it?"

Kathy pulled at the ragged tissue. "I thought about it once in a while, but I couldn't bear the thought of never being able to talk to him like that again! He made me feel pretty and smart and fun to be with. He was interested in me in a way Robert wasn't."

"Yet you haven't seen him since the incident. Whose decision was that?"

"Partly mine, partly Robert's. But I had already made up my mind not to see him again. There's nowhere our relationship can go."

"And how do you feel about that?"

The fragile facade of control crumbled completely. Tears gushed down her cheeks as sorrow and longing deluged her. When she could finally trust her voice, she whispered, "I feel so lonesome!"

"Do you love him?"

She managed a crooked smile. "I don't know. I . . . loved the fact that he loved me."

"Are you considering leaving your husband for this man?"

"No! That would mean leaving my family and the Church. I'm not willing to give all that up for love," she said, attempting lightness.

Bishop Mangus was not smiling. "You would stay with Robert in a home without love, then?"

She nodded.

"You would lose all you long for in such circumstances. There is no home or family or gospel without love."

"What should I do?" she asked pleadingly. "I'm willing to do anything."

His round cheeks seemed to have sunk during the interview, and he looked infinitely sad as he said, "Considering what you have told me tonight, Sister Montgomery, I have no other recourse but to convene a bishop's court. There are circumstances in this case that need careful consideration. Are you willing to meet with me and my counselors?"

Blood began to seep where Kathy's nails drove into her flesh. "Yes," she managed.

He came to sit beside her and took her hand. "It sounds quite frightening, I know. Bishop's court! I think that's because we associate the word *court* with punishment. But the purpose of such a court is not to punish. It is to determine the seriousness of the offense and what course of action will help the person to complete the process of repentance. The whole object, in fact, is to assist in the repentance process."

"But there is a punishment. People get . . . disfellowshipped or even excommunicated!"

"Yes, I suppose that could be looked at as a punishment. Actually, it is a blessing. A person whose transgression is of such a nature that disfellowship or excommunication is indicated would only make his situation worse by continuing to take part in Church ordinances as if nothing were wrong. For those who have a real desire to repent, it offers a chance to wipe the slate clean, to put things right with the Lord and to come back with a pure heart to full activity."

"It still seems like punishment to me. The gift of the Holy Ghost being taken away, for instance."

"Kathy, the Spirit leaves all who transgress. It's the unavoidable consequence of sin, isn't it?"

She couldn't speak, feeling all too keenly the truth of his words.

"When a person is excommunicated, the gift of the immediate presence of the Spirit that he receives at confirmation is forfeit. However, that doesn't necessarily exclude all contact with the Spirit during the probation time."

She sighed. "How many people make it through the probation time and are reinstated?" she asked. Her real question was far more personal: Do you think I'll make it through this?

He sensed the question she had not asked and replied carefully, "The percentages are not good, Kathy. But you have come to me on your own initiative, which is in your favor. If you will humble yourself and accept whatever is required for complete repentance, you will one day sit in this office with a smile on your face. I promise you."

Eight

"Well?" Robert asked as she walked into the family room.

"There's going to be a bishop's court," she said in an exhausted voice.

"I thought as much."

"And can you predict the outcome?" She was too tired to be sarcastic.

"Yes. I think so."

"Well, what will it be? Tell me now and save me the bother."

"I imagine you will be excommunicated."

She dropped into the nearest chair. "Why that instead of being disfellowshipped?"

He hesitated only slightly before saying, "I think the bishop will have to take that action because you were warned that you were heading for trouble. But the fact that you went to him yourself is a good sign. Most of the time, the person who has transgressed doesn't come at all."

"Oh. What if I hadn't gone in?"

"I would have," he said flatly.

"It can get started that way, too? I didn't know."

"Most cases are brought in by the person's family, actually."

She put her hands behind her head and stared at the ceiling.

"Brad will hear it announced in priesthood meeting, won't he?"

"No. Excommunications are no longer announced."

Robert had been looking at the cold ashes in the fireplace; now he looked at Kathy. "But he does need to know what's happened, and he needs to hear it from you."

She sat bolt upright. "Robert! I can't tell him! How could I possibly tell him?"

"Is the alternative of having him find out from someone else any better?"

"No." She hesitated. "You won't . . ."

"Absolutely not!"

Kathy closed her eyes and leaned her head on her hand. "It gets worse and worse, doesn't it?"

"For me, it will never be worse than the moment I knew you had betrayed me!"

Something in his voice caught her attention; she raised her head to look at him. His blue eyes were directed right at her, the contact immediate and searing. She could feel hatred flowing across the room, and she crossed her arms in a gesture of protection. He had not allowed himself any show of feeling while the children were present, but now the full force of his emotion filled the room.

"You know, I did everything I could to make you happy. I've worked night and day to get where I am, just so I could provide for you and the kids. I never once thought of myself. And what do you do in exchange? Make love in the back seat of a car!"

Anger and guilt made her reckless: "Wrong. But I can tell you the exact time and place and all the details if you really want to know!"

The sound that came from between clenched teeth was half groan, half growl. "You're unbelievable! When you first told me, I thought we could work it out somehow, but now I'm not sure. Maybe the best thing for you to do is to pack your bags and leave. I'm sure Jay would take you in—it is Tuesday, after all!"

She blanched. "At least he cares about me!"

"And all I've done in the last eighteen years doesn't count as caring?" He swore, slamming his fist down on the arm of the chair. "I wish you had told me that before!"

"You would have done it all, married to me or not. You have a picture of what life is supposed to be like painted on your glasses! You're so blinded by that picture, you can't see the real world!"

"I think I see much more of the real world than you do. Your idea of what's real comes from 'the 3-Gs' and soap operas. In fact, this little scene would fit nicely in any one of your favorites!"

"At least there's a little love in my world! Yours is made of stone-cold commitment!"

He didn't respond at first, then answered slowly, "Yes, I guess I do live my life by my commitments. My commitment to the Lord, to the Church, and to my family. And my commitment to you," he finished. The rage had dissipated; the eyes were no longer blue but grey and lifeless. "That's the one thing that gives purpose to going through this hell you've made for us both: the commitment we both made at the altar in the Salt Lake Temple. You may have decided to disregard those promises, but I haven't. Forget what I said about leaving. It doesn't even come into question. We're going to get through this even if it kills us!"

Kathy had the distinct impression that it probably would.

Long after Kathy had gone up to bed, Robert sat alone in the family room. His speech about commitment was still warm in his mouth, but that warmth did not radiate to the rest of him. Her taunt about "stone-cold commitment" had stuck in his craw because, right now, it was accurate. He did feel stone cold. All his life he had worked hard, moving forward unswervingly, doing what he felt was required of him as husband and father and priesthood holder; and now she was telling him all his efforts had been worthless! He could hardly comprehend that they didn't mean to her what they meant to him. If there were no value to the way he had provided for his family and the way he had performed every Church job he had been called to, then what was of value?

He was stunned that his whole life's work should be called into question just when his goals were finally within reach. He had begun quiet negotiations with a west-coast company that wanted him to join them at a substantial increase in salary; his oldest son, a fine student and athlete, was planning on a mission; his own calling to the high council had opened up a new realm of spiritual experiences and brought him into close contact with men whose association he valued. The thought that he might have to tell President Sheehey that he must resign was crushing.

As he surrendered momentarily to the feeling of loss, an inner gate cracked open, and he felt something alien move within. "What?" he gasped as the unfamiliar force of pure emotion rushed through him. He struggled against the onslaught, marshaling his intellectual forces and issuing commands until he could finally breathe normally again. Then he relaxed his white-knuckled grip on the arms of the chair, rose, and moved toward the stairs. He had to get some sleep—he had a full schedule in the morning. But he got only as far as the steps before a strange tightness between his shoulder blades stopped him. It extended across his left shoulder and down into his left arm, where it faded into a tingly feeling not unlike that caused by jamming one's funny bone. He held his breath and waited, but instead of increasing, the tightness relaxed into tingling and faded away. Then Robert Montgomery went up to bed.

Jay Enders was disappointed. He stood on the steps of Old Church and watched the members of the Parker-Jeffry Chorale as they left the building. He wasn't sure why he didn't go directly to his car; there was no reason to stay any longer. Kathy hadn't come, that was all there was to it. Standing on the steps was foolish—as people stopped to ask about Kathy, he found it necessary to answer, "Yes, I'll tell her you missed her," or "I'm sure she'll be here next Tuesday." They thought of him and Kathy as a pair—he would surely know why she hadn't come.

But I don't, he thought. *I have no idea what's been going on, except that she's been to her mother's.*

He knew that, because Sue had told him. He had talked to Sue quite often in the last few days—Kathy never answered the phone anymore and never returned his calls. He couldn't understand why she didn't want to talk to him or see him.

It's up to her, now, he thought angrily. *And it looks like she's going to leave me hanging!*

So why was he waiting, hoping that she might appear at the last minute? He started down the steps two at a time. The group he and Kathy had once gone with after rehearsals came out just then, and one of them called to him, "Hey, Jay! Why don't you come with us tonight?"

"No, thanks," he said, waving his hand.

"Looks like you'll get home earlier than usual," another said, smirking.

He carefully avoided turning back, keeping his pace easy and normal, but once he got into his car, he finally let go, slamming the steering wheel and swearing. He started the Audi and pulled away from the curb much too quickly, leaving tire marks behind. The signal light turned yellow before he got to the intersection, and he accelerated to make it through before the signal turned red. He kept his speed up through several lights, then took the entry ramp to the freeway too fast, tires squealing.

The evident collapse of the house of cards he had built for himself and Kathy wasn't the only thing bothering him; there was also the inescapable fact that he had set up housekeeping in it. Incredible, that a person his age could be just as vulnerable to the tyrannies of love as the young.

"I promised myself that I wouldn't get involved again. I should have kept that promise!" he muttered to himself. He had hoped that that night with Kathy would be the beginning of a new life for the two of them, together. Instead, he felt used and rejected. He swore grimly and resolved to put her out of his mind, but he was still thinking of her as he drove up to the parking lot of his apartment building. Then, as he climbed the stairs to his apartment and unlocked the door, the reality of his single life hit him with this one fact: no one was there waiting for him; the apartment was empty.

He had always liked his apartment. Rented and decorated right after Donna had announced that she wanted a divorce (she had packed her bags first and had told him as she stood at the door), he had spent money in a careless fashion, buying everything that caught his fancy. He had chosen furniture in the modern style, with lots of clean, curved metal in tables and chair frames. The brown leather couch and chairs from Germany added comfort to the combined living/dining room that was otherwise rather hard and cool in appearance, and bright framed prints brought in color and design. He had liked the spare, open atmosphere of the finished room up to now. At this moment, though, it seemed cold and sterile. He didn't even want to enter, but there was no place else to go, and nothing to do.

He knew he wouldn't be able to sleep, at least not now, so he turned on the TV, but the images irritated rather than soothed him. He crawled through the disarray of his mind in an attempt to understand what was happening, but no matter which direction he took, his thoughts kept meeting barriers. When he conjured up any one of the evenings he had spent with Kathy, he found himself aching so much with loneliness that he couldn't hold the image long enough to examine what she had actually said or, more importantly, what she had actually communicated.

"I've missed something somewhere," he said, beginning to chew on the nail of his right index finger. He bit at the corner of the nail and chewed across it without being aware of what he was doing, but when he started on the next nail, he stopped short. "No way! I'm not getting into that again!" he said brusquely, as he got up and began pacing the room. He had been a compulsive nail chewer until high school, when he had overcome the habit by sheer force of will. He had learned to take pride in having well-groomed hands and manicured nails, but even now, when he was nervous or under stress, he found himself unconsciously at it again. This chewing of his nails was like a frenzy, and he knew that if he didn't do something different right now, he would continue until all his fingernails were mutilated.

Little hot points of nervous energy pricked at his muscles as he strode into the bedroom and put on his jogging suit. He ran down the stairs to the empty street and set off in the direction of White River. He ran and ran, without really noticing which direction he was taking, until overcome by exhaustion. Then he began turning the corners and taking the streets that would lead him back home. But he had gone farther than his physical condition was prepared for, and by the time he stumbled up the stairs, he was drenched and weak. He showered and fell into bed and found it blissfully easy to close his eyes and sleep.

PART THREE

Nine

The mound of washing was almost intimidating when Kathy descended the stairs to the washroom the next day. She began to sort, tossing the whites here, the coloreds there, the towels in their own pile. Suddenly, she grabbed an armful and threw them into the air, so that they landed willy-nilly.

"Can you believe it!" she laughed harshly. "My life is falling apart, and here I am doing the wash! Stupid! But I'm doing it because it has to be done. Congratulations, St. Kathy-of-the-Washroom!" St. Kathy-of-the-Washroom. Well, she had learned how to keep up with the wash. She knew how to keep white things white and how to iron Robert's shirts just the way he liked them. She had become an excellent cook as well, despite the fact that she had never cooked much while she was at home. Surprised that she enjoyed cooking so much, she had embarked on a self-directed course that had resulted in her being a recognized expert in Lemburg. She had learned a lot about nutrition as well and had developed many recipes using the basic foods recommended for storage. Add St. Kathy-of-the-Kitchen.

Then there were the classes she had taught in church, with people coming up afterward to tell her how inspiring she had been, and there was the record of 100% visiting teaching she had set three years ago. The bedtime stories she had read, the noses she had wiped, the reports typed in the middle of the night for a procrastinating teen. She should be rewarded with sainthood for all of that.

Here's a question for you, she thought. *What about all the things I've done that were positive and loving and dutiful? Don't they count anymore?* Had this one mistake, no matter how serious, discounted all the good she'd ever done? Erased everything as if it had never been?

Me and "Doctor QBVII," she thought. She couldn't remember the name of the doctor who was the central character or many details of the made-for-TV movie, and she had never read the book, but the face of Anthony Hopkins, who had played the role of the ill-fated man, was still clear in her mind. She had been haunted by that face and by the question of who the doctor was, ultimately: Was he the kind, dedicated doctor who had spent years of his life serving desert tribes; the loving husband; the adoring and adored father? Or was he the brutal surgeon who had performed hideous operations on Jewish prisoners in a concentration camp? How was it even possible that the former could also be the latter? And then, how was it possible for him to have repressed the remembrance of that part of his life so completely that he felt justified in bringing a slander suit against the reporter who had discovered his past? Did he have such an enormous blind spot that one part of him was unable to see another?

She remembered how overcome with emotion she had been at the end of the movie, seeing him ruined by his decision to work in the camp surgery, a decision made under extreme pressure, pressure that at least one other doctor had resisted, though at a cost. He was still the same husband, the same father, the same doctor as he had been before the trial. But now he was also a recognized war criminal. Did that part of him invalidate the rest? Yes, if one were to judge by the reactions of his wife and son, among others.

Now Kathy had a new case to consider, less spectacular, to be sure, but the questions were the same. Who was she, in the aftermath? Kathy-of-the-clean-shirts, Kathy-of-the-fresh-baked-bread, Kathy-of-the-inspiring-lessons, Kathy-of-the-bedtime-stories?

Or was she Kathy-with-an-A?

Did that last cancel out all that she had ever been or all that she might yet become? Or perhaps she had always been Kathy-with-an-A, had always had some blind spot where, hidden away, the wicked witch—Kathy visualized a witch with hairy tarantula legs—spun thread, enough to make the scarlet letter when the time was right? And if she had always had such a blind spot, how could she have prevented what had happened, the nature of the spot itself precluding that?

She took the wash from the machine and threw it into the dryer, then put another load in and started the cycle. *I guess I know the answer to that one,* she thought ruefully. *Others can see the blind spot. Family, friends, and the Holy Ghost. Both Robert and Mom tried to tell me, only I couldn't hear what they were saying.*

Looking back was so difficult. She felt that her mind had always rearranged facts to form justifications. Given that, how could she ever discern the truth behind the facts to really see the true progression from beginning to end?

She drove those thoughts from her mind and began ironing with quick, jabbing motions. She didn't want to look back. It just made her feel more acutely the sense of loss that pervaded her. She was so lonely—she missed Jay, the Jay of her daydreams as well as the man himself, so much.

But not that way. Not that way. How could she possibly explain to Robert that although she had wanted nothing else that night, the incident had brought little satisfaction?

"One miserable hour of my life and everything's changed!" But then the nagging thought reappeared. Was it just one hour or the work of years as the witch of the blind spot sat spinning?

Later her mother's words "No wonder he fed you on fairy tales and dreams" came back to her. She wondered for the first time if perhaps her dear, dear father had somehow contributed to what had happened by setting her on a pedestal. It hurt to think of Judge Adams as having done anything wrong or misguided. She loved the large, square man so, and she had basked in his open adoration. She remembered her brothers asking, "Hey, Kathy, go ask Dad if we can drive you swimming," when they thought he would be disinclined to give them permission. They knew he would if she asked. She had been aware in a naive way of the power she had over him and had always returned, a smiling six-year-old, dangling the keys.

She had used that power at first intuitively, then consciously, then habitually. As she grew into a young woman, she became aware that she was the object of a struggle between her father and her mother. To her father, she was someone special, a wonder, a child to be handled delicately, to be spoiled, to be catered to. When he read her fairy tales—and he really had fed her on fairy tales—he always called her his princess and told her that one day the knight or handsome prince would be coming for her and would whisk her away into a wonderful future. He never said what that future was; it was as if the prince himself were the goal to be achieved. If life after that was hazy, it definitely had a rosy tint.

After she had outgrown fairy tales, he told her almost daily how special she was and that she could do anything she set her mind to. Never mind that she didn't really do much, he always had the conviction that *if* she tried, she could be an astounding success. When her mother complained that she wasn't doing as well as she could in school, her father would say, "She'll come into her own, wait and see. When she gets to college, she'll buckle down." When her mother complained that she was useless around the house, her father said, "Don't be so hard on her, she's just having fun. Let her enjoy being young!"

Once, when she was standing in the same room feeling as if she were an uninvolved observer, she became aware that her mother resented her and didn't really like her. But she was aware of something else as well. The conflict between her mother and father rested on the fact that while her father saw her as a dream child, her mother saw her as a real teenaged child—spoiled, conniving, lazy, and unskilled. For a split second she had wondered in panic if that were really what she was, but her father had turned to her at that moment and said, "Princess, it's a great day. School will be starting soon, so take advantage of it. Go ride your horse, go swimming with your friends, go read a book."

And she had gone, reassured by her father's warm smile. She didn't have to do anything to be loved or accepted but to be herself. All she had to do was wait for the man who would one day take her father's place on the throne. It made her laugh now to think that she had ever believed that Robert would. Was that what she had wanted from Jay as well?

But I'm a different woman now, she thought. *I have a lot to my credit. I'm an intelligent, capable person. If Jay admired me, it was because I've done something with my life since I married Robert.* And then she wondered how much of what she had become was due to Robert.

The summons was hand-delivered to her on Saturday. She had been expecting it; the bishop had called to say that his first counselor and another priesthood member would be bringing it.

"I wanted you to know they would be coming."

"Thank you. I appreciate your thoughtfulness," she had replied with a steadiness that belied her weak knees.

"The date for the court has been set for early Sunday morning. I'm sorry that it has to be at such an inconvenient hour, but we couldn't seem to find another time when we could all meet. And it's important that we meet as soon as possible."

Her heart was pounding painfully. "I understand. I'll be there."

They left the house at six that Sunday morning. Robert was driving; he had insisted on coming. The children would come later, Brad driving her car.

"Do you want me to speak on your behalf?" he asked as they turned onto the freeway.

"Is there anything you could say that would change the outcome?"

"No. I don't think so."

"Well, then." After a moment she asked curiously, "What would you say, anyway?"

"That you are a good mother and a dedicated Church worker. That you have a testimony of the gospel and that you will have the support of your family during this time, no matter what the outcome."

"You can't say that, Robert. We haven't spoken to the children yet. They're going to be devastated!"

"Yes."

"And as far as you supporting me, I think you'd like to. You probably think you must. But be truthful—you can't stand the sight of me right now. And after today . . ."

They finished the rest of the drive in silence.

When they reached the chapel building, they walked in without speaking. As they parted, however, Robert did pat her back in an awkward attempt at reassurance. Then he remained behind while Kathy entered the bishop's office alone, where the bishop, his counselors, and the ward clerk were already assembled. The presence of the clerk, Paul Fuller, made her doubly thankful that the proceedings would be confidential—Paul was the husband of her close friend Myra.

In essence, the proceedings of the bishop's court were not so different from the talk she had had with the bishop Tuesday night. After stating the charges and asking if they were true, to which Kathy replied in the affirmative, the bishop asked much the same questions as he had asked previously. His counselors also questioned her, seeking clarification. As they probed, Kathy realized more and more that there had been many points along the line where she could have said, "No. That's far enough": the first time they had gone to eat alone; the first time he had put his arm around her; the first time she had spoken about intimate details of her marriage; the first time she had responded to his "brotherly" kiss.

She couldn't avoid the fact that she had been warned. This time she added the information that her mother had warned her as well, qualifying her statement by adding,

"But I honestly don't remember her ever saying anything like that."

She spoke clearly, answering questions in a quiet, controlled voice. She had a tissue in her hand, but she didn't use it until the bishop asked her how she felt about the Church. Then the tears came, not because of overwhelming feelings, but because of an overwhelming lack of feelings. "I know in my head that the Church is true," she said, crying. "I know because I can remember how it felt to have the Spirit. I know the Book of Mormon is scripture because I can remember the day I gained a testimony of it! But I can't feel those things anymore!"

Before she left the office she asked the bishop, "Whatever you decide, please don't say anything to Brad or Susan. I haven't talked to them yet."

"I won't," he assured her. "Please wait in the foyer."

She found Robert sitting on the couch by the south entrance.

"They're deciding now," she said.

"It won't take long," he replied, looking out the door. "I'll have to resign from the high council, I suppose."

"But why?"

"I can hardly go from ward to ward telling other people what they should be doing, considering our circumstances now, can I?"

"No. I suppose not."

"I'll call the stake president tonight."

She didn't know what to say, so she began counting the bricks along the bottom of the wall. Unable to comfort each other, they sat silently until the bishop appeared. Robert was right—barely fifteen minutes had passed.

As they walked back to the office, Kathy noticed that people had begun to arrive. The librarian was coming in the door; Sister Clarens was taking an armload of things to her classroom; and a couple of young children were running in the hall. It was a typical Sunday morning.

"I'm sure you know how difficult it was for us to hear this case," the bishop began, after they were seated side by side. "Robert, you have been in attendance at high council courts. You know how carefully evidence is weighed, how prayerfully a decision is reached." He paused, hand to nose. "I am aware of the consequences this sort of action has on the relationship between a husband and wife and on the family in general. I am deeply concerned about you both, as individuals, as a couple, and as parents in a family. I am truly distressed by the necessity that now faces us all."

He focused on Kathy. "There was only one decision possible when all the facts were before us, Sister Montgomery. The decision of the bishop's court is that the transgression you have committed is sufficiently serious to warrant your excommunication from the Church."

She had known it was coming, nevertheless she gasped and collapsed against Robert, who put his around her in support. She leaned against him, grateful for his presence.

"Let me explain exactly what that means to you, Kathy."

He picked up a booklet and turned to the page he wanted, folding the booklet front to back and creasing it flat. "I'm going to read directly from the handbook to you, Kathy. I realize that in your present state you won't grasp all that I read, but don't worry about that too much. We'll go over it again together sometime during the week." He paused, grasped the end of his nose and twisted it once or twice before giving it a final tug, then began to read.

The words rolled over Kathy and echoed in her ears, but she found that what Bishop Mangus had said was true. She couldn't clearly understand the meaning the words would have for her or what their lasting effect would be. They seemed to her like wind that stirs leaves and bends branches as it passes but leaves the trees unchanged. She was no longer a member of the Church, that she knew. And what he said next seemed reasonable, obvious in fact, given her present status: she was no longer able to give public prayers or give talks in any Church meetings; she was no longer privileged to partake of the sacrament; she could no longer tithe or give other contributions under her own name, although she could under Robert's.

Up to this point, she had been able to sit unmoving (and unmoved) but then the next sentence hit, coming with unexpected force and snapping all the inner fiber. She could no longer hold a temple recommend.

She jammed her fist against her lips, driving them into her bottom teeth, cutting them so that the salty taste of blood was on her tongue. Only as her breathing gradually slowed and the burning of her cheeks began to cool did she become aware that time had stopped only for her; the bishop was still speaking.

"This is a drastic step, I know, but it's necessary to the process of repentance that lies before you. We'll be sending you a letter outlining the decision of the court and its recommendations, and, in addition, I'll be wanting to talk to you often. I'll also want to talk to you as a couple from time to time." His gaze shifted to Robert.

"Robert, these things don't happen in a vacuum. Your wife is not the only one who will have some soul-searching in the next months. I think it might be helpful to you both if you considered seeing a family counselor. We can provide the name of a suitable counselor through the Church social services."

Kathy stirred eagerly. Here was something that offered hope!

"No," said Robert with finality. "This is something we have to work out ourselves!" He said it through gritted teeth, hurriedly, because that odd tightness between his shoulder blades was back again.

Bishop Mangus looked at him thoughtfully. "You don't have to go through this alone, Robert. I appreciate how you must feel, but your family faces a major crisis. There is nothing wrong with seeking appropriate help."

"This is our problem," Robert reiterated, moving uncomfortably in his chair.

"Oh, please," Kathy begged. Robert shook his head.

"If we find we can't do it ourselves, we'll let you know," he said, rising quickly. He barely paused to shake hands with the bishop, then made for the door, rubbing his left arm above the elbow.

It seemed years later that the meetings were finally over and Robert and Kathy got back into his car and headed home. Grant had wanted to ride with them, but Robert had sent him back to the other car, saying, "I need to talk to your mother."

"What an awful day. I wasn't sure I could make it through all the meetings!" Kathy said, slumping down in the seat. She had tried to look normal, if not exactly cheerful, during the meetings that had followed their interview with the bishop, but her face had betrayed her. Several times in the course of the day, she had noticed sisters looking at her with quizzical expressions, and Myra had asked the question straight out, saying, "What's the matter with you? You look like death!"

The worst part had come during the passing of the sacrament. By some fluke, Brad was the one who had brought the tray to their pew. He noticed immediately that neither partook of the bread. She had quickly turned away, afraid to meet his questioning glance. He was there again as the water was being passed, but she kept her eyes on her hands.

"Brad already knows something is wrong," she said. "He noticed that neither one of us took the sacrament."

"I know."

"I can't take the sacrament now, but why didn't you?"

"I wasn't in the proper frame of mind, that's why. That shouldn't be too hard for you to understand." After a time he said, "You have to tell the children."

"Will you be there when I tell them?"

"If you want me to."

She wasn't sure she did. And there was the problem of Grant. "What'll we do with Grant? He doesn't need to know."

"We can wait until he goes to bed."

Kathy snorted. "You know how he is. The minute he gets the feeling he's being hustled in that direction, he stays awake for hours. Maybe it would be better if you took Grant for a bike ride or to the park. It's a nice day and he'd like that."

As it happened, Kathy took Susan and Brad on a picnic while Robert "picnicked" with Grant at home in front of a sports broadcast. The sun was low in the sky as the three left the house. If Brad and Susan thought it strange that they should be picnicking so late in the day or so early in spring, while the park grounds were still spongy from the rainy season, they didn't mention it. They were aware of the tension between their parents, had seen the looks that passed between them, had heard the strain in their voices, had noticed the way they avoided touching. They knew their mother had a reason for this outing beyond her invitation to enjoy the lovely evening together.

They had just left the subdivision when Brad said, "Listen, Mom, why don't you just drive over to St. Joseph's Lake. That's not too far."

"Okay," she said, remembering how they used to laugh over the name, saying that the person who had named the lake must have been a Mormon without even knowing it.

"That way you can tell us what you have to say and get it over with," he continued roughly. "I'm not really hungry, Mom, and I doubt if Sue is either. Somehow it occurs to me that this isn't going to be a picnic."

Kathy's fingers ached with the tension of her grip on the wheel. "You're right," she said when she felt she could trust her voice.

The usually short trip to St. Joseph's Lake seemed to go on and on. But finally they arrived, and Kathy pulled into the parking lot on the east side.

"There's a table over there in the sun," she said, pointing. She took the picnic basket with her in spite of what Brad had said and put it on the end of the table when they reached it. Brad and Sue sat together on one side, Kathy sat across from them. They looked as if they were expecting a blow but didn't know which direction it was coming from.

"Sure you don't want a sandwich?" she offered, jockeying for time.

They both shook their heads. "Come on, Mom," added Brad. "You know we're not here to eat."

Kathy drew a breath. "Something happened in church today. Something that's going to make the coming months very hard for all of us."

Now the look of dread was plain in Susan's frightened

eyes and Brad's clenched jaw. *Quick,* thought Kathy. *Get it over with.*

"I've been excommunicated," she said quickly, tonelessly.

Both faces registered shock.

"But why?" Susan cried.

"I've had a relationship with another man," she said. Even as she spoke, she wondered if she could get a spot in the *Book of World Records* for figuring out the most ways of saying, "I have committed adultery," without really saying it.

"Oh!" Susan buried her head in her arms and began to sob. Kathy was afraid to look at Brad. He was like his father in so many ways. He was closer to Robert than to herself, and he had adopted his father's mannerisms and attitudes. She knew he would feel the betrayal twice, once for himself as son, again for his father.

"You what!" he demanded harshly. "Could I have possibly heard right?"

"You heard right," said Kathy softly. Her gaze was directed between Brad and Susan toward the circular beds where the early varieties of tulips and daffodils were moving slightly in the evening breeze. Seeing the flowers so cheerful in their primary colors, she longed to join them instead of going over and over the same story. She suddenly grew angry. Why were they all so shocked? Didn't they know she was human? Had they expected her to go through life always doing the proper things, never making a mistake? Her eyes blazed.

"Yes," she said, her voice no longer timorous or apologetic. "I found someone who cared for me, who liked the way I looked, who complimented me on the things I did. Someone who thought of me as a person, not as a robot preprogrammed to take care of everyone else's needs! And you know what? It was the most wonderful thing that ever happened to me in my life!"

The minute the words came out of her mouth, she regretted them, but she was so tired of being responsible for the shocked looks and the sorrowful faces. She was so tired of seeing disappointment.

"No, don't leave, Brad! You don't understand what I mean! I only meant it felt so wonderful to be a *person* again! Brad!" She grabbed at his sleeve, but he jerked away and ran across the grass.

Susan was still crying, but quietly now. Kathy touched her shoulder tentatively, and she looked up with accusing eyes. "It was Jay, wasn't it!"

"Yes." There seemed to be no point in denial, but the admission only seemed to distress Susan even more.

"And I thought he was so nice . . . Mother! That was what all those phone calls were about, wasn't it!"

"Yes."

"Then all the time you were talking to me about what real love is, you were guilty of . . ." She seemed reluctant to go any further, but her eyes narrowed, and she asked coldly, "You only get excommunicated for adultery, isn't that right?"

Kathy nodded.

Knowing with certainty devastated Susan. She seemed to crumble. Her mother had committed adultery! The very word sounded ugly, but the images that rose up before her, mysterious and awful to her young mind, were uglier still. "Go away!" she cried. "Go away and leave me alone! I don't want to talk to you again for the rest of my life!"

"Sue, let me drive you home," said Kathy, worried by the intensity of her reaction.

But Susan only turned her back in response.

Kathy looked in the direction Brad had run, but he wasn't anywhere in sight.

There's no reason for me to stay here, she thought. She picked up the basket, still full of sandwiches, chips, and pop.

Who was I kidding? she asked herself. On the way to the car she stopped at a trash can and dumped the contents of the basket into it. Then, as if the basket itself were somehow offensive, she jammed it into the can as well.

When she got home, she heard voices in the kitchen. Grant was telling his father the latest episode of "Spiderman," and Kathy stood quietly in the doorway for a moment, listening. She must have moved, however, for Robert looked up and saw her.

"You're back," he said.

Grant turned to her with an excited smile. "Mom, do you want to hear about this neat adventure Spiderman had?"

"Not now," she said, giving him a hug. "Why don't you put on your jacket and go for a walk while it's still nice outside? You need the fresh air. Then you can tell me all about it when you come back inside, okay?"

"Do I have to? I was right in the middle of telling Dad. I was right at the exciting part!"

"You can finish it when I come to kiss you good night," Robert told him. Satisfied, Grant put on his jacket and went out into the yard. They could see him from the kitchen window as he wandered down the creek, picking up sticks as he went.

"Where are Susan and Brad?" Robert asked.

"I don't know." She pulled up a chair and sat down.

"You told them then."

"Yes."

"Do you have any idea where they might have gone?"

"Susan was still at the park when I left. She didn't want to come home with me. Brad just disappeared. I have no idea where he is now."

"Sounds like you had a real nice picnic."

"Don't be so hateful! You sound like you're glad they're taking it so hard!"

He opened his mouth, but she said the words she could see on his lips. "That's just another consequence of my behavior, right? Well, la-ti-da!"

"Isn't it?"

She turned away.

"I think I'll go see if Susan's still there," he said finally.

She made no comment. After he left, she went to the cupboard and got out a loaf of bread. She ate honeyed toast and drank milk until she felt like throwing up.

Ten

She regretted the toast the next morning when she got into the shower. *I must have gained five pounds since I was at mother's,* she thought in disgust. She began the familiar litany *Why do I do that?* but suddenly stopped herself. *What difference does it make? Who cares if you're fat? Brad didn't say a word after he came home last night, and neither did Susan. Robert acts like you're not even there.* But Grant was still around, the dear loving little boy. At least he still gave her his good night kiss, hugging her warmly.

She got dressed and went downstairs to make the kids' lunches and get breakfast as usual, but neither Brad nor Susan came down until the last minute and then only to pick up their lunches before leaving. Robert read his paper and drank his juice in silence. When the same thing happened on Tuesday, Kathy resolved to stay in bed until it was time for Grant to get up.

"They can fix their own lunches and pour their own juice!"

So a new routine began to evolve. Brad and Susan left without seeing their mother in the morning and always scheduled something to keep them out of the house until late, spending time with friends or in after-school activities. On Wednesday night Brad didn't come home until very late, and Kathy, who had already gone to bed, was awakened by the sound of harsh male voices in the family room.

"And just where have you been all this time?"

"Around."

"That's not an acceptable answer, young man. What were you doing? You've been gone for hours!"

There was silence. Kathy imagined that Brad had shrugged.

"You're not going to get away with that sort of an answer. Tell me right now where you've been and what you've been doing!"

"Nothing. Just walked over to the shopping center. I met some of the guys from school in the arcade, so I watched them play a few games. Then I played a few myself and walked home."

"That's a long time to be playing video games, don't you think?"

"Playing video games is a pretty safe way to spend time compared to what some other people have been doing," he said bitterly.

"Brad—" began Robert, but Brad interrupted.

"Dad, don't say anything. I don't want to listen to a lecture right now. But there is one thing I want to know. Are you going to go to church on Sunday?"

Kathy, who had moved to the top of the stairs, stood still. Her heart was slamming.

"Yes," he said after a moment's pause.

"You're really going to go and sit there with everybody wondering what Mom has done?"

"Brad, besides our own family and the members of the bishop's court, hardly anyone will know what's happened. And they would only know that your mother's been excommunicated—they wouldn't know why."

"Really!" said Brad sarcastically. "They aren't stupid, Dad. She hasn't committed a crime, she doesn't have connections with any apostate groups, and she hasn't lost her testimony and asked to be removed from the rolls of the Church. There's only one thing left, and everyone will know what it is!"

"You've been doing some reading, I see."

Brad ignored the comment and again asked the question that was plaguing him, "Are you really going to go?"

"Brad, I can't let what your mother has done alter the

things I do. I go to church on Sundays, and I intend to be there this Sunday as usual."

"How will you be able to stand it!"

"I'll try to keep my mind on the purpose of the day, which is to worship God." Then he added in a voice so low that Kathy almost missed it, "And I'll try to remember that it's nobody's business what Kathy has done to get herself excommunicated!"

"They'll make it their business, you just wait and see! I wish I could bash Jay Enders in the nose! I'd like to bash everyone I see in the nose, including those snoopy, gossipy Relief Society ladies!"

"That's not at all fair, Son! Watch what you're saying!"

"They'll talk about her, Dad. They'll put her on the dissecting table!"

"No, I don't think so. You're being too harsh. Your mother has many friends among the sisters. They'll do all they can to help her."

"And talk when her back's turned."

That was enough; Kathy didn't want to hear anymore. She had harbored the hope that Brad would calm down as the days went on, but he hadn't. Not only that, his words had aroused doubts about the reactions her sisters in the Relief Society would have when they found out. *They aren't that way, they aren't!* she reassured herself, but the times she had heard sisters comment about someone who was having trouble came to the front of her mind and tortured her. With a sinking feeling she turned and went back to bed.

In a few minutes she heard Robert and Brad walking up the stairs, and then Robert came in the bedroom. She could hear him take off his clothes in the dark and hang them up. Then he sat heavily on the edge of the bed for a moment before sliding carefully under his half of the covers. Because she had been listening so intently, Kathy was immediately aware of the artificially measured breaths he drew. *Odd*, she thought before falling asleep.

Robert lay next to her, concentrating on breathing long, slow breaths. How many times lately had this strange feeling settled in his shoulder? Sometimes it was only a faint tingle, sometimes it was a tightness reaching to the middle of his back, sometimes it seemed to grip his shoulder from behind with long, hot fingers that extended down to his chest. For the hundredth time since he had learned of Kathy's affair, he wondered, *How can this be happening to me?* It was crazy, like the song his grandfather had loved to sing, where he'd recite a long litany of terrible mishaps only to deliver the clincher: "And then I got dandruff!"

Dandruff was an innocent irritant, though. This strange new symptom was far from innocent—it could very possibly be deadly.

In the early afternoon of the next day, Kathy walked into a nearby department store and stepped rather uncertainly in the direction of the underwear department. That morning she had stood before a virtually empty lingerie drawer—she had already folded and packed away her temple garments. Now, as she stopped before the counter, she hesitantly selected some merchandise. *Why not?* she asked herself suddenly. *If I have to wear these things, I might as well get nice ones!* But even as she made her decisions and paid the sales clerk, she had to bite her lip to keep it from quivering.

Later that day, she found that preparing for her Tuesday and Thursday classes helped alleviate some of her misery. In front of her "ladies," she felt confident and sure. She knew she was well prepared as she set up the materials necessary for her presentation of elegant desserts. She had special large-print recipes on laminated poster board and photocopies of the same for each participant. She put the posters up where they could easily be seen and laid the copies on the table. She had extended the table to make room for the ten participants. There was actually enough room for twelve, but she limited her classes to ten people since everyone had to have enough room to chop or whip or grind.

How ironic that Robert's industry and perseverance had provided the lovely home with a kitchen large enough to accommodate her classes. It was well outfitted, sunny and warm. And the oak antiques she had collected (mostly with his money) lent a definitely cozy atmosphere. Many women took one of her classes every fall and spring just because they liked her lively way of presenting ideas and the atmosphere in her home. She had developed a following of sorts, and last fall a suburban newspaper had even published the article "Cooking with Kathy: Oakridge Woman Makes It Fun" about her and her cooking classes.

Despite his stated disapproval, Robert had also financed over a period of years the classes she had taken to increase her knowledge and skill. At first she had taken extension classes at the high school, and then at the local trade school, and more recently at the U. of I. branch in Lemburg. Her goal was to take a few classes each semester until she could get a degree in nutrition.

He was proud of her success, she knew that, although he had never said so and she didn't expect that he ever would. But he was plenty vocal the day she had told him she'd opened an account of her own.

"Why must you have a separate account?" he had demanded, taking the proudly offered checkbook in his hand. "I don't hang onto my money. Everything I make is used for the family. Your money could go into the same account."

"Yes, but then you would be in control of it, and I'd be right back where I started."

That was really the part he didn't like about her having her own checkbook: he didn't like the idea that she had funds available for her own use, that she could make plans and carry them out, telling him about them as accomplished fact rather than asking him for permission. It had caused friction between them before, but this time Kathy was not willing to be the one to give in.

All these thoughts went through Kathy's head as she finished getting ready, but when the doorbell announced her first arrival, she put on a smile and put all other thoughts on the back burner where they simmered away during the class and bubbled over when she had time to think again. She had had a particularly successful day, but as she contemplated it, the words of President McKay popped into her mind—"No success can compensate for failure in the home"—and she wondered uncomfortably if her classes had been worth it.

It was the second week that Kathy had not gone to rehearsal. Jay had found himself thinking about Kathy more than usual, wondering if perhaps she would be coming to rehearsal in the evening. In spite of his determination to forget her, he had been waiting hopefully for a call. But when it came late that Tuesday afternoon, he was taken entirely by surprise because Robert was on the line, not Kathy.

"Hello, Robert," he said cautiously while thinking, *Of course, he knows.*

"I don't suppose you were expecting to hear from me."

"No. I rather expected and hoped to hear from Kathy."

"You won't. That's why I've called. Kathy's told me everything, and she's begun the process of getting her life back in order. That means you have to stay out of it. No calls, no contact of any kind."

"Isn't that up to Kathy?"

"It's her wish" was the cold reply.

Jay's thoughts went back to the last time he had seen her. He still didn't understand what had happened, how things between them could have changed so completely. But he remembered her desperate plea, "I have to make things right, and to do that, I have to say good-bye to you. This has to be the end!"

"I would have preferred to hear it from her," he said, still not wanting to accept her words as final.

"You'll have to take my word for it. Any contact with you would seriously jeopardize Kathy's progress. I don't want it interrupted or blocked by you. You don't understand Kathy very well," Robert continued, his voice rising. "In fact, you don't understand her at all, or you'd have realized that you have put her in an untenable position. She will never be happy again until her life with her family and her standing in the Church is what it was before."

"She wasn't all that happy before, I know that for a fact!"

Robert didn't reply immediately. When he did, his voice was less certain. "That may be so; but I know her. She could never live with herself if she threw away everything she's stood for all her life. She wouldn't be the same person; it would be like taking away her bones . . ."

A pain that had begun to be familiar settled in Jay's consciousness. Perhaps Robert was right. He must not have understood her. But that was not entirely his fault, he reminded himself. The basic conflict inherent in their meetings had never seemed to bother her. Whenever he had tried to sound her out, she had either complained about Robert or had changed the subject completely. He had finally come to the conclusion that she was not strongly committed to her husband, in spite of the high-flown sentiments of her church, and had taken her silence on the subject as encouragement. And she had accepted his attentions gladly, or was that just his imagination?

"All right," he said resignedly. "I won't call her, and I'll keep our contact at rehearsals to a minimum, that is, if she's going to start coming again?"

"Kathy won't be coming anymore."

So that's that, Jay thought. *It's all over.* Aloud he said, "It looks like you've taken care of everything."

"I try to be thorough," Robert replied in a dry voice. Jay thought he could sense a smile behind the words, and he had the distinct feeling he had heard this conversation before. On TV? In a movie?

"Then there's nothing more to be said."

"No. I don't think we'll need to speak to one another again."

Without saying good-bye Jay slowly hung up the phone, leaned back, and sighed deeply. After the days of waiting and wondering, it was all over. And there was one thing that he was finally sure of in the whole mess: Robert was right when he had said, "You don't understand Kathy very well; in fact, you don't understand her at all."

And that other statement about "getting her life into order"—what a strange thing to say. What had Robert meant by it, actually? It implied some plan, some pattern that demanded conformation. He was referring to their church, no doubt. And Jay realized that despite all their hours together, he knew virtually nothing about her religion. *I'll look it up when I go to the library today,* he promised himself. *Maybe then I'll understand. I have to understand.*

He was still running in the evenings, but he had taken up going to the library several nights a week as well. He found that reading helped him to keep Kathy from the center of his thoughts, and by going to the library he postponed the inevitable, unpleasant opening of the door to his dark apartment. Besides, he liked reading, liked learning about all sorts of exotic places, and found a certain humor in knowing obscure, useless facts. Normally, he would wander through the stacks, picking up such books as caught his eye, but that evening, when he stepped through the library doors, he went directly to the section marked "Religion" and picked out a book on religions of the world.

He read the section "Mormons (The Church of Jesus Christ of Latter-day Saints)" in that book, then a section in another. After that he looked up "Mormons" in the card catalogue. He spent several hours reading, his brows drawn together. Sometimes he frowned, other times he shook his head. Then again, he would lay the book down on the library table and gaze at the wall vacantly.

She believed in this religion? In a tangible god? In immutable laws of behavior? Any good scientist could tell her that even the most relied-upon laws of nature weren't as immutable as once thought; the theory of relativity applied to more of the universe than most people would be comfortable with. And then there was Joseph Smith and his visions. And polygamy, for heaven's sake!

He was more confused by his reading than he had been before and taken aback that any thinking person could actually be drawn into what he felt was a web of nonsense. But he did understand something that had been a mystery to him before and that made his reading worthwhile. The

Mormon doctrine of eternal marriage and the continuity of the family unit had opened up the door to whole conversations he had had with Kathy. He knew with certainty that she did believe in that, even though she had sent a double message in the way she had smiled at him and leaned into him as he had kissed her forehead. That was what she had meant when she said that she was bound to Robert.

He found himself hating Kathy's husband. He wasn't worth her loyalty and commitment, the robot. Robot Robert. How could she have married that creature? What malevolent quirk of nature had set it up so that Robert had found her first? And now that he was married to her, this religion and Kathy's belief in it said that she would be bound to him for eternity . . .

Even if it's an eternity of pain? he questioned. It didn't make sense. But she would never leave Robert, that was clear to him now, because she believed in this odd notion of eternal relationships and in the strict moral code of her church. He shook his head unbelievingly. Absolutes had never been part of his thought patterns; he had been reared by parents who believed in relative morality and alternative life-styles long before those words had become part of the public consciousness.

"Make your choices based on what you want, that is the only criterion," his father had been fond of saying.

"But what if that means you break a law or hurt somebody?" he had asked, confused.

"Then you take the consequences," his father had replied. But his eyes had softened as he added, "The consequences may have a lot to do with your decisions about what you really do want."

Jay knew that there was something sobering in the accepting of consequences, but nevertheless, he had had his doubts about his parents' philosophy that everything was open and allowable, providing one was willing to accept responsibility for the outcome. To Jay, this world without bounds was frightening in a way he couldn't articulate, enormous in the millions of possibilities.

At any rate, what his father did was a more potent explanation of his beliefs. Jay found himself close to tears as he thought of his father, the tall, thin, and very gentle man who had walked through life making the daily choice to live ethically simply because he wanted to, not because there was a god somewhere poised to reward or punish. So in the end, though Jay's parents had left him to formulate his own code of ethics, Jay had drawn his set of values from their example.

There had come a time, though, when he had lived by their words alone. His marriage to Donna had been the most painful period of his life. Before their marriage it had been easy to mouth a willingness to let each other be "free," but afterward he found that he actually wanted boundaries and a real commitment from her. He had watched her lead her own life, touching his only when they were both home at the same time, and then with a casualness that was appalling. He had retaliated by behaving in the same callous manner, but his unhappiness had only increased. He realized that accepting responsibility for destructive behavior didn't make the behavior any less destructive. He found that he wanted something he could hold onto, something clean and solid.

But his wife hadn't moved in the same direction he had moved; instead, she mocked his "weakness" and continued as always, until the day he had come home to find her at the door, bags in hand. She had been able to leave easily, with a smile, telling him that he had turned into an old stiff. "You know what your problem is?" she had asked him, and then she answered her own question. "You've forgotten how to go with the flow."

Well, maybe he had. He only knew that he had felt a vague, disturbing need for something permanent in his life, something he could count on. But he didn't know where to find it, for any organization that demanded a commitment had no power to draw him into the fold—in that respect, he was too much his parents' child. So he had turned back to their way of life, trying his best to be honest for honesty's sake, caring for caring's sake, though the feeling of unease had persisted. Until he met Kathy.

Kathy. He had thought for a time that she would fill the void. But the very force that had formed her life was the force that had taken her away from him. What was the draw of that kind of value system? *Is there something inherently positive in living the so-called commandments?* he asked himself as he shifted position on the hard library chair. *Does it bring a certain strength and beauty?* Perhaps the beauty he had seen in Kathy was partially the result of the way she had conformed to the set of absolutes espoused by her church. Maybe that was why she had to "get her life into order." Maybe Robert was right—without her belief, she would collapse inward. She wouldn't be the person he loved.

That, however, brought him to the point of swearing. Her involvement with him was inconsistent. Had she made a conscious decision to go against her very fiber? No. Was it a momentary rebellion against the strictures of her church? Not likely. An act of revenge against Robert? Perhaps. Or simply a moment of weakness and need?

He knew he needed her. His divorce from Donna after seven difficult years had left him committed to bachelorhood—he hadn't wanted another woman in his life. *But I do now,* he admitted reluctantly as he took the pile of books back to the shelf. *Maybe that's what it was all about. Two people in need . . .*

The thought was anything but comforting.

Eleven

At midweek, the bishop called Kathy in for the first of their promised meetings. As he helped her to her seat, he asked whether she were all right.

"I guess so," she replied.

"You look a bit tired and pale. You don't have a cold, do you?"

"Don't I wish. I had no idea how exhausting negative emotions can be. Between bawling my eyes out and worrying about what's going to come of this, I feel like my head's going to burst."

He nodded sympathetically. "Be sure you take good care of yourself, Kathy. You need to avoid any extra stress, and you need to make sure you get enough rest."

Her laugh was bitter and short.

"What's funny?"

"Nothing, really. It's just that you represent the Church, and the Church is as offended as my family by what I've done, yet you don't seem to be personally offended. As far as that goes, you seem to be the only one who cares whether I'm okay or not."

"By that, are you telling me that your family doesn't seem to care?"

"You got it." Kathy leaned her head on her hand. "The worst part is feeling that they've never really known or cared about me as a person; what they liked most about me was the way I fit the image of a 'good mother.' Now that I've muddied that up, they don't have much use for me."

"Kathy, your family is suffering from a severe loss—the loss of the mother and wife they thought they had. Every loss is accompanied by a sense of anger and betrayal; but believe it or not, those feelings are often the first step in the grieving process that every individual must work through. Give your family time to work through it. They have to if they're ever to complete the process."

Kathy sighed. "Well, I hope you're praying for us, Bishop, because we are going to need your prayers if that's ever going to happen."

"I am, every day. Now, is there anything you want to ask me, or anything I can do for you or your family?"

"You can wave a magic wand and make it better," she said with a ghost of a smile.

"I wish I could."

At the door Kathy paused, and the strange smile flickered as she said the words that were for most members simply another way of saying good-bye: "See you on Sunday."

She had a fatalistic turn of mind Sunday morning; she felt as if the events of her life had taken on a strength of their own and that she was powerless to alter their course. She rose and showered, noting her increasing size with a grunt. "Well, look at that," she muttered cuttingly. "Little Kathy is eating herself into obesity. But it really doesn't matter. Nobody cares." Her hot tears were lost in the hot spray. Nobody did care. Robert had found it possible to be more impersonal than ever, and Susan and Brad had subjected her to that brand of superior disgust possible only in teenagers. And Jay? Jay hadn't called or sent a note. He had virtually disappeared. That she was not to see him anymore was of no importance. She needed to know he still cared, that somebody cared!

She finished with her shower and used the blow dryer on her hair. *It's getting too long,* she thought. The weight of the extra length had pulled out some of the natural curl of the usually springy locks. She did the best she could with her hair, then went in to dress. Picking out something to wear was not easy—she had to find something that would hide the newly added pounds. She chose a navy blue suit with a dirndl skirt and a deep pink blouse. She knew they would enhance her own coloring and enliven her eyes, and she needed that extra help today.

She applied her makeup, dressed, and stood before the mirror, surveying the results. "Not too bad," she assured herself. But nothing had altered the flat expression in her eyes. They mirrored clearly what she was saying inside, over and over again: *It doesn't matter—doesn't matter if you're getting fat, if your house is clean or not, if your clothes look attractive. It doesn't matter what happens today. Nothing matters any more.*

As she walked down the hall, she could hear Grant conversing with his teddy bear. She opened the door and looked in. "Grant, time to get ready for church," she said, endeavoring to be cheerful.

"Don't have to go to church today," he informed her brightly.

"What?" She was surprised. He was a dedicated churchgoer.

"That's what I heard Daddy tell Brad. He said Brad didn't have to go to church today. I looked in his room. He's still in bed."

"Oh."

"Do you have to go, Mommy?"

"Yes, I have to go," she said.

"Then I'll go too," he decided, climbing out of bed.

"Oh, Grant!" she murmured, clasping him to her. "You're a good little soldier." Then she smiled at him. "Get into the tub, kiddo, and I'll lay out your clothes."

After putting out his things, Kathy stood in the hall, looking at Susan's closed door. Robert had probably given her permission to stay home as well. It looked as if that was exactly what she had decided to do. Kathy knocked softly on the door, but there was no answer. She opened it slightly. The room was dark, the curtains drawn shut against the light, and the digital numbers of the clock radio cast a reddish glow in one corner. She crossed the room to the bed. Susan had wadded the covers about her so that only the top of her head was visible.

"Susan?"

Susan pulled the covers completely over her head, muffling her response, "What do you want?"

"Are you all right?"

"What do you think?"

Kathy sat down at the foot of the bed. "Sue, I'm sorry, I'm truly sorry for all the mess this has caused."

Susan neither spoke nor moved.

"Please believe me when I tell you that I love you very much. I wouldn't hurt you for the world!"

Susan pushed herself up out of the covers. Her face looked bizarre in the dim red light. "Then why did you do it, Mother?"

"I'd like to explain it to you, but I can't. I feel all my reasons, but the minute I try to put them into words, they sound so . . . so meaningless."

"Maybe they are meaningless."

"Maybe. Are you coming today?"

"I don't know. I'm not sure I want to. It's so embarrassing! I'd like to crawl in a hole, but then I keep reminding myself that I don't have to be embarrassed, do I? I'm not the one who's been excommunicated!"

"No." Kathy looked at her hands.

"I'm surprised you're going, to tell the truth. Aren't you embarrassed?" Susan's voice was vibrant with emotion. "It's so disgusting! Really, it's the most disgusting thing I've ever heard! How can you look at yourself in the mirror? How can you stand looking at Dad, knowing what you did?"

Kathy rose heavily and began to walk toward the door.

"I've decided to go, after all," Susan called after her. "Dad is going to need all the support he can get today. Maybe I can give him some; you certainly can't!"

Kathy didn't turn around. *The ranks have closed,* she thought. They would stand together—Brad, Susan, and Robert, the injured parties—and she would stand alone. Her steps were leaden, her heart was stone, and the weight of pain dragged her down. *It doesn't matter,* she told herself. *Nothing matters anymore.* And to her surprise, she found the pain was gone. In its place was a dark and frightening emptiness.

In the end, they all went to church that day, but the family that got into the car had no sense of togetherness. Grant kept looking from one stony face to the other, asking what was the matter. Getting no answer, he tried to cheer them up by telling jokes and stories, but finally he, too, fell silent. Kathy was relieved to arrive and escape the forced closeness.

Between the car and the building, Kathy caught up with a vigorously striding Brad and asked quickly, "Why did you come? You didn't have to."

"Didn't I? If I don't come today, when will I come? This Sunday or next, it doesn't make any difference. All my friends will know, and I've got to face up to that." He quickened his pace to leave her behind.

Her sense of dread distorted time the way water distorts shapes. Walking up the hall took forever. The opening portion of sacrament meeting sped by; the passing of the bread and water was drawn-out agony. She learned to know the shape of every fingernail and every wrinkle on her hands (*that's how I know I'm thirty-eight, by looking at my hands!* she thought). Fading in and out, the minutes went by. First sacrament meeting, then Sunday School.

All through those meetings, Kathy felt as if the eyes of the bishopric and Paul Fuller were unswervingly fixed upon her. She told herself it wasn't true—and indeed it wasn't—but that didn't change how she felt. In fact, probing glances seemed to fall upon her from all sides. By the time that gospel doctrine class was over, she could stand it no longer. She touched Robert's arm. "Let's leave," she whispered urgently.

"What's the matter? Are you ill?"

"No. I just don't want to stay any longer."

"Why not? You've made it this far."

"I know, but I can't stand the feeling that everybody's looking at me. Please, can't we just leave?"

She was so caught up in her need to convince him that Kathy forgot to keep the carefully composed expression she had worn all day. At the sight of her suffering, Robert felt compassion opening up within like a spring of water. He was on the point of acceding to her wishes when an inner voice said, *She deserves to suffer; it's the consequence of sin.*

"I'll meet you at the car when it's over," he said shortly and turned to face the front of the room.

Somehow she made it through Relief Society, although afterward she couldn't remember anything that had gone on because she had been preoccupied with the question of how to get away from Myra Fuller after it was over. Well-meaning but sometimes insensitive and blunt, Myra would insist on knowing why she looked so pale and distraught for the second Sunday in a row. She started for the door almost before the final amen had been said, but Myra, who had been sitting next to her, called out, "Kathy, slow down! I haven't seen you all week!"

Kathy turned in exasperation, but she managed to smile and kept her voice bright. "I'd love to stay and talk, Myra, but I've got to find Robert. I'll call you this week, promise!"

Again she started for the door, but this time, the Relief Society president addressed her.

"Kathy, may I have a moment with you?" Beth Hubbard asked.

The moment Kathy looked at Beth's face, she knew Bishop Mangus had told her of the excommunication. "I see you've been talking to the bishop," she said.

"Yes. And I'd like to talk to you, if I may."

"I'm not sure what there is to say, Beth."

"Nevertheless, I would like to come and visit with you this week."

"Tell you what. You give me a call, and we'll see about it."

"All right," said Beth, and she gave a Kathy a quick hug. "Please take care of yourself. We love you."

Kathy was in no mood to hear those words; she walked quickly into the hall where she came face-to-face with a crying Myra.

"Oh, Kathy! I just asked Susan what in the world was the matter with you, and I know she shouldn't have, but she told me! I had the oddest feeling all last week that something was wrong, and that I ought to call, but somehow there just wasn't enough time. Oh, I wish I had! I should have been with you!" She threw her arms around Kathy, too caught up in her own emotions to notice that Kathy, who felt angry and betrayed, didn't return her embrace.

At just that moment, Kathy looked over Myra's shoulder down the length of the hall and saw Robert. He was alone. She broke away from Mrya with a hurried excuse and went quickly to him. His eyes were blazing with bitterness. The scene at the other end of the hall had not escaped him.

He smiled sardonically. "Sharing your escapades with Myra?"

"No!" she cried, shocked. "Of course not! She was just . . . letting me know she would stand by me."

"I'm sure she was. Maybe your sin appeals to the romantic streak in women."

"That is an absolutely disgusting thing to say!"

Hostility crackled between them. Robert took her by the arm, none too gently, and said "Let's get out of here. The last thing we need is a scene in the foyer."

She couldn't have agreed more. They hurried through the door and to the car. Grant was playing happily in front of it. The welcoming smile on his face wavered, then faded, then disappeared altogether.

"Get into the car," ordered Robert. The little boy obeyed.

"Brad and Susan rode home with the Beverlys," he offered hopefully, but no one said anything.

The drive home was much the same as the drive to church had been. If it differed at all, it was only in the level of tension and in the finality of the silence. Kathy felt like screaming or pounding the dashboard with her fists. She did neither. When they arrived home, she changed her clothes, told Grant to change his, and went into the kitchen to fix Sunday dinner. That was what good sisters were supposed to do, after all.

So began the task of daily survival. The confrontations Kathy had dreaded were behind her, but as awful as those confrontations had been, they were not nearly so bad as the meals eaten in silence, the avoidance of physical contact when passing in the hall, the hostile stares caught when she looked up suddenly from a book.

Okay, she thought. *If that's the way they want it.* If they could shut her out, she could shut them out. Turn about is fair play. Except for Grant.

Since she had stopped getting up early to fix breakfast for Brad, Susan, and Robert, Grant had begun climbing into bed with her after his father's wake-up call. Sometimes she was still asleep, sometimes she listened to him through lowered lids as he talked to his teddy bear. When it was time for him to get ready, she would move slowly down to the kitchen and fix him breakfast, which most often just involved putting cereal and juice and milk on the table. Then she would sit and listen to him talk through a mouthful of cornflakes. It twisted her heart to see him try so hard to cheer her up. For him, she would smile; for him, she would pretend nothing was different. But the fervor with which he would say, "You're the best mom in the world!"—told her that her smile wasn't convincing.

Not much was left now of the routine that had governed her life for so many years. No early breakfast, no early morning start on the day, no good-bye kiss from Robert ("You are going to get up today, aren't you?"). If they didn't care, why should she? Forget cleaning the house and going down to the "dungeon" to wash (funny, she hadn't called it that for years). Forget fixing a tasty, attractively served meal. They could do it themselves. Given the casseroles, fruits, and vegetables she had frozen, it should be easy enough.

When Beth Hubbard called, Kathy told her that she didn't particularly want visitors but that Beth could pick up the supplemental materials for the Social Relations class since she wouldn't be able to teach it anymore.

"May I stop by tomorrow?" the Relief Society president had asked.

"Yes. I'll leave it out on the front porch, where you can find it."

"I'd much rather have you give it to me in person, Kathy. I would very much like to talk to you."

"I really don't think there's anything we need to talk about," replied Kathy.

"I hope you're not cutting yourself off from us. I wouldn't like to see that happen."

Kathy felt a moment's doubt. Her sisters were her friends. They had stood by one another in crises and in sorrow; perhaps they would stand by her now. But then she remembered Brad's late-night comment about gossipy sisters, and even as she felt the poison of the suggestion, she was helpless against it.

"I hope you'll understand," she said, "but I'm not really in the mood for company. I've even asked my own mother to postpone a visit she was planning. It's just not something I can handle right now."

"Yes, I understand."

"And that includes my visiting teachers," continued Kathy with a rush.

"Are you sure you want to be that isolated? I can tell them to make their visit very short, and I'm sure they won't bring up any uncomfortable subjects. Please let them come by, if only for a minute."

"No. I really don't want them to come. I don't want anyone to come!"

"Not even Myra?"

"Not even Myra!"

"Oh, Kathy, I think you're making a mistake. We all have our own problems, and it's by supporting and strengthening each other that we make it through! Not one sister in Relief Society is without some heartbreak, some you would be surprised about. You're not as alone as you think."

"I don't want to hear about anyone else's problems, and I don't want anyone else worrying about mine! I don't want anyone to come. And when you stop by tomorrow, Grant will give you the materials."

"May I call you now and then?"

Kathy sighed in exasperation. "If you must!"

"I really wish I were with you now, Kathy. I feel the need to tell you how much I care about you and want to help you, but I would rather tell you when we're together, not over the phone."

"I don't think that would make any difference," said Kathy, who lately had found herself responding with anger when she heard people saying how much they loved one another. Maybe those feelings were authentic, but she doubted it, especially when someone said it to her.

"If you change your mind, will you let me know?" Beth persisted.

"I suppose so, but now I really must hang up. Goodbye!" And she almost threw the receiver back onto the cradle.

Once contact with the Church and with friends had been cut to a minimum, Kathy began going back to bed again or lying down on the couch in the family room during the day. She wasn't sure how the time passed; she was always surprised when she heard the sound of laughing, of children walking home from school, chattering and calling to one another. Sometimes she didn't even get dressed until she heard them, and then she threw on whatever was within easy reach or whatever was easiest to zip up. She rarely bothered with makeup. She rarely left the house, and then only to walk around the yard to see which bulbs were blooming and which perennials were putting up shoots.

She was standing by the bare plot that was the family vegetable garden one evening, watching the mauve and purple twilight descend, when Robert came up beside her.

"Are we going to have a garden this year?" he asked.

"I don't know." She knelt to pick up a handful of earth. It was still cool but not so wet anymore. It crumbled easily, perfect for planting.

"But that's not your real question, is it?" she asked, straightening. "Your real question is, 'Are you going to get the garden planted this year?' The answer to that is, probably not. Not if it's up to me alone. If you and the kids can stand to be in my presence long enough to help, then okay. Otherwise, the answer is no."

The garden didn't get planted. Neither did the house get its spring cleaning or the neighbors their May baskets. The library books lay unread and unreturned on her bedside table, next to the scriptures, which also hadn't been opened in weeks. Sometimes she thought she ought to be doing one thing or another, but she couldn't seem to translate that thought into action. She would sit for hours looking out the family room window. Sometimes birds would come to the feeder, or squirrels would dart from tree to tree; once an arrogant pheasant cock strutted across the lawn, but her expression never changed. Her eyes saw the shifting patterns and colors, but her mind was too preoccupied to acknowledge any meaning in them.

She went through Sundays with the same vacant gaze; it was the only way she had to protect herself from the painful underscoring of her present position. With agonizing slowness she would dress, help Grant get ready, and perhaps put something in the oven for Sunday dinner. Then they would all ride to the chapel in the same car, something they hadn't done in years because of Robert's various Church responsibilities. Kathy remembered with irony how often she had wished they could go to church together, as a family. Now they were together and she hated it! Every Sunday she wished that she would break her leg falling down the stairs or that she were terminally ill—anything to stay home.

But she went, giving in to the inevitable. She automatically smiled and shook hands, saying "I'm doing fine, thank you." She sat through the meetings, unmoving, unhearing, and had reached such a point of detachment that she could pass the sacrament trays from Robert to Grant without a pang. She was relieved to know she could retreat to an empty place within herself; the path there was becoming well worn, the password almost always on her lips: "It doesn't matter. Nothing matters any more."

Mother's Day was a torment. She had not even thought about the coming holiday and didn't realize it was Mother's Day until Grant came bounding in Sunday morning to give her a big kiss and to present the brightly colored, ribbon-festooned card he had made in school. She had thought there were no more tears to cry, but she was mistaken.

"Hey, didn't Sue fix you breakfast in bed like she always does?" he asked, surprised and disappointed.

"No. But don't worry about it, it doesn't matter."

Grant didn't pay any attention but ran around to Robert's side of the bed. "Dad! Dad!" he cried, shaking his father's shoulder. "It's Mother's Day, and nobody has made breakfast for Mom! Come on, let's go do it!"

"I don't want to get up yet," mumbled Robert.

"But Dad! What about Mother's Day!"

"Your mother just said not to worry about it!"

Grant's face fell momentarily, then he brightened. "I'll just have to do it myself!" he declared.

Quite a bit later he came struggling up the stairs with the tray. He had tried to do everything he had seen his sister do in years past. There was dark brown toast, juice, watery scrambled eggs, underdone bacon, and canned peaches. He was triumphant.

"See! I even got a flower from the garden!"

He sat on the bed beside her, watching her eat, chattering away in that compulsive fashion that had become usual for him. Robert lay on his side of the bed, unmoving, although he was not asleep.

So he's going to act as if it weren't Mother's Day at all, thought Kathy, remembering the lovely cards and the orchids that had been his gifts to her every year since the first Mother's Day after Brad's birth. It would be awkward to go to church without the orchid—that sign that she was loved and appreciated—like a court-martialled officer being forced to appear before his troops, untidy threads where his stripes had been.

That Sunday presented a special challenge to her ability

to retreat from what was going on around her, but she managed to block out most of the program until the bishop asked all mothers to stand. Then she stood as well, thinking she would be even more conspicuous if she didn't. With shaking hands she accepted the pink carnation that was the bishopric's tribute to all mothers.

Grant never once paused in his efforts to normalize things, asking Kathy on the way home if she would make "some of that good rice stuff you used to make on Sunday." Behind the words she heard the plea, "Please make the good rice stuff, Mommy, then it will be like it used to be." To please him, she did make the casserole.

Late that evening she called her mother. Clarice immediately said, "Kathy, I don't like the sound of your voice."

"I'm sorry if I don't sound like you want me to sound. Things aren't exactly hearts and flowers around here."

"I know that, and I don't expect you to put on an act for me. All I want to do is to help you any way I can. I can be up there tomorrow if you want me to come. Please don't say no again, dear."

"Mom, I don't know how to say this without upsetting you, but I don't think it's a good idea. No, listen!" she exclaimed as her mother started to protest. "You know we're just starting to have a good relationship for the first time in our lives. I want that as much as you do, but I have too many things to work out right now. I don't think I can do it with you here. I'd feel obligated to say things I didn't feel like saying and to do things I didn't want to do."

"I don't know why."

"Because you're my mother, that's why! I want you to be proud of me. The best way you can help me is by not coming."

Kathy paused, but Clarice said nothing. "Now I've hurt your feelings! See, that's just what I'm talking about."

"So I won't come," said Clarice in a tear-thickened voice.

"And to think I only called to wish you 'Happy Mother's Day!'" said Kathy bitterly.

"Well, thank you for that. Now, I do think I'll go to bed; I'll call you later in the week, if that's not intruding too much."

"Mom, you're not intruding, but a person just has to go through some things alone. Please try to understand."

"I do, I guess."

"Keep praying for me."

"I have no intention of stopping," said Clarice.

PART FOUR

Twelve

It was a day later, as she sat alone, that the thought came to her, *I'm not going to make it.* She spoke the words aloud, her voice heavy with conviction, as her scriptures, bound in white, with the name Kathy Adams Montgomery embossed in the lower right-hand corner, lay on her lap unopened. The holding of her scriptures was a strange ritual. Bishop Mangus had encouraged her to read them daily, and daily she picked them up, but she couldn't bring herself to open them. Instead, she would sit by the window, tracing her name, feeling the grain of the leather, or holding them to her.

She was having the same difficulty with the prayers she had been encouraged to say daily. Just to get on her knees was a victory, but once on them, she couldn't bring any words past her lips: she couldn't praise, thank, or plead. But now, as she talked to herself, she was really talking to the Lord, and most of what she had to say wasn't pleasant. The anger she couldn't express to her family (how could she get angry at them—she was the guilty one?) was directed at the Lord; he became the scapegoat for all that had happened.

After all, if it hadn't been for the fact that as a nineteen-year-old she had knelt in prayer concerning Robert and had been convinced that the Holy Ghost had answered that prayer, she might not have been so quick to say "yes" when he asked her to marry him. Not that her inclination wasn't already in Robert's favor, but her secret, on-the-knees prayer asking, "Is Robert the one for me?" and the subsequent burning in the bosom had been the seal of certainty. From that point on, she had had no question in her mind that they would marry. And later, when she had become the object in her dorm of the "pass the candle" ceremony—the candle stops when it reaches the newly engaged girl—she had told of her prayer and the answer to it.

But I never would have married him, Lord, if I hadn't really believed that we were meant for each other! The burning is no self-created condition, as I ought to know, considering my present situation. So it had to come from thee.

But why did it come? I wouldn't be in the middle of an unhappy marriage if you hadn't answered that prayer the way you did! Or did I interpret the burning wrong? Perhaps it didn't mean "yes" at all. Perhaps it meant, "Daughter, you are seeking me in prayer and that is pleasing to me." But then, how can one know exactly what a spiritual experience means, unless actual words are spoken? How can one ever be certain?

She felt as if she had broken loose from moorings that had kept her safe in inclement weather. She was adrift, rolling out to sea on waves of doubt. *Then again, maybe we were meant to marry and go through this as a means of learning something. But what a lousy way to learn! Does learning always have to be connected with suffering? Is there no other way?* Something about Christ suffering and descending below all tried to push its way up into her consciousness, but she was too frantically involved in her accusations to acknowledge it.

By now, she was seething. The idea that suffering was necessary for growth infuriated her, and she lapsed from the language of prayer, saying aloud, "If this is your way of helping me reach some exalted state, forget it! I don't want this. I didn't ask for it. It sure doesn't feel like a blessing, in disguise or otherwise. If this is your way of telling me you love me, thanks a whole bunch!"

Even though in her anger she was almost beyond hearing or seeing, she could still hear the inner voice chiding, *You can't really blame God for your suffering.*

She sat ramrod-straight in her chair. *Who is responsible*

then! You can't blame me! I didn't ever want anything like this to happen!

The answer was disturbing. *Perhaps not, but you believed the idea that the one, true love of your life would make you happy forever, and when it didn't happen with Robert, you looked for another rescuer.*

You mean I set myself up? she asked herself.

Perhaps I did, she mused, answering her own question, *by holding onto cherished dreams and fantasies. Perhaps I brought it all on myself.* She thought of the witch-spider, the hideous, hairy creature, crouching in the blind spot of her mind. Had she invited the spider in herself? The thought was repulsive.

"No. I don't accept responsibility for that!" she said grimly. There were too many things the individual had no control over, such as the kind of parents one was born to, one's place in the family, the color of one's hair and eyes, one's talents and inclinations, and one's health. These factors determined much of a person's future. Added to them was the influence of the country the individual was born in, of the language learned as a child, of the social strata, and of the culturally determined ways of perceiving and feeling that shaped perception of the world. What could be done against all of that? How much freedom of choice did anyone actually have?

On the other hand, one couldn't possibly function in a world where there were no givens; there had to be a place to stand. A new, startling thought entered her mind: *Perhaps our marriage is a given, and what faces us now is the real arena of choice!*

She pressed her hands against her temples. All her thoughts were leapfrogging, going around in a circle, and she couldn't stop them. *If that is true, where does love come in? What did I mean when I said I was in love with Robert? Was it a case of rampaging hormones, or compatible neuroses? Most likely the latter. But what about my prayer and the answer to it?* She had come back to where she had started.

I was certain I had received inspiration from you; I trusted my feeling, and this is where I end up! Are you laughing, Lord? I'm not. But then, maybe I should. After all, it might be nothing but a big joke. Or it might not have been inspiration at all—it might have been nothing more than a "bit of beef, a blot of mustard, a bit of an underdone potato," as Scrooge said.

Her tumbled thoughts had moved her from apathy to rage. *What do you want of me? Do you want me to submit to all and yet praise your name? Okay. I submit. But don't expect me to praise!*

She raised her face upward and cried, "What do you want of me? What *do* you want of me!" Then the momentary surge of anger and energy abated. All this effort so useless, so senseless, so impossible! She sank down into her chair, her hand hanging limply over the side.

"How can we get through to Kathy?" Beth Hubbard asked Bishop Mangus when they had a private moment one Sunday. "I can see her slipping away, and I don't know what to do about it. I've called her repeatedly; I've even gone over to her home, but she won't let me in. She doesn't want her visiting teachers, either."

"I know. I'm as worried as you are. The home teachers have gone twice, but Kathy excluded herself both times, and the rest of the family avoided talking about themselves. They can't seem to hear what we're saying. Or if they do hear, they don't believe what they hear, and no amount of talking—or doing—will help under those circumstances. Somehow, we have to reach them."

"Have you spoken to Robert?"

"If you can call it that. We've had several brief, highly unsatisfactory conversations in the hall; he has never actually responded to my invitation to meet with me in the privacy of the bishop's office." Bishop Mangus shook his head. "It amazes me that such an educated man can make a virtue out of intransigence. He is absolutely convinced that the problems they are facing must be handled alone. It's the pioneer self-reliance taken to an extreme. Like so many good saints, he is sure that determination mixed with prayer can solve any problem."

Beth smiled. "It does, in many cases."

"Of course. But not when the problems are so severe that true prayer—humble, heartfelt prayer—is for the moment beyond the capacity of the individual. A person who gives his angry feelings free reign drives the Spirit away. On the other hand, a person can repress his negative feelings so thoroughly that he renders himself incapable of experiencing spiritual feelings. I'm not sure which is true in Robert's case, but I think he's forgotten that hearts are healed and forgiveness is granted through grace and the ministration of the Spirit. Eventually, he'll come to the inescapable conclusion that he can't do this alone; when he understands that, the Spirit will soften his heart to the point that we'll be able to help. I just hope it isn't too late by then."

"Isn't there anything we can do?"

Bishop Mangus interlaced his fingers. He had always viewed the bishop's responsibility to his ward, aside from the business aspect of running a smooth organization, as that of a facilitator. That is, he was willing to help whenever necessary, to counsel when the situation required it, to encourage always, and to love, but he was not a pusher. This case, though, obviously required his intervention.

"I have a feeling that this is out of my reach, Beth. In most cases, I'm confident in my ability to counsel ward members, but in this situation, I think specific help is necessary. I'll call Randy Green."

"I don't think Robert likes Randy very much."

"I'm not surprised, but we need to have Randy actively participating in this effort."

Sometime later that Sunday, Randy, a member of Bishop Mangus's ward and a psychologist, sat in the bishop's office, listening to the bishop's assessment of the Montgomery situation. Then he said, "From what you've told me, I'm reluctant to become involved at the moment. Until Kathy and Robert want to be helped, there isn't much I can do. Intervention before that point is reached is pretty fruitless, to tell the truth."

"But I'm very concerned about what may happen if we don't intervene, Randy."

"I can certainly understand that. But professionally, I can't justify getting involved unless the Montgomerys want me to. However, I will be glad to meet with them when they're ready."

"I appreciate that. We'll try to keep as close contact as we can and let them know we're always here to help. I still have hopes that Robert will meet with me. We'll get through somehow!"

As Robert walked from the plane into the terminal of the Twin Cities International Airport, he wondered why he had ever envied those of his business associates who flew to New York one day and Dallas the next. He hadn't wanted to go on this three-day, three-stop trip for his company, not now, not with things the way they were at home. His private life, he admitted, if only to himself, was a shambles. His house was a mess. His children seemed to be off in another place and time. No matter what he did, he couldn't seem to make contact with them. His frustration was intensified by the uncomfortable suspicion that this estrangement wasn't the product of the present situation only; he had been out of real contact with them for months. Or could it possibly be years?

And what about Kathy? He tried to remember a recent moment of intimacy, but he couldn't, not without reaching back so far that it didn't count anymore. But was that all her fault?

Suddenly a pain so sudden and sharp that he almost cried out wiped out the necessity for answering. He felt as if an expert with a whip had sent it coiling around and around his chest with one flick of the wrist. He gasped and leaned against the smooth, white wall, grasping his left arm tightly to him. He was only marginally aware of other passengers moving by him; all his energy was focused on one thing only: to breathe away the pain. It seemed to be hours later when a cart stopped by him, and a skycap asked, "Sir, can I be of some assistance?"

"Get me out to where I can get a taxi," whispered Robert.

"We have an excellent first-aid facility right here in the airport, sir. I'd be glad to take you there."

"No. Just get me a taxi."

"Okay. Do you have any luggage to claim?" asked the skycap as he helped Robert to the cart.

"No. I only brought my carry-on suit bag," said Robert, moving his head to indicate the bag, which was lying on the floor. The skycap retrieved it.

"You're sure you don't want me to take you to our first-aid station? You look pretty bad, if you don't mind my saying so."

Robert grimaced. It was meant to be a grin. "The taxi will be fine," he said, as he closed his eyes and drew another artificially long, even breath.

The breathing technique he had developed was working for him now. Eight counts in, eight counts out, slowly. As he breathed in and out he said to himself, *I feel all right now. There's nothing the matter with me. I'll make it to tomorrow's meeting right on time. Everything will go fine. I'm all right.*

But he wasn't. He was sick and he knew it. He wondered every time the dreaded signs appeared whether the attack would be "the big one." He knew that if he didn't get help, "the big one" was inevitable. Everything that had ever been said by his co-workers about angina and heart attacks had come back to him in the last weeks with startling clarity. But he was even more frightened by the prospect of going to a doctor. He knew what the doctor would say: "Take it easy. Get some rest. Change your life-style." Oh, he knew the whole line, he'd heard it enough in the office. But what would happen if he ever stopped moving forward? Would he be able to lift up his burden again once he dared put it down? Someone had to keep going on in a world that was crumbling. How else would there be any hope of halting the disintegration?

The need to keep on as always was what had recently prompted Robert to accept the bishop's call to be a part of the ward activity committee. But it wasn't a calling he enjoyed, not so much because of the extra drain it put on his faltering energy supply, but because he could hardly stand to go to a meeting where Randy Green was in attendance. And Green was the committee chairman.

Just the sight of Green raised Robert's hackles. Green, with his woodsman's beard and his inevitable plaid shirt, chinos, and hush puppies. Robert always felt stiff by comparison in his suit. True, they rarely met on Sundays, and there was no real need for Robert to wear a suit, but Robert always felt it appropriate and resented Green's casualness. But the resentment went deeper than that. Green's casualness in dress wasn't the only thing Robert disapproved of—he also disapproved of Green's casual approach to life.

He was a fine Church member, Robert conceded, but he had a live-and-let-live acceptance of other people and their foibles that seemed exaggerated to Robert. He had taught Brad's Sunday School class for a time, and while Robert could find nothing to fault in Green's understanding of the gospel or in his teaching of the principles, Green was always willing to let the teenagers in Brad's class decide how to translate principle into policy; he himself only gave suggestions.

How did Green think the world would operate if someone didn't give definite directions and draw boundaries, Robert wondered. He had not been surprised as he heard Brad's enthusiastic reports week after week. Of course teenagers would like any class that allowed them so much freedom. But Robert felt that Green was taking a terrible risk in assuming they could learn the value of living gospel principles by their own experience. That was leaving too much to chance; no one could ever be sure what moral might be drawn from any given experience. Green's viewpoint wasn't unexpected, however. He was a psychologist, and his attitude was typical psychologist drivel.

But something was even more disturbing about Randy Green—the expression his eyes took on when he looked at Robert. They were full of compassion, understanding, and, incredibly, pity. Pity! That enfuriated Robert, and the more he glared at Green and clipped his words, the more he could see of it in Green's eyes.

The jolt of the cart as it went through the automatic doors interrupted Robert's thoughts. Then the weight of the heat and humidity slammed into him, and all the gain from his rhythmic breathing evaporated as he gasped for breath.

"Hang on, sir. I'll get that cab right there, and we'll have you off in a minute!" said the skycap, waving his hat to get the attention of a driver who had just dropped off his passenger.

Carefully Robert slid off the seat and began to walk in the direction of the cab. The skycap rushed to assist him, then ran back to get the suit bag, which was still lying on the seat.

"Really, sir, you ought to see a doctor," said the concerned fellow as he handed the bag to Robert.

"Thanks, I believe I will," Robert said, smiling weakly. And though he really hadn't any intention of doing so, he heard himself tell the driver, "Take me to the nearest hospital." Still, as the taxicab whisked him off, Robert felt betrayed. It was bad enough that his marriage and family life was out of control, but his own body was betraying him as well. And because of that, he had to go through the ignominious poking and prodding of an emergency room doctor and nurse.

Once in the emergency room, the hospital personnel made him take an EKG. As he feared, the little premature spikes, which he thought could only be seen with a magnifying glass, made the diagnosis official: angina.

"You understand that this is serious, don't you?" asked the emergency room doctor brusquely. He had dealt with this sort of patient before, men who were so convinced that the whole structure of society would collapse if they weren't holding up their corner, that they would risk death to keep their appointed rounds.

"Yes, yes," replied Robert wearily. They had already given him a nitroglycerin pill, and he felt better now, although he was exhausted. "I'll get some time off when I get back home. Maybe we'll go to the company cabin. It's here in Minnesota, up near Split Hand Lake. But you can't really expect me to cancel all my meetings because of a little twinge!"

The doctor shook his head disgustedly. "You don't understand, do you. The choice is to let the business world function without you for a little while or have it function without you permanently. Which it could do very well!"

In a moment of revelation, Robert realized that it could do exactly that. His company could function without him, the Church could function without him, even his family could. Kathy had done a marvelous job of running the household and taking care of the kids in his absence, he admitted now. They could get along fine if his absence were permanent. It would probably be no different than if he had gone on an extended business trip. They might not even miss him.

And that was why he couldn't stop. If he did, then they would all understand that he was dispensible.

"I want you to stay here overnight," the doctor was saying. "That way, we can be sure you're stable before you go rushing off to your meeting."

"Yes. All right," said Robert, to the doctor's surprise. His own mortality had been revealed to him, and the need to be protected against that finality was stronger than his need to prove he was invincible.

The next morning, when Robert left the hospital he felt immeasurably better—furthermore, he was reassured by the pills the doctor had prescribed for him as insurance against any repetition of yesterday's episode. Thus Robert reviewed the points of the coming meeting with outward confidence as a taxi conveyed him to his destination. Underneath it all, however, he was uncomfortably aware that an inner solidity had been compromised; he no longer had the pleasant sense of controlling his own life.

Thirteen

The depth of the depression that was sucking Kathy under could be measured by the fact that even her classes were a burden to her now. The task of finding something to wear and working up the energy needed to wash her hair and put on her makeup was overwhelming. She tried to clean the kitchen the way she used to, but she would find herself standing with something in her hand, not sure what to do with it. Throw it away, put it away? She couldn't remember where it should go.

Fun with Foreign Favorites, Good-for-you-Goodies, Diet Delights, the classes came and went. Diet Delights was particularly difficult to present. Kathy, in her loosest dress, was uncomfortably aware of how she must look to her "ladies." Diet Delights indeed!

How did I ever manage to do all the things I used to do? she asked herself one day as she lay on the couch, unable to move. *I was usually halfway through my list long before noon!*

That was it. Lists, lists, and more lists. Lists and charts and the blue notebook. Kathy's eyes ran down the rows of books on the shelves and pulled the notebook out. She opened it up to the index (an index, yet!). Gospel Living, Family Preparedness, Missionary Work, Homemaking, Teaching Children Gospel Principles, Personal Growth, Service. She sat down and began turning the pages.

The notebook had not been her idea. Robert had insisted that she use one to keep track of her life goals.

"Life goals?" she had said with a slightly bewildered

smile. "I filled my life goal when I married you!" She had meant it to be a compliment, but he had only grown angry.

"You don't know what you want to achieve?"

"Of course I do!" Her eyes were filling. "I want to have a happy home and a half-dozen kids."

"Six kids! How do you think you'll manage things with even one? You can't seem to keep the house clean now! We've had the same three casseroles over and over again since we've been married! And what about washing? My white clothes have turned every shade of the rainbow! Look, I can write out a list of goals for you in five minutes!"

And he did, beginning with "1) I will be a good homemaker." Under that heading he wrote "A) I will get good, nutritious meals to the table on time" (If he had known how she would use that later as a justification for the classes she took, he might have never written it); "B) I will keep the house neat and clean; C) I will keep the wash up." Then he had made numerous listings under the subheadings. He wrote quickly, almost maliciously zeroing in on all her weaknesses. He didn't stop to think of how he must be hurting her.

If anyone had asked Robert on his wedding day what had attracted him to Kathy in the first place, he would have said, "She's so much like my Aunt Emma. She's easygoing and happy. She's got the same sparkle in her eyes my favorite aunt has." Now he seemed to have forgotten the things he had admired in her. He may have wanted the girl he courted to be like his Aunt Emma, but he wanted his wife to be like his mother.

"We have to start with basics," he said briskly, showing her the list. "By the way, how is it that you never learned to keep a house clean?"

"But it is clean! There's nothing on the floor and the dishes are washed. What haven't I done?"

"Look here. There's dust on the books. The windows above the sink need to be washed. You haven't vacuumed under the buffet. And look at this!" He rubbed his fingers across the refrigerator top and held them up triumphantly before her. They were covered with greasy dirt. "Every day I have to look at this mess! Why don't you take care of it?"

"But Robert," she cried, devastated. "I'm not as tall as you are! I can't see what's on top of the refrigerator! I didn't know it was dirty!"

"Everyone knows that junk like this gathers on top of refrigerators!"

He was berating her because she didn't do the same things that came naturally to him. To be sure, she was unskilled in matters of housekeeping, but Robert's orderliness was compulsive. He didn't say, for example, "Today I must arrange my shoes in the closet," or "Now I will hang all my shirts facing east and my pants next to them and my suits last." For him, they were reflex actions, as were washing out the sink after his morning ablutions or scraping bits of mud from his shoes. In fact, he wasn't conscious at all that anything was unusual about his combing his hair at night, but Kathy was.

"What are you doing?" she had asked in amazement one evening.

Combing my hair," he had replied, the tone of his voice implying that what he was doing was obvious.

"But you're in your pajamas! Why are you combing your hair before you go to bed?"

"I just am, that's all," he replied, irritated by her question and her laughter. "What's so funny about that? I always comb my hair after I brush my teeth!"

But it never occurred to him that they perceived things in intrinsically different ways. He assumed that all she needed was instruction, and instruction he could certainly give. Some of the sparkle went out of Kathy's eyes when he assumed the role of teacher. She accepted his judgment that she was incompetent as a homemaker, and a sadness crept into her heart. She felt young and inexperienced, inadequate, unworthy of her husband. She tried to do everything he set out for her to do, even though he devised a very thorough training schedule. Under the goals, he enumerated steps she had to follow to reach those goals; he even made lists of what she should accomplish each day and showed her how to do things to his specifications. Though she tried hard, she could never quite do them well enough, and now and then he held an interview with her in the evening, sitting behind his desk, which had been his first purchase after their marriage.

Still, even though cleaning according to Robert's standards filled more of her day, their basement apartment on Capitol Hill in Salt Lake wasn't that big, and the afternoons stretched out before her. She had wanted to take singing lessons at the University of Utah to fill her spare time, but they didn't have a piano, and she had no place to practice. She thought she might take some classes at the BYU Extension Center, but he had rejected that idea as well. "You'd only have to quit when you get pregnant." So she wrote letters to her parents in Bancroft and to his mother at the ranch. Now and then she would write to her brothers, though she rarely heard from them in return.

She also learned to crochet in Relief Society, where she was the only younger woman. Even though she was in the heart of Zion, she felt the same as she had back in Bancroft, where she was the only MIA-aged girl. The women were sweet and helpful, but they were mostly mothers of grown children or grandmothers. She went faithfully, but being among all those experienced women only heightened her sense of inadequacy.

Using her new skill, she started working on a baby blanket in the evenings while she watched TV alone—Robert often brought work home—but she still found herself lonely and bored most of the time. It was then that she took to borrowing great piles of books from the library, most of them escape literature. She was a fast reader and would often read a book in an afternoon. Putting herself into the role of the heroine, she would let herself be carried out of her little world for a time. Those books were to her what food is to a hungry man, because Robert had become very businesslike since their marriage, and her need for tender attention and consideration was left unfilled except vicariously. Once her father's princess, now she felt like a forgotten Cinderella in a fairytale rewrite.

However, Robert had taken a sentence from a long-forgotten class on marriage and made it into an axiom: they were always to go to bed at the same time. They seemed able to talk to each other at those times in a way otherwise impossible. Lying there together in the dark, Robert let down his guard somewhat and became more like the man of their courtship. They would talk about anything that came to mind, the weather, the news, how his mother and her parents were doing, what they would name their first child. At those times the intimacy that they shared extended to their physical relationship as well.

There was one other shared experience that bound them closer in those early months. Living close to the Salt Lake Temple, they went together to an early morning session at least once a week. The part she liked best of all was coming into the Celestial Room, where her husband greeted her with a softened expression radiating love. Then she knew they belonged together and the doubts of the lonely hours would disappear.

She had been thrilled when she found she was pregnant. Thrilled but sick. All day long her head ached and she felt nauseous. The changes taking place in her body disturbed her, the coming birth frightened her, and although she wrote to her parents and called home often, she felt far away from sympathetic ears. She needed comfort and reassurance, but Robert was not in the mood to give either. He had seen his mother working in the garden during her pregnancies, her ungainly body moving slowly down the rows. She had kept house, and cooked and sewed as well. She had even driven the truck on hot, airless days when they needed someone to help with the haying. Life had gone on as usual during the nine months, and at the end of that time, nothing had changed except for one more presence in the household.

He doesn't love me anymore, thought Kathy one day as she lay in bed, sucking on dry bread to calm her stomach. *I've been such a disappointment to him!* She was determined not to let him down, so she struggled out of bed. When Robert came home later in the day, he found her up and dressed. A pot of soup was filling the kitchen with a delicious aroma.

He sat at the table, saying, "See, I knew you could do it! All you have to do is get out of bed!" With those words, he took away her triumph over illness and a coddled past. She felt more isolated than ever before and longed for the birth of the baby. Then she could hold and draw comfort from someone.

But Robert had noticed the pallor of her cheeks and the way she would wipe the cold sweat from her brow with an unconscious gesture, and he wondered whether she really were sick. He decided she probably just wanted sympathy; however, he did begin helping a bit around the apartment, and once in a while he brought flowers home, which always seemed to brighten her day (and increased his conviction that it was all in her head—she didn't complain as much when he babied her a little).

He brought her more flowers the day that Brad was born.

"The first boy grandchild in the family," he said, dialing his mother. "I can't wait to tell her. We'll have him blessed in Beaver, of course. You probably won't feel like the trip this coming fast Sunday, but the next for sure. Oh, Mom! Good news! Yes, and it's a boy, your first grandson!"

Kathy's mother arrived the day she and the baby came home from the hospital. Kathy had never been so glad to see her before. She let her mother take charge, although she had learned to do more than her mother would have believed. Clarice responded by rearranging the porta-crib and the change table so they were more convenient and checking through all of the things Kathy had so loving folded.

"I see there are some things you still need," said Mrs. Adams. "If you don't mind staying home alone for awhile, I'll just run downtown and pick them up. I can probably find everything I want at ZCMI."

"Of course I can stay home alone with the baby, Mother! We have to get used to each other sometime!"

But Mrs. Adams ignored her protest. She acted as though Kathy were incompetent and she and Robert together were a real team. She washed, cooked, and managed as she had done in her own home, moving around Kathy as if she were a piece of superflous furniture, even when it came to the baby. She did everything except feed Brad, since Kathy was breast-feeding, but she had an inexhaustible store of advice on that subject as well.

As much as Kathy had been grateful that her own mother had come instead of Robert's, she was very glad to see her go. She was a mother now, and she could take care of the baby herself! But never having been around babies much, she was honestly uncertain and in need of help, so she enrolled in some classes in baby care offered by the hospital. It was a delight and a relief to be among other new mothers. She not only learned what she needed to know, she also received the commiseration only those experiencing the same things can give. That helped her over the early stage and gave her confidence a boost.

But the self-confidence she had gained in the first few sessions was not strong enough to stand up to the whole Montgomery clan, all of whom were present at the fast meeting in which Robert blessed Brad and at the family dinner held afterward at the weathered ranch house. Lanky blondish men and thin intense women seemed to be everywhere, and fair boys and girls ran in and out of the house, letting the screen door slam behind them. Even those who had married into the family seemed to be mostly fair to Kathy—they weren't really; she was just somewhat paranoid about blond Montgomerys—and equally as intense as the Montgomerys themselves. Kathy felt extremely uncomfortable as she sat there with her dark-haired, dark-eyed son on her lap.

"Takes after his mother, doesn't he?" they said to each other, as if she weren't there at all.

"In looks, yes. But Robert's the most Montgomery-ish

of us all. He'll make a Montgomery out of him in spite of the color of his hair!"

They couldn't seem to sit, any of them, for more than a few minutes. Up and down, in and out, calling to each other, laughing together, saying a word or two to her as they passed by; they were too involved with each other to sit down with the increasingly quiet young mother. *Where is Aunt Emma?* she wondered to herself. At least she got along well with Aunt Emma.

Finally Emma came. She advanced slowly, walking in an odd, stiff manner; the arthritis from which she had been suffering for years had made walking a painful process.

"Let me have a look at that boy," she said, smiling warmly at Kathy. She sat down beside her and took Brad in her crippled hands. Marion sat at her feet and observed the baby with childlike eyes.

"How are you feeling, new mother?" Emma asked.

"Right now, mad!" said Kathy. "Robert acts like the baby is some accomplishment he did all by himself. He shows us off like a couple of . . . I don't know what! Then off he goes and doesn't think about us at all!"

"That's typical. They're a very close family, dear. And they aren't really excluding you. They just expect that you'll join in if you want to. They'll never ask you, as I can say from many years' experience. You just have to take the bull by the horns and make a place for yourself in the family."

"Do you think I'll ever be able to?"

"Sure. It'll take time, but you will."

"Have you?" Kathy wasn't aware of how frank and critical her gaze was as she looked at Aunt Emma. She looked so out of place among the conservatively dressed Montgomerys. Although she had gained a little weight in the last years, she still preferred bright colors—this time she was sporting a lime-green ruffled blouse and a long skirt in a slightly darker shade—and her hair was elaborately done up. (Because she had had limited use in her hands, she had done her silvery hair over and over again with Marion at her side until the girl could follow the same process exactly.) And beyond the striking outfit and the impractical hair-do, she had something foreign about her, an air of energy and—could it possibly be?—mockery.

"Well, when I'm with my own family in my own house, I'm happy and I think my family is too. But when we get together, the whole bunch of them, I'm an oddity, I admit. But I don't mind the job. I have been able to lighten up several sober Montgomerys. At one time, I thought Robert was one of my successes. But then . . ."

"I wish I could feel comfortable with them!" Kathy said longingly. "They all seem so purposeful, even the young ones! They know where they're going, and they're in a hurry to get there."

Aunt Emma leaned toward Kathy as if to tell a secret. "There's more than one way to live a life, child. Each of us has his own tempo, his own way of seeing things. Take Marion, here." She touched Marion's face, the bony, malformed finger soft against her cheek. Marion, who was the same age as Kathy, smiled at her mother—a sweet, uncomplicated smile. "Marion was brain-damaged at birth. It happened a lot before doctors were advised not to use forceps regularly. So she has to take things slowly. And her old crippled-up mother has to take things slowly as well. Together we make a great pair! We have a lot of fun together, don't we, sweetie?"

Marion nodded, her eyes full of love for her mother. Kathy could imagine that among the nearly hyperactive cousins, there was precious little of the understanding that Marion needed.

"Find out what makes you happy and content, and make sure you get planty of it your life," Emma continued.

"I like to sing," Kathy said shyly. "I took singing lessons at the 'Y' the year before I married Robert. My teacher thought I had possibilities." Her eyes lightened a bit, and her voice became animated. "Actually, I know I can sing! If I could have lessons, I could get good enough to be a soloist. It would take a lot of work, but I know I could do it." Her voice dropped to a confidential level. "What I'd really like to be is an opera singer!"

"Really!" Emma was delighted. "And I wanted to be an actress."

"You did?"

"Yes. I was quite well known in my day for dramatic readings. I still love reading poetry and plays aloud."

"I guess there's not much of a possibility for acting in Beaver."

"No. And in my condition . . ." Her upraised hands were more eloquent than any words. "But Marion and I play a little game together, don't we, Marion?"

Marion nodded excitedly.

"I teach her the lines of a certain character—she has some trouble with reading—then I take the other lines, and we put on a play, don't we! We have such fun, and Marion loves it."

"I like the sounds the words make," Marion said, and began to quote "The quality of mercy is not strained" from the *Merchant of Venice.* Her voice changed subtly, took on a richer, deeper quality, and her delivery was astonishing.

"That was wonderful!" Kathy said.

"Very good, Marion," commented Robert's mother.

"She can really quote up a storm, can't she," said Uncle Alma, who had also stopped to listen.

Marion was complimented, of course, but Kathy could see that most people gave her compliments as if she were a dog trained to jump through a burning hoop. They didn't realize how the girl strained to grasp beauty in sound. Kathy realized something else as well: Marion was a perfect mimic. She was even able to present the richness of emotion and experience that came from Aunt Emma's soul.

"Are you sorry you never pursued acting?" Kathy asked.

"No. I'm content with my life. I wouldn't change anything that has happened to me through the years."

"Not even the sad things?" Kathy couldn't help looking at Marion.

"No, not even the sad things."

Kathy was overwhelmed.

Later, on the way home, Robert accused Kathy of being

a stick-in-the-mud. "You didn't talk to anyone but Aunt Emma!"

"I like talking to her—she's the most wonderful person I've ever met! Besides, nobody else wanted to talk to me, as far as I could tell."

"Well, you just can't sit there and expect everyone to come to you like some princess!"

"At home, my dad calls me 'Princess,'" she said with a toss of her head.

"Well, you're not home anymore, and you're no princess. You're Mrs. Robert Montgomery, and I don't want you sulking in the corner the next time we go down to the ranch!"

"Who says I want to go down to the ranch? It's ugly and dry and dusty. It's not like the well-kept farms in Iowa, with the house and barns painted and the lawns green and trees everywhere. You can keep your old ranch!"

The ranch, ugly? He was so shocked by the idea that he actually considered it. The weathered-wood house and outbuildings; the patch of grass before the front steps, unwatered except by rain; a few trees that gave welcome shade; and the distant mountains—he loved them, but he could see how it must look to her as he remembered the beautiful, prosperous farms he had seen in Pennsylvania. It was then that he first contemplated the possibility of looking for work in the Midwest, near Kathy's home. "I guess it is different from what you Easterners are used to," he admitted. "But it's my home, and I won't have you talking about it that way."

"I'm sorry," she said, subdued.

"Listen, I know you feel pretty much the odd person out, but next time please try to get better acquainted with my relatives."

"I'm sorry, Robert," she said. "I'll try next time, I really will."

The rest of the trip home they were both lost in thought.

After they had arrived back in their apartment, Kathy wisely waited until Robert was in a good mood to bring up the thought she had been considering since her talk with Emma. "Robert, do you think we could afford a piano? An old one, a used one would be okay. I'm sure we could find one that wouldn't cost too much. Please?"

"We can't afford it."

"How can you say that when you don't even know how much a piano costs? Here, I looked in the want ads. There's an old high-back here for only 126 dollars. That's not too much, is it?"

"Well, maybe not," he said reluctantly, "but how would we get it down the stairs?"

"I don't know, but we could, somehow! Would you consider it, please?"

He folded the newspaper and dropped it into the magazine rack by the chair. "Maybe," he said shortly. But he had seen the excitement in her eyes, and he remembered that Uncle John had said of his Aunt Emma, "She loves music, just has to have it."

The day the men brought the used Baldwin spinet, Kathy was in a state of shock. She couldn't believe they had the right address, but they showed her the invoice: "Deliver to Mrs. Robert Montgomery." She nearly danced as they struggled down the steps with the heavy instrument, and she could have kissed them as they left. She kissed Robert instead, flinging herself at him the moment he walked past the door. She had prepared a special meal and had used the last of her food money to buy flowers for the table. With Brad asleep in the porta-crib, they had an evening of rare togetherness, relaxed, warm, and tender.

There were more practical matters to face in the upcoming days, though. To help Kathy get back into the swing of things, Robert helped her to fill out a daily schedule in her notebook, beginning with getting up at 5:30 and doing her sit-ups—"You've got to get rid of that baby fat!" he told her—then showering and dressing before breakfast.

She sighed. The way he put it down on paper made it all seem so easy. "You're not thinking about the baby," she said. "I can't schedule in diaper changes and feedings."

"See here," he said, proud that he had allowed for that contingency. "I've actually given you some discretionary time every hour. Fifteen minutes to be exact. That ought to give you enough time to work in Brad's little emergencies." He smiled at his son and chucked him under the chin.

Kathy had to smile too, looking at them. Robert was fascinated by the dark-haired child and spent more time playing with him than Kathy had ever expected. He often took the baby on walks in the pram—he had actually bought the big English-nanny variety!—and read to him from picture books; he loved to buy toys or clothes for his son. Kathy picked up the list. She decided she would give it a try, especially after she noticed that the schedule included time for "Kathy's music."

She had barely gotten a grip on her new situation though, when she became pregnant with Sue. This pregnancy was even more difficult than her first. Kathy could hardly manage to get out of bed to take care of her own needs, much less those of Brad. Cleaning, cooking, and washing were nearly impossible. She couldn't seem to stop vomiting, and she could barely keep Seven-Up and dry bread down. Finally, Robert took her to the doctor.

"Well?" he demanded when the doctor invited him into his office.

"Your wife is severely dehydrated. I recommend immediate hospitalization."

It was simple survival that ruled their days after Kathy came home from the hospital. Never once during the nine months did she feel really well. Although the ward Relief Society did much to relieve Kathy of the burden of housework and laundry, and though Robert's mother arrived every weekend to blitz-clean the apartment and offer her brand of encouragement (*Lecture is a better word,* thought Kathy), both Robert and Kathy had a miserable time. The only occasions that lifted Kathy's spirit were the rare visits from Aunt Emma and Marion.

Whenever Uncle John had business in Salt Lake, Aunt Emma and Marion would come along. Having them for even a few hours was a joy. Marion would do some cleaning while Emma sat with Kathy, listening to her litany of troubles; but Kathy never could take her own suffering so seriously when Emma with her clawed hands and smiling Marion with her child's mind were there. Emma's gentle encouragment did much to motivate her, while Faye's chiding only made her feel like a stubborn child.

The experience took its toll. After Susan was born, Kathy announced, "That's it, Robert. I don't want any more children. I can't handle it!"

"What about the dozen you used to talk about?"

"I must have been crazy!" There was a determined set to her jaw that was new.

In spite of all that Robert did to change her mind, Kathy held to her decision. He had counseled her, sitting behind his desk, reminding her that having a large family was something they had agreed on before their marriage.

"But there must be some consideration of the mother's health!" she insisted. "I'm worried about my physical and mental health!"

"You'll change your mind when you're feeling better."

"That may be, but look how quickly I got pregnant again after Brad! I've got to have time! I'm not saying I'll never want another baby; I'm just saying 'not now.'"

Robert kept at her, and so did his mother. That enraged Kathy even further. "How dare you tell your mother about my personal problems!" she had cried. But Robert had not let up.

Aunt Emma, though, didn't push. "Pray, child," she encouraged her. "When you know what the Lord's will is for you, be strong in carrying it out. That's why I never had any more babies after Marion, you know. I knew without a doubt that the Lord was with me in my decision. And now I know why. With Marion's problems, and my arthritis getting worse all the time, he knew I had all I could handle."

Kathy prayed and prayed and then went to Robert again. "I'm following through with what we talked about," she said. "I'm positive the Lord understands and supports me."

Robert retaliated to her firm stand by refusing to have

any physical contact with her. "If you're going to take measures against conceiving, there's no reason for us to take chances at all," he said coldly. But his resistance did soften after time, as she had known it would.

That year brought many changes in addition to the ones that come as children grow and as husbands and wives set aside courtship illusions. One morning Kathy was awakened by the phone: her father had died of a stroke. It was a terrible, unexpected blow—he had never been much for writing letters or making long-distance calls from Bancroft, but Kathy had always depended on the fact that he loved her and was sending good thoughts her way. The feeling of abandonment overwhelmed her.

Another development soon after softened her sense of loss. Kathy had not been back from Bancroft long when Robert told her he had been offered a job by Industrial Investments, a firm with a major branch in Lemburg, Iowa.

"Lemburg!" she shrieked. "I can't believe it! I'll be close to Mother, right when she needs someone! Oh, Robert, I never thought I'd get back to Iowa, back where it's green!"

"Well, just wait a few months and you can start setting up housekeeping in your new house." He said it without any emphasis and waited with a satisfied expression for her reaction.

"A house! We're getting a house!"

"Why not? We've saved up a little, and I've decided to sell my share of the ranch to my brothers for the rest of the down payment." He sighed richly and put his hands behind his head. "I. I. is a growing company, and Lemburg is a growing town. I've been looking for just this sort of opportunity—I can really show what I'm made of. We're on our way!"

So they moved from the dry, mountain-ridged valley to northern Iowa, where the fields were green and lush and the horizon low and long. Kathy stood in the treeless back yard of her new, three-bedroom house in Lemburg, less than a day's drive from Bancroft, and looked with satisfaction at the sky, which arched overhead like an inverted bowl that came down to meet the flat line of earth. Only then did she realize how hemmed in the mountains had made her feel.

Kathy had more to do during her day now. Her new ward was full of young married couples, a wonderful change from their ward in Salt Lake. She loved going to Relief Society, especially to homemaking meetings. She learned to sew, to quilt, to grow a garden, to bottle fruits and vegetables. She learned to make homemade bread and to cook with soybeans. She made some hesitant starts in genealogy work. And for each of these new skills, there was a page in the blue BYU notebook: schedules, charts, graphs, dates of genealogy letters written and of answers received, planting dates for the garden each year, records of yields and numbers of quarts bottled, food storage lists, and rotation charts.

She learned CPR, she made a kit of emergency health needs, she had an evacuation suitcase packed. Her garage was lined with labeled boxes à la Daryl Hoole, and her bookshelf was lined with how-to books: *How to Be in Control of Your Time and Your Life, Work Smarter Not Harder,* and a host of others. She bought a yogurt maker and a wheat grinder. She studied health-food books. If there was anything a good Mormon mother was supposed to do, she did it. After hearing a talk by the bishop in Relief Society, she even agreed to have another baby. That was in 1976—Brad was 11, Susan 9½.

Her resolve wavered, however, when she approached Robert about the possibility—the memory of those miserable months still frightened her: "It seemed so right when I was listening to the bishop," she said. "It didn't seem hard or frightening, but now that I'm home and not so strongly prompted by the Holy Ghost, it seems impossible!" But she stuck to her resolution, to Robert's immense satisfaction.

This time, after she had become pregnant, she felt well and strong and confident in her sense of self. Looking around her home—a new, larger home in a more prestigious neighborhood—she could see the results of her efforts and was satisfied that Kathy Adams Montgomery was a woman to be taken seriously. She was confident in her role as mother, also, but most important, she had a circle of friends who were going through the same nine-months waiting—"Looks like we all took the bishop's talk to heart!" they'd say, laughing.

That sense of well-being lasted through the pregnancy and up through Grant's first birthday. Then, in late 1977, Robert was called to be on the high council, which meant many evenings away from home and many Sundays spent in other wards without his family. He also began traveling a great deal for his firm. These new developments left Kathy to run the house and to take care of the children alone much of the time. During those hours and days without Robert, she managed the affairs of the household the way she chose to, making all necessary decisions herself. She became capable of dealing with repairmen, paying the bills, and getting the car serviced, things she would normally have left to Robert.

When he would come home, though, he would immediately step into his role as head of the household and begin criticizing her for what she had or hadn't done.

Finally, she lashed back. "Listen, we do just fine when you're not home! I'm a grown woman, Robert. You may have married a child who needed to be taught how to count to ten, but I'm not that person anymore. I'm quite capable, in case you hadn't noticed. I know how to run this household as well as you!"

"Well, you haven't done too bad," he admitted grudgingly, "but now that I'm here, it's up to me to make the decisions."

"Why?"

"Because that's the way it is! A man is the head of his family. He has the last say."

"Why?"

"Because men have the priesthood and women don't. It's the eternal order of things!"

Kathy had been on the verge of saying something, but her mouth snapped shut. She was enraged, but she couldn't speak. In a flash she had remembered her father saying the same thing to her mother, and like her mother, she could think of no reply more articulate than a scream.

They began to drift apart then, Robert increasingly burdened with business and Church responsibilities, Kathy beginning to find interests beyond Church and family. She started to teach cooking classes now and then for neighbors and friends. She had been taking vocal lessons, but she also auditioned for and was accepted into the prestigious choral group that practiced Tuesday nights in Old Church. She had been taking community education classes off and on, then decided to enroll at the University of Iowa branch in classes that would lead to a nutrition degree.

She checked off her lists, worked on her charts and goals, and endured her interviews with Robert, as before. But the sense of accomplishment that in recent years had motivated her work in the notebook was no longer there. She had supposed that by doing all those things, she and her family would be happy and they would be together forever. She didn't ask herself if she wanted to be with Robert forever—that was too dangerous a question.

The blue notebook had thus accompanied her through the years, sometimes a helpful companion, sometimes a reproach. Sometimes she had abandoned it altogether, leaving it on the shelf to gather the dust Robert hated, but she had always come back to it. In it could be read her good times and her bad times, but whatever the situation some progress could always be seen. Until now. Now in her thirty-eighth year, Kathy Montgomery had slid right off the chart.

She touched a page of the notebook with her finger. "I thought you said your yoke was easy and your burden light," she whispered. "I listed all the shoulds and oughts. I had it all written down, codified, just like the biblical Jews with their laws. They were so sure of what they were doing, and you rejected them." She laughed softly, bitterly. "Didn't do me much good either." Sounding brass and tinkling cymbals—that was what all her effort was worth. Duty was like sawdust in her mouth. She put the notebook back on the shelf and went back to her place on the couch.

Fourteen

The vulture that had taken up residence in the desert of Kathy's heart had an enormous wingspan. The shadow cast as he stretched his wings extended to the four men in her life, so that they walked in gloom on even the brightest of days.

The shadow was visible in Robert's face, so much so that one day his secretary ventured to say, "I wish you'd see a doctor." She herself was appalled that she would risk being so personal, but the pallor of his face and the unguarded moments when the lines around his mouth twisted in a grimace of pain motivated her to speak.

"See a doctor?" His voice had risen in surprised response.

"I don't mean to be out-of-line, Mr. Montgomery, but I've noticed that you don't feel too well lately, and I'm worried about you."

His eyes widened, and he burst into laughter, a raucous, unpleasant sound. Then, noticing her face, he stopped and said in a normal tone, "Thank you, Janice. I'm grateful that you are concerned about me. And you're right. I haven't been feeling too well. But it's easy to put off doing something about it till another day."

"I hope you don't put it off too long, sir."

"No, I won't. Don't worry."

He wasn't just saying it to pacify her; he knew that he had to go. He knew by the frequency of the episodes and by the diminishing count of tablets in the vial he carried in his breast pocket (his hand reached up to touch the vial, just to make sure). He felt keenly that his body was susceptible to disintegration. The specter of fatality that had entered his consciousness in the curtained cubicle of the emergency room had never left—it had taken its position quietly and simply waited, gaining power.

Robert was not the only one to cause his co-workers to worry, however. Jay's recent behavior had also sparked concern among his colleagues. He had gone from a state of confident anticipation to a state of irritability, moodiness and depression. The flow of witty repartee that had been his trademark had suddenly stopped; his hands, always so well groomed, showed signs of furtive nail-biting. He had lost ten pounds he could ill afford to lose—the effect of his now-habitual evening run and his recent lack of appetite. His face was a spare construction of angles and planes; his eyes were dark, deep-set pools of suffering. He seemed sparked by some inner disquiet that led others to remark, "He's been so strange lately—as if he were possessed!" And indeed he was.

He was driven by the need to assign some meaning to life: life in general and his own life in particular. He wanted to believe that there was something more than the time spent on earth between birth and death, but that implied there was some entity in the universe great and glorious enough to be God, and there his mind balked. He couldn't imagine pure intellect managing the universe, nor could he comprehend the Mormons' personal god. His trips to the library took on purpose. He was searching, reading with fearful hope book after book in the section marked "Religion." Because he had never read the Bible, Jay had no knowledge of the verse that so aptly described the yearning in his heart: "Lord, I believe; help thou mine unbelief."

But while Jay was actively searching, Brad was faltering. Since his mother's admission of guilt, he had lost interest in everything that had been important to him during high school. He felt singled out from his comrades for a special burden of sorrow. He knew that other teenagers had problems too—not enough money, poor grades, trouble with parents, drinking problems. Some were doing drugs, and a few he knew even suffered from abuse. Those were definitely more difficult situations to deal with than his, but he knew that only in his head. He couldn't talk himself out of the feeling that his own problem was unique and that his suffering was greater than theirs.

After all, how could he tell them what had happened? It would have been simple enough to say, "My mom's had an affair"; but the words themselves were not the problem—it was the thought of what they meant. He had heard the guys talk about their escapades with girls. He didn't like hearing that sort of conversation and almost always left when it got started, but he had heard enough to have some pictures in his mind. And now, the face of the girl in those pictures was his mother's face.

It was hardly surprising that he began turning away from the girls he had been friends with for years. He had never had a steady girl, although he had always had many girl friends with whom he had attended dances and school functions, girls with whom he could flirt without being taken seriously. But now, even the light banter was too much for him. There was nothing he could say or do that didn't have some awful possibility connected with it. A casual arm around the shoulders was no longer casual. A simple remark about looks was no longer simple. So Brad stopped talking to them, isolating himself in an aura of melancholy.

Brad's little brother, Grant, was not melancholy, however. He was cheerful, much too cheerful, perhaps. He had become rather hyperactive, always talking, always laughing, trying to tickle others into laughing too. He was so determined to make his family smile again that he had become a nuisance, a fly to be swatted at. But in true fly fashion, he kept coming back.

"For heaven's sake, Grant! Don't you ever stop talking?" Susan would ask him, exasperated.

Brad was more blunt: "Shut up! I've had all I can take of you!"

But Brad's rudeness had no more effect on Grant than his sister's pointed question or his father's preoccupation.

(Grant would buzz around Robert trying unsuccessfully to find a place to light, and every time he tried, he was absentmindedly shooed away.)

His hyperactivity extended to his class as well. He was disruptive in the classroom, teasing girls into tears and destroying the atmosphere by loud laughter at totally inappropriate moments. But there was a desperate quality to his cheerfulness that his teacher was wise enough to catch. She disciplined him when necessary but with kindness; she recognized a deeply disturbed child.

So Robert, Jay, Brad, and Grant carried their private sorrows day by day, handling them the only way they knew how. Four men with this in common: they each had a place in Kathy's heart and because of that could not escape the shadow of the vulture's wing.

Although Kathy's insistence that she not be visited was respected, her visiting teachers had been sending cards and calling her at least once a month—despite the fact that she was shamelessly rude. When a florist delivered a bouquet of lovely flowers from them one day, she almost threw them into the trash, but her need for beauty surfaced long enough to change her mind. She put them in a vase and set them on the table by the baby grand, absently running her fingers over the dusty keys as she passed by.

Myra however, finally got angry at being rebuffed when she called and being ignored on Sundays. They had been friends too long, and she wasn't about to let something step between them. So she appeared at Kathy's door at eight forty-five one morning and pushed her way in even though Kathy seemed about to shut it in her face.

She had prepared a speech, but the condition of the house drove it from her mind.

"Good grief! What's going on here, Kathy! I knew things were bad, or you wouldn't have cut me off like this. But I sure never expected to see your house looking like mine!"

"You don't need to worry about the condition of my house, Myra. Nobody asked you to."

Myra looked straight at Kathy, who avoided her glance. "I'm not worried about the house, and you know it. I'm worried about my friend. And I've been praying for that friend," she added softly.

"Don't bother," said Kathy despairingly.

"You can't mean that!"

"Oh yes I do. Forget trying to cheer me up. Consider your errand of mercy completed and leave me alone."

Instead, Myra looked around the room, taking in the dusty table tops, the pile of newspapers by the kitchen door, and Kathy herself—face pasty, hair dull and matted, still in her bathrobe.

"Listen, you may not have wanted me here, but I'm here now. And I'm taking over. You go up and take a shower, right now. You'll feel better right off if you shower and get dressed instead of sitting around in that ratty old robe. I'll take care of all this." She waved disdainfully at the accumulated mess. "Then I'll fix you a cup of peppermint tea."

Kathy obeyed. It would have taken far too much effort not to. She smiled a little as she walked up the stairs, thinking about Myra and how she managed to bully people into doing what she considered to be the right and proper thing to do. *Or bullies the Relief Society president into assigning it to someone.* Like the clothing exchange. Everyone was so pleased with it. The program had filled a real need in the ward. "Why didn't we do this before?" sisters asked one another, as if it had been their own idea. But Myra had been the one who had engineered the whole project, seeing the need in a ward where so many were struggling and so many others were well-off.

The hot water pouring down on Kathy felt good. She washed her hair and then just stood there, clouds of steam rising to fill the bathroom. With effort she finally turned off the water and stepped from the shower, slowly drying and dressing.

I must have gained fifty pounds, she thought, *I didn't realize a person could gain so much in so little time.* She stepped on the scales and watched the numbers roll, then steady twenty pounds higher than usual. She shrugged. "So what?" But she felt a weak struggle within that she suppressed. *I don't care. I don't care!* she told herself.

Still, she had to admit that she felt better clean and dressed. The house looked better, too. Myra had certainly been busy. The family room was brighter, the furniture had been dusted, and the curtains were moving in a light spring breeze. The kitchen was brighter too and smelled clean and fresh. Myra was standing at the sink, washing the last of the dirty pans.

"How did you manage to get all this done in such a short time?" Kathy asked her.

Myra smiled. "You went upstairs an hour and a half ago."

Kathy sat down, uncomprehending. "I was gone that long?"

Myra poured boiling water into a pot and put in some peppermint leaves and two tablets of artificial sweetener. "It'll be ready in a moment," she said. "You sit there, and I'll finish up these pans."

What's happened to me? Kathy wondered. She should be the one shining up the kitchen, brewing tea from mint leaves gathered from her own garden the summer before.

Myra brought cups and saucers to the table and poured the steaming liquid. They sat there quietly, waiting for it to cool, Kathy warming her hands on the cup. The tea was strong and good, tasting rather like the smell of spearmint gum. Relaxed by the hot shower and now by the warm, sweet tea, Kathy felt herself wanting to talk. She reached across and took Myra's hand. "I'm glad you came."

"I am too," said Myra with an answering squeeze.

"Does everybody talk about me?" Kathy asked hesitatingly. "Do they know what I did?"

"Kathy, let's get one thing straight. Your excommunication is not a topic of conversation! Nobody even knows about it! Listen, sweetie, the only thing I've heard anybody say is that they're concerned about you. And no wonder! It's not hard to tell that something is wrong, even if they don't know exactly what. But I'm not going to tell them, I promise you!"

"Do you know what I did?" Kathy wanted yet dreaded to hear the answer.

Myra looked into her cup. "I can guess," she said finally. "We've always had our private talks, you and I. We know each other quite well. I've listened to your complaints about Robert. And I've heard you talk about Jay."

"But you still came."

"Why not? You're still the Kathy I love."

"Am I? Everyone looks at me as if I had suddenly sprouted snakes in my hair."

Myra scrutinized her friend, noticed the rounded jawline and the clean but still unruly hair. "If you see anything different in people's faces, it's only concern, believe me. No one is anywhere near as hard on you as you are on yourself. You're seeing something that isn't really there."

Kathy shook her head. "I know what I see. All you have to do is stay until Brad and Susan come home. Or Robert. Yes, that would be best; then you'll know what I'm talking about!"

"Give them time, dear. They love you. I know they do. But I also know that this has been a terrible shock for them as well. They need time to work out their feelings."

"They can have all the time they want. But time's running out for me."

Myra looked up, startled. "What do you mean?"

"I don't know. It's just that I have this year in front of me, and I don't see it as a road going anywhere. I see it as a dead end. I'm supposed to make things right, but I don't know if I can or even if my own family really wants me to."

"Of course they do, Kathy! So do I! And even if you can't believe in that, God wants you to succeed. That's for sure!"

But Kathy only shook her head.

"I have to go now," said Myra, looking at her watch. "Are you going to be all right?"

"I don't know. But thanks for all you did."

"No problem," said Myra, hugging her friend. "And no more shutting me out, understood?"

"Myra, I'm glad you came, but please don't presume on our friendship. Next time call first, okay?"

"And have you tell me you don't feel like company? Not likely!"

"I can't promise I'll let you in."

"Well, let's cross that bridge when we come to it."

Kathy was back in the newly cleaned kitchen, enjoying the cheery atmosphere, when Brad came in, home from school at an unusual hour. Startled by his unexpected appearance, she forgot that he didn't talk to her anymore and asked with concern, "Brad, why are you home so early? Don't you have a baseball game this afternoon?"

With his dark eyes he stood staring at her as if deciding whether to answer or not. Finally he said, "I'm not playing on the team anymore."

"What?" She couldn't believe her ears. Her tall, athletic, energetic son was really saying that? "Brad, you love baseball! And this is your last year on the team!"

"So what. Baseball's stupid."

"I can't believe you're saying that! You never missed a practice or a game last year!"

"Well, this year's different, isn't it!"

She ducked her head. "Yes, it is. But believe me, I would give anything to have our lives back the way they were." She caught herself short. They were nice words, and the sentiment was perhaps expected under the circumstances, but she knew they were not true. She raised her head and tried to speak steadily. "No. That's not exactly true. I don't want to go back. We weren't all that happy."

"Speak for yourself!" he retorted.

She felt a knot twist in her stomach. "All right. I wasn't all that happy, and I don't think your father was either. But until now we were willing to go along with the way things were. Now everything's on the line. Our survival as a family is at stake, don't you see that? If we can't learn to love and forgive one another, we're lost!"

She was about to say more, but she could tell he wasn't really listening to her. "Brad?" she questioned.

His eyes met hers, cold and frightening, and then the dam burst.

"Do you have any idea how it feels to know that your own mother has slept with someone besides your father?" He slammed his fist down on the table top. "I sit and listen to the same talks every year in Mutual, all about self-control and being clean and staying close to the family. I guess they think we really need it, that otherwise we'd jump right in bed if they didn't tell us over and over what Church standards are! It seems to me they need a standards night for adults! Don't you agree?"

"Yes," she whispered. "I guess the biggest mistake is thinking it can never happen to you."

"You know," he continued as if she hadn't spoken. "I can't imagine you and Dad together. But the thought of you with someone else makes me want to throw up! How could you do it?"

He was leaning over the table so close to her, his eyes so full of hatred, that she couldn't hold his gaze.

"I know what it feels like to want someone," he said, his voice harsh. "I'm not a kid anymore. But I've never done anything that was against Church standards. And I never will. In fact the thought of sex makes me sick. The thought of you makes me sick! So is it okay with you if I leave, now that we've had our mother-and-son chat?"

Without waiting for an answer, he turned sharply and strode from the room. Kathy felt herself going down in a whirlpool of emotion, but she frantically repeated to herself, "It doesn't matter, it doesn't matter . . ." Then she opened the package of cinnamon rolls lying in the cupboard.

Fifteen

Myra's blitz had taken care of the surface cleaning in the family room and kitchen, but the Montgomery house was definitely neglected, its sorry state only emphasized by the work she had done. Robert had not said anything, hoping that Kathy would snap out of her depression and that things would improve. His own vulnerability had made him more aware of hers, and he was determined not to ride her about it. But the contrast between the rooms now clean and those untouched set him off. As she came down the stairs the next morning, still dressed in her robe, he said what he had not intended to say. "When are you going to clean up this place? And when are you going to get dressed?"

"Probably never," she replied.

"Listen, Kathy, we've got to keep going if we're going to make it through this. But you're letting everything fall apart!"

"Just what is your understanding of 'getting through this?' Do you mean we should go along as if nothing has happened?"

"Well, you could at least get dressed and comb your hair. And clean things up a bit. What you're doing only makes things worse!"

"Oh, I see. It's all right to be dying inside as long as I don't look like it, right? Well, I don't care if the place is a mess. I don't have enough energy to do more than one thing at a time—all I'm trying to do is survive. Trying to figure out if I want to survive, for that matter. Everything else is just going to have to wait."

She put some bread in the toaster and got out some milk. "Are you sure you want to do that?" he asked, trying to be helpful.

"What's it to you? Why do you want me to stay, Robert? Can you tell me that?"

He didn't answer.

"You say you want me to stay, for commitment's sake. But you can't stand the sight of me. You say we have to sleep in the same bed so the children won't think anything's wrong! What a laugh. We aren't fooling anyone, not even Grant. Why don't we just call it quits! I can pack and be gone this morning!"

"Where would you go?"

"Mother's. I don't have anywhere else to go."

"No?"

"No."

"You said once you didn't want to go."

"That was before I knew how much you hate me. How can I get my life in order when everybody around me wishes I were dead?"

Her words were like a sword, cutting, because he knew they were true. Brad had said those very words just the night before. Susan had even said them once as well, adding "I wish I were dead!" But neither one meant them—they were only a figure of speech, something blurted out when no other words could express their anguish. *You said it yourself!* an inner voice accused. *But I didn't mean it, either,* he silently defended himself.

"You hurt us, you know," he said aloud. "Do you really expect us to welcome you with open arms and kill the fatted calf?"

She pounced on that, eyes glinting. "But that's exactly what you're supposed to do, isn't it? That's what Jesus taught! If you were the good Church member you profess to be, Mr. Robert Montgomery, you would kill the fatted calf and proclaim the feast!"

He felt blood rush to his face. She was right! But that made repentance too easy for her. They were suffering, all of them, because of her. Yet the gospel required them to forgive! That was hard, unfair! She should suffer, she should descend to the very depths, and then, perhaps . . .

"See! See!" she gloated, pointing at him triumphantly. "You can't do it, can you! Jesus said we should forgive one another, but you can't do it! Oh, you need help as much as I do!"

He glared at her, furious. "It's not my fault! Any of it!" he hissed. "I haven't done anything wrong! Remember that!" And he fled. Once outside the door, he took a pill from the container with trembling hands and laid it under his tongue.

He had not been in his office more than half an hour when his secretary buzzed him.

"Mr. Montgomery, Mrs. Adams is on the line. Will you speak to her?"

Why is she calling again! he thought irritably, but he knew he couldn't avoid talking to her. He picked up the telephone receiver.

"Hello, Mom," he said.

"Oh, Robert, I'm so glad I caught you. I'm really worried about Kathy. I just talked to her on the phone and she sounded so depressed!"

"She is depressed. I think under the circumstances that shouldn't be surprising."

"No, of course not," retorted Clarice. Then in a softer tone she said, "Listen, I know you have reason to be disillusioned and angry. This is awful for you. But please don't let your own unhappiness blind you to the unhappiness of others. Kathy needs you now."

There was no response.

"Robert, stop tuning me out! I think I should be up there with you, but every time I suggest to Kathy that I come, she says not to. I'll come anyway, if you think I should."

"That's very nice of you, Clarice. I appreciate your offer, and I'm sure Kathy does too, but we're doing as well as can be expected." *Sounds like we have a terminal disease,* he thought. Aloud he said, "I don't think there's any reason for you to come. Kathy is glad that you call now and then, so just keep calling. That's about all you can do."

"I'm not so sure about that." Clarice's voice carried a challenge. She had the strong impression that she should go to Kathy, although Robert sounded so certain, so in control.

"Clarice, you'll be the first to know if we need you." Robert then used his standard "this-is-the-end-of-the-conversation" line: "Now thanks for calling and keep in touch."

Clarice's mouth settled in a hard line when she realized that Robert had hung up on her. *I don't care what he says,* she told herself. *I'm going to Lemburg as soon as I can.*

But Robert, as he replaced the receiver, thought, *Another person worried about Kathy. I would like to get one phone call, just one, from someone worried about me!*

Clarice had been calling him weekly since Kathy had been to Bancroft. He had also had calls from home teachers and visiting teachers, who wondered what they could do to help Kathy. Though they had asked, "What can we do to help you?" they had really meant, "What can we do to help Kathy." Not one of them had ever asked what they could do for him; not even the bishop, who had taken him aside on Sunday, saying that he was very worried about Kathy. Then there was Myra. She was the worst, cornering him every time she had the chance, telling him what she thought Kathy needed. "I'm so concerned about the way she looks," Myra invariably said.

No wonder! She goes about so hangdog! he thought angrily. *Why does she wear her miseries so obviously that a blind man could see them? Hoping to get sympathy, probably. And she has certainly succeeded there. Maybe I should start walking around like a zombie. I could gain fifty pounds, stop washing my hair, and wear unpressed suits to work. Maybe then someone would ask if there was something they could do for me!*

And if they did ask, he could tell them! He had a legitimate illness, something measurable and menacing in his body, something that could lead to disaster if he didn't take care of himself. Obviously, it was up to him to take care of himself, just as he always had. He still had some nitroglycerin tablets left; he planned to call his doctor for an appointment when they were close to running out.

I'll just go on doing what I've always done, he assured himself. But as that thought went through his mind, he could see his father, plodding along, doing what needed to be done. There he was, pitching hay, then stopping for a moment to rub his left shoulder.

As Robert zeroed in on that gesture, a thought struck him. He began to recall other memories, looking for something specific, and he found it again and again: his father saying, "Rub right there between my shoulder blades, will you?" or his father saying, "Gosh, my arm's asleep again!"

Then Robert knew without a doubt what had happened in that dusty draw in Southern Utah. His father hadn't been caught by the flash flood alone—he had been caught by the weakness in his heart. It had struck him right when he needed his full capacity the most, right as the wall of butterscotch-colored water was coming down the draw at him. He had let go of the wheel to clutch his chest, and that had cost him the moment's lead he had had.

The picture was so clear and intense that Robert instinctively shut his eyes, though that had no effect. He almost cried aloud as he saw the rolling water engulf the pickup. He felt himself being inundated and swept away as well, and his mouth opened and closed in dry sobs that brought him no comfort. He realized he wanted Kathy, wanted to press himself against her warm softness and tell her about his father and weep with her over his loss. But he couldn't; he had spent too many years avoiding such intimacy.

But if anything, Robert Montgomery was a practical man. The insight into his father's death had shaken him deeply; he knew he had to make the call he had avoided up to now. He looked up the doctor's number, then he reached for the phone.

*****

Clarice moved with great rapidity once she had made up her mind. She arrived in Lemburg the next morning after a highly uncomfortable night trip by bus. Kathy, who had been able to keep most of those concerned about her at a distance, hadn't counted on her mother's determination. She answered the door that morning to see Clarice Adams standing on the porch, overnight case in hand.

"I told you I had learned how to fight," Clarice said. "I'm here to fight for you. I don't intend to let my own daughter sink, not if I can help it."

"Mother!" was all Kathy could say in reply.

With Clarice in residence, things seemed to improve with remarkable rapidity. Kathy got up the first morning, showered, and even put on a bit of lipstick.

"Doesn't Kathy look nice today?" Clarice asked Robert in Kathy's presence.

"She looks more like herself," agreed Robert.

Kathy felt the pressure; she showered and put on some makeup every morning.

"Come on, let's help Susie give this house a good turning-out. With the three of us, we can get it done in no time. And I know you'll feel better if the house is clean."

So Kathy cleaned.

"We ought to take a little walk around the block every morning, Kathy. It'd do us both good. Oh, come now! If these old bones can do it, so can you!"

And Kathy walked.

"This visit of yours is the best thing that could have happened," said Robert after several days. "It's just what you needed, isn't it, Kathy?"

Kathy agreed, and even Beth and Myra, who saw Kathy on Sunday, felt relieved at the miracle Clarice had worked.

But Kathy wasn't better; she was in fact worse. The effort to be "okay" for her mother was keeping her in an artificial state of activity that was draining her remaining energy. Clarice finally noticed the desperate quality in everything Kathy did; thus, when she came upon her daughter gazing pensively out the window, she sat down quietly beside her. "What's wrong, dear?" she asked.

Kathy's eyes filled as she shook her head.

Clarice wiped her own eyes with a corner of her print apron. "I guess I haven't helped much. I don't understand exactly what's happening or how it's ever going to be resolved, but I can see that my presence has only put more strain on you."

"Don't blame yourself, Mom. It's not your fault," said Kathy, turning back to the window.

After waiting a moment or two, Clarice quietly withdrew to the guest room, where she spent the next half-hour in prayer. When she left the room, she had reached the conclusion that she would help Kathy most by going home. But first, she was determined to talk to Robert.

The moment he entered the house she drew him aside. "Robert," she said earnestly, "Kathy needs more help than I can give her—I'm talking about professional help."

Robert bit back a retort. Instead, he said as reasonably as he could, "But look how much more cheerful the place is. And Kathy's done so much more recently than she has for the past month. She looks better too." But even as he said this, he remembered how she looked in unguarded moments and was inclined to take Clarice's observation seriously.

"She's close to a breakdown. What she has isn't going to respond to a little encouragement, a clean house, and a diet, no matter how comforting it is to believe that."

Robert thought for a minute. "Yes, I guess you're right," he agreed reluctantly. "I'll look into it."

"Is that a promise?"

"Yes, that's a promise."

A day later Robert repeated his promise as he said goodbye to Clarice at the bus station. His intentions were good, and after she left, he even went so far as to get a list of names from his doctor. However, the thought of revealing to an outsider what was essentially a family matter was, in spite of the present conditions, still too hard for him to accept. *I'll give it another couple of weeks,* he told himself. *Then if things haven't improved, I'll definitely make some calls.*

PART FIVE

Sixteen

Susan stood looking out the window at her mother, who was sitting on the patio, so pale and still. She had watched Kathy's cheeks like a sheet in the summer sun bleach out under the strain of the last months, and she had been secretly glad. Now she was frightened. Her mother had become a stranger, a ghost who moved lethargically from room to room. Sue had been able to ignore her mother while school and friends had kept them apart most of the time, but now that school was out and she was home all day, she couldn't help but see how serious the situation had become.

She had talked to her father about finding herself a summer job when Brad had started looking in May, but he had asked her to wait. "It looks like I'm going to need you to stay home and keep things going this summer. I'll pay you for your work, as well as you would get paid at a restaurant or in a secretarial pool. But somebody's got to get this place in shape, and it doesn't look like your mother's going to do it."

She had objected at first, angry at her father for even suggesting such a thing, but she had changed her mind as she watched the dust thicken on the baby grand, the plants in the dining-room window lose their leaves, the soap scum build up in the tub. She was amazed at all the things they had simply expected Kathy to do. *We're a bunch of slobs,* she thought. *We don't know how to do anything for ourselves.* She was embarrassed to think that Myra instead of herself had been the one to muck out the kitchen.

So she had tackled the job head-on, relying more on memory of what she had seen her mother do than on actual experience. She vacuumed and dusted, washed the windows, cleaned out under chairs and behind couches. She made inroads into the piles of dirty clothes and tried to keep the kitchen counters clean. But since her grandmother's visit, Susan had realized that she would have to do something more direct to help her mother. Only one thing would really make a difference: she would have to break her silence.

After weeks of tight-closed lips, it was difficult to find a way to begin. What could she say? "I'm sorry for the way I've been acting?" That was true, but she wasn't sure she could bring herself to admit it. She could hardly start discussing the weather. She finally decided to fix lemonade and take some out to her mother. That would give Sue a reason for joining her, and perhaps things would simply develop from there.

Kathy lay half-asleep on the chaise lounge, the afternoon sun warming her now always-cold limbs. She looked up, startled, as Sue asked, "Want some lemonade? I just made some and thought you might like a glass."

Kathy took the glass from Sue questioningly. After such a long and bitter silence, this normal, everyday question was unnatural. She sipped the tangy drink, her eyes watching Sue warily over the edge of the glass.

Gee, I'm not going to bite, thought Sue. "Did I make it sweet enough?" she asked aloud.

"It's very good," whispered Kathy.

"The irises sure look pretty."

"Yes, they do."

"And those poppies, what are they? I keep forgetting."

"Islandic."

"They always bloom like crazy, don't they?"

"Yes."

"Uh, I thought I'd make tacos for supper tonight. Does that sound okay?"

"Sure."

Impatience overrode Sue. She was trying to hold a conversation, but her mother preferred one-word replies. Suddenly, without really thinking, Sue found herself blurting out the question that had been lurking in her mind for weeks.

"Why did you marry Daddy in the first place, if you were going to . . . do what you did?"

It was as if a cloud had passed over the sun; Kathy rolled down her sleeves and buttoned them before answering.

"I married him because I loved him. At least, I was sure of that at the time."

Susan's face mapped her anxiety. "That will never happen to me," she said loudly. "I'll never have to ask myself after I get married if I made a mistake. I'll never question myself or my husband!"

Kathy was taking a sip, but a hysterical laugh choked her. When she managed to control herself, she said, "I hope with all my heart that it turns out that way, Sue. But I really don't think there is a married couple on earth that goes through the rest of life without a moment's doubt."

"That's cynical," Sue shot back.

"No. I think it's a realistic viewpoint. Believe me, I never thought things would turn out this way. I thought we would live happily ever after!" Kathy could see herself and Robert as they had been during those courtship months: the perfect couple, the manual personified, the returned missionary and the sweet young innocent.

"After all, he fit everything on my list," she said with a humorless chuckle, more to herself than to Sue.

"List?"

"You know. The list every seminary teacher worth his salt has his students write at least once before they graduate: 'Qualities I want in my future husband or wife.'"

"Oh, I wrote one this year. Only it wasn't my seminary teacher, it was my Young Women's teacher, Sister Brimhall."

"What did you put down?" asked Kathy curiously.

Susan looked at her mother, not certain she wanted to discuss something so personal. And yet, she herself was asking Kathy to do the same. "It's upstairs in my jewelry box—one of my prized possessions," she said in a slightly mocking fashion, then got up. "I'll go get it. It'll only take a minute."

In the dull space around Kathy's heart, a yearning for such innocence flared up—her daughter still had so much hope! When Sue returned, Kathy took the list her daughter handed her and unfolded it carefully, conscious of the honor she was receiving. Her eyes scanned the list. "Just about like mine," she said, cocking her head.

"Really?"

"Yes. Of course, the basics will be the same on almost every list: returned missionary, honorable priesthood holder, dedicated servant of the Lord, things like that."

"What else did you have on your list?"

"Do you really want to know?" Kathy searched Susan's eyes.

"Yes, I do. I want to understand."

"There's a box on my closet shelf, over on the right-hand side. I think it has 'Keepsakes' or some such thing written on it. Bring it down."

Susan again walked quickly toward the house, and Kathy held her daughter's list to her bosom, clasping it as if it were the child herself. "Oh Lord, oh Lord," she kept saying over and over again, "Let it be real. Let it be a beginning, please!"

It seemed a long time before Susan returned to the patio, the box in her hands. She handed it to Kathy, who took off the lid and began riffling through yellowed papers. Finally she identified the page she wanted and drew it from the pile.

"Here it is," she said. "The list I wrote when I was eighteen."

Susan took the offered paper and began to read.

"You see, the first things are the same. The wording is maybe different, but the basics are there."

"Mom," said Susan, "you put 'loves music' on your list. Daddy doesn't love music, not the way you do."

"You're right; I do have things on my list that your dad doesn't match, but I didn't think they mattered as much as other qualities, such as having a testimony. I still don't."

Susan's voice was anguished. "What happened then?"

"I felt lonesome," Kathy said simply.

"Did you ever tell Dad you felt that way?"

"I tried, but he didn't really listen. He had too many other things on his mind."

"But that doesn't justify what you did."

"No, it doesn't."

"I'm sorry, Mom, but I have to understand! Everybody thought we were such a perfect family, a 'forever family'; I thought so too. I'm so mixed up, I don't know what to believe, and I don't know what to count on anymore!"

"Susan." Kathy made a move toward her daughter, fearing that she would run away, but instead, Susan flung her arms around her mother and sobbed on her shoulder. Kathy held her tightly, pain and joy a heady mixture.

"I wish I could say you can count on me," Kathy said, feeling repetitious: she had said those very words to her mother.

"I looked up to you, you know," said Susan tearfully. "You were supposed to teach me what it means to be a woman."

"Well, I've shown you the whole spectrum, haven't I."

"Oh Mom, I don't care what you've done, I love you. I tried to hate you, but I can't! Will you forgive me for the way I've been acting?"

Deep in Kathy an almost stifled belief in the future stirred. "Oh, Susan," she cried. "I love you—whatever happens, don't forget that!"

"I won't, said Susan, wiping her wet cheeks. Then she looked at her watch. "I guess I ought to get the tacos made," she said as she stood up. "It's getting to be that time."

"I'll help you," said Kathy, swinging her feet off the lounge.

"Are you sure you feel like it? I can do it myself, I think."

"Susan, there's nothing wrong with me that a hug or two from the people I love won't cure."

Susan grinned broadly. "Well, I guess I'll just have to give you another hug, then!"

She did; then they went in to fix supper.

Seventeen

The days seemed elastic that June. Kathy had to reach far back to her childhood to find such open, endless days; days when she and school friends packed lunches and went on all-day horseback rides; days when she sat in a cool, shaded, flower-scented corner of the screened-in porch and read and read, lifting her head now and again to listen to the soft, lazy call of cooing doves.

But these were not delicious days like those she remembered. She was not filled with a sense of luxurious anticipation when she awoke mornings, but with a sense of betrayal—the nights were not long enough. Sometimes she would pull the covers over her head in an effort to pull night back over her and then retreat into a heavy, restless sleep that shut out all signs of living.

When she did get up, it was only because Grant and Sue wanted her to. Even then that one act used up all her energy for the day. Only when Susan gently chided her or Myra prodded her, did she bother to shower. Her wardrobe consisted of her robe and a couple of caftans. Her schedule for the day included eating (mostly bread, rolls, or cookies), sitting in front of the television set, and walking sluggishly in the backyard a bit. She wanted to smile for Susan and Grant, wanted to cook and clean and laugh and go to the beach and be her old self, but it was literally impossible. Her center of command seemed divorced from her body.

She was glad that her cooking classes were over, and she

did not consider offering any during the summer. She couldn't bear to see what was happening to her mirrored in the faces of her ladies. She had tried to keep up her spirits for the last classes, but she knew she looked awful, and she hadn't been able to muster enough concern or energy to get her hair cut or to put on makeup. Then there was the ever-worsening problem of finding something to wear. She had easily imagined her ladies whispering, "What's the matter with Kathy, do you know?"

"No, but something is, that's for sure."

"No doubt about it. She looks terrible! Even her house doesn't look the same—it doesn't sparkle like it used to!"

At the same time, she was frightened by her decision to take the summer off. She realized that the end of classes had severed one more connection with the world outside her front door. She was still adamant that her visiting teachers not come to her, but she had counted on the notes, calls, and plates of cookies and flowers they had sent. She received a call from them now and then, but their preoccupation with her and her situation was gradually giving way to other, more pleasant summer thoughts. She found that she missed those signs of their concern, and she feared that it would only be a matter of time before the calls stopped altogether.

Early on she had told Myra harshly, "Don't you go organizing a 'Get-Kathy-out-of-the-house' campaign! I won't have it!" The abashed look on Myra's face had told her that she had hit the mark. But now her self-imposed exile was taking on ominous dimensions.

How is it going to end? she thought one day as she sat slumped on the edge of her bed after Susan had roused her. *Am I just going to shrivel up and blow away? Heavenly Father, canst thou not say, 'Go thy way and sin no more'? Canst thou not say, 'Thy sins are forgiven thee, rise and walk'? I need to be healed, Lord, body, mind, and spirit. Please help me!*

No answering rush of warmth, no comforting feeling of assurance came to her. "I need to know you're there!" she cried. Then she began to rock, beating her knees with her fists. She hardly knew why she was crying. She longed for her father, but Judge Adams was not the only father she wanted to see, his arms were not the only arms she needed to feel around her. "I want to go home," she sobbed, rocking. But whatever she had hoped for did not come. Finally she lifted her face and said accusingly, "You don't even care about me anymore. What's the use of trying!"

Only a few days later in the evening Susan fell while playing ball with Grant and twisted her ankle badly. Though she quickly applied an ice pack, the ankle swelled and turned dark. Brad had some elastic bandages with which he wrapped it, then he drove her to the hospital emergency room to get it X-rayed.

"How are you? What did the doctor say?" asked Kathy anxiously when they returned.

"It's not broken, just pretty badly sprained. The doctor said it will take a few weeks to get back to normal. In the meantime, I'm on these," Sue said, indicating with a nod of her head the crutches upon which she was balancing.

"I'm so glad," said Kathy, giving her a hug. "Thank you for taking her, Brad."

"Yeah" was all he said in acknowledgment.

It was because of Sue's incapacity that Kathy got up the next morning, dressed in old maternity jeans and one of Robert's shirts, and drove Grant to the YMCA for his swimming class. She noticed that the car was low on gas and decided to fill it at a nearby station while Grant was swimming. This chance decision was what brought her face to face with Jay.

He had already put gas in the tank and was about to get back into his car when she drove up. He observed the car with idle curiosity, thinking that it looked familiar. Then Kathy stepped out, and he frowned, momentarily perplexed. Something about the heavy, unkempt woman sparked a feeling of recognition, but what was it? Who was she? Her head was bent as she fumbled with the gas cap, then she looked up, right at him.

Horror was like an electric shock. Kathy? Kathy! But how could this graceless, sloppily dressed woman be Kathy?

His mind reeled as reality snatched from him the assumptions upon which he had based his actions for the last few months. If this was Kathy, then all he had gone through was worthless!

In recent weeks he had drawn comfort from the belief that by letting her go, he was making it possible for her to reorder her life. Jay felt he had been offering her a purer love than the love he had held for her before; but now he realized he had been offering it to a mythical Kathy, a Kathy grown stronger and more beautiful by virtue of her penance. He had been unwilling to believe in an unfallible god, but instead had fastened all his need to believe on a fallible human being. His shocked surprise gave way to deep disappointment, then bitter anger.

"Kathy," Jay said harshly, stepping toward her.

The sound of his voice brought her head up with a snap. Her hand moved automatically to smooth her bedraggled hair, to straighten Robert's shirt. She tried to speak, but only an embarrassing croak escaped her lips.

Jay took the Lord's name in vain and said, "Kathy, what's been going on?"

His demanding tone reminded her so much at that moment of Robert that anger replaced her embarrassment. Her eyes flashed as she retorted, "Nothing's been going on, at least nothing that has anything to do with you!"

But he knew better. Their lives had been inextricably entwined since that night, and even though the spool of time would roll out the threads of their lives in different directions, they would feel the effects forever.

"That's not true," he said with soft intensity. "It has everything to do with you and me . . ."

"I find it extremely odd that you insist you have some part in my life when you haven't called or even sent a note since . . . then!"

"But don't you know why?" he asked earnestly. "You told me to go away that morning and to not come back. Have you forgotten that? Then when Robert called to tell me the same thing, I thought that made your feelings pretty clear."

"Robert called you?"

"He said you were getting your life back in order and that I should stay out of it. But it doesn't look to me like things are 'getting back in order'!"

Kathy blushed with shame. "Did he tell you I had to go through something called a bishop's court? That I've been kicked out of my church—excommunicated?"

"That's . . . barbaric!" he said, finding no other word.

"It's supposed to help me repent," she said hopelessly.

He swore explosively. Anyone could tell by looking at her that she was in torment. He had never seen a person change so completely. He felt anger rush through him, as much against her as against Robert. "I'm going to talk to your husband!" he said curtly.

"Oh, no! Please don't!" Kathy cried. "It's not as bad as you think it is, really!"

He looked at her narrowly.

"Truly!" she insisted, her face suddenly bright. "It's almost over!"

The words chilled him. "Just what do you mean by that?"

Her face fell. "I'm not sure. I don't even know why I said it. Please, please, don't talk to Robert!"

"Sorry," he said shortly. "Maybe he can't see what this is doing to you, but I can." He jerked open his car door, slid onto the seat, and roared away. Kathy felt nothing as she watched him go. If the incident had happened earlier, she might have felt glad or grateful or comforted. But it was too late for that.

Jay swore again and again as he sped down the road toward the building that housed Robert's firm. The horror of her metamorphosis was still upon him, and he couldn't drive fast enough to suit the force propelling him. The car squealed around a corner and screeched to a stop in the parking lot. He paused in the lobby only long enough to ascertain where Robert's office was, then took the stairs two at a time. His running had resulted in better physical conditioning, so he was not affected by the two flights he took headlong. He did stop for a moment before going into the office, however, long enough to collect himself for the sake of Robert's secretary.

The buzzer on Robert Montgomery's intercom sounded, and he leaned slightly forward as he pushed the button and answered "Yes."

"Mr. Jay Enders to see you," said his secretary.

"Jay Enders?" he echoed unbelievingly.

"Yes. Should I send him in?"

"All right," said Robert, wondering why Jay was coming to see him now, so many months after his call.

The door opened and Jay strode in, his whole body tensed in challenge. He came right to the point. "What are you doing to Kathy?"

"You don't have any reason or right to inquire about Kathy," Robert replied smoothly.

"Yes, I do. I care about her, and it doesn't seem like anyone else does, or things would have never gotten this far!"

"I'm not sure what you're talking about," Robert said, gritting his teeth against the familiar pain.

Jay leaned over the desk, intruding on Robert's territory. "I'm talking about Kathy, about the way she looks, the expression in her eyes, or more precisely, the lack of expression. You're killing her, but you don't care!"

"That's a rather exaggerated view of things, don't you think?" said Robert, leaning back in his chair. "Besides, when have you seen Kathy? It can't have been recently."

"I saw her today at the gas station on the corner of Wood's Crossing and Pine Hill, and I couldn't believe my eyes! Maybe you haven't been paying any attention to her lately, maybe you're too close to see how she's changed, but I haven't seen her for weeks, and let me tell you, I couldn't believe it was really her! I don't know what you're made of, but I couldn't sit back and watch another person die a slow death when I could change everything with a little compassion!"

Robert moved in his chair. He knew Jay was right. He had seen her vacant eyes this morning and for a moment, hadn't been sure she could even make it across the room.

"Forgive her," Jay said in a raw voice. "For her sake

and your own. And mine," he finished unsteadily and sat down, his hand over his eyes.

"Yours?" Robert was incredulous.

"Yes, mine." The moment had passed; Jay's eyes were steady. "I love her. Whatever you may think, my intentions were honorable." His lips twisted in a wry smile. "I wanted to marry Kathy."

Robert's composure crumbled. "What?"

"So she didn't tell you? She made the decision to stay with you and her children. And her church. I honored her decision because I really thought you were right, that she wouldn't be the same person if she were forced to live outside her church. But now I don't know. She's going through hell for you and that religion, but it seems to me it hasn't been worth it. I'm giving you fair warning that I'm going to keep an eye on her!"

"This is none of your business! As the head of my family, I'm doing what I think is necessary. What goes on between me and my wife is of no concern to you. If you're worried about the effect of your little fling, just remember that you're responsible for it, not me!"

"Mr. Montgomery," Jay began, and his tone chilled Robert, "before you go any further, you need to examine what you call your family. Go back over the last years and ask yourself what kind of a relationship you've built with your wife. You have some responsibility to bear in this as well!"

Robert started to protest, but Jay stood up and leaned over the desk threateningly. "And hear this. If I don't see some change in Kathy in the next couple of weeks, I'm going to visit your priest or pastor or whatever you call him myself!"

Jay was not the only one goaded to action by the course of events. Ever since Sunday, Bishop Mangus had been haunted by the way Kathy had looked that day. Perhaps she had thought her face was neutral, a nonexpression to cover negative feelings. Instead it had been a ghastly, slack arrangement of flesh and muscle with flat eyes staring out.

Seeing that face before him again, the bishop reached for the phone and dialed Randy Green's office number.

"Hello, Bishop," said Randy. "I was expecting to hear from you."

"You were?"

"You're calling about the Montgomerys, aren't you?"

"Yes, I am."

"I expected as much. I think the crisis is very near."

"Well, I want to avoid that crisis if possible. I'm calling the Montgomerys in."

"I thought you said Robert has 'respectfully declined' any such interview."

"This is going to be a 'command performance,' as it were."

"That extends to me as well?"

"If necessary. I'll set up something and call you back. I hope we can meet tomorrow or the day after."

"Fine. You just let me know," said Green. To himself he said, "I bet Kathy won't make it till then."

Eighteen

"How long has it been since you've been out?" demanded Myra when Kathy finally responded to her vigorous jabs on the doorbell.

"Believe it or not, I went out today," said Kathy. "I drove Grant to the 'Y' and back. Susan can't drive right now—she sprained her ankle and she's on crutches."

"What! When did that happen?"

"Last night."

"Just what you needed. Who's going to keep the house clean now?"

Kathy, however, was not embarrassed by Myra's bluntness. She only shrugged her shoulders and stood aside so that her friend could come in.

"No, I don't want to come in; I want you to come out! That's why I'm here. We haven't been down to White River Park in ages. Not since last summer. Let's drive over there, okay?"

"Are you really asking? Do I have a choice?"

Myra laughed. "No, not really!"

White River Park held a special meaning for them both; they went there whenever they needed a break from the nonstop rush that until recently had governed both their lives. The atmosphere of the park invited relaxation; they enjoyed the lovely paths that followed the river, the broad-armed trees that beckoned one to sit in their shade, and the congenial mix of joggers, roller skaters, bikers, lovers holding hands, and mothers with children.

Kathy felt that a trip to the park might help, so she allowed Myra to drag her there. About fifteen minutes later, as they walked along the river a way, Kathy actually found herself admiring the flower beds and watching the boaters. Then they sat on a bench that faced the sun. Kathy bent her head back, her skin tingling in its rays.

"Thanks for thinking of this; it's just what I needed," said Kathy. "It's perfect today; the only thing that's missing is a couple of Sunfish on the river. I love to watch them—their sails are so bright and pretty. They look so free."

"I know what you mean. I've always thought it would be nice to have a boat, any kind of boat. No telephone, no unexpected visitors."

"For me it's sailing and hot-air ballooning," said Kathy. "I love to watch the balloons. They seem to rise and drift away so effortlessly. I'd like to take a hot-air balloon ride into infinity."

"Escape seems to be on your mind," said Myra with a smile.

"It's true," replied Kathy. "I would like to escape—to run away from it all. No, that sounds too strenuous. More likely, I'd just like to fade away and disappear altogether."

"You could escape if you wanted to."

"What?"

"You could leave, if you really wanted to."

Kathy was silent for a moment. "I guess I could, if I had the strength," she said slowly. "But what would I do? I've always wanted to be married. Assuming Robert and I got a divorce, I'd be lonesome, and I would probably want to get married again. I'd want a family. Most likely I'd end up with essentially the same bunch of problems I have now!"

"Even with another man?"

"You mean Jay?" She thought back to her meeting with Jay that morning and shook her head ruefully. "I used to think about that, about how nice it would be. But if I married Jay, what's to say that in nineteen years I wouldn't be in exactly the same position I am now? What's to say I wouldn't turn into a nag, that I wouldn't get tired and bored. Maybe the things I thought were so awful are just part of the package. What a waste to go through all the pain of divorce and separation from my children just to end up in the same place!"

Myra nodded. "I wish someone would write a sequel to Cinderella with a prince who always says 'Uh' between every sentence or who likes to use a toothpick in public and wears white socks with dress clothes!"

Kathy couldn't help laughing, an unaccustomed sound. "You better watch out! I recognized Paul just now!"

"It drives me nuts!" said Myra. "The more I bug him about white socks, the more he says 'Nobody even notices my white socks but you!'"

"So Paul has irritating habits too. But you haven't gotten yourself into the mess I have."

"I could have," said Myra quietly.

Kathy's eyes went wide. "I had no idea," she faltered.

"Well, it actually isn't anything to talk about. But there was a man in our ward back in Nevada. We got along so well, and we had so many things in common. And how we could talk to each other! For hours, literally hours on the phone. Of course, we always had a good reason to call each other, but long after that was taken care of, we would go on talking. I would even take the phone into the bathroom where I wouldn't be disturbed . . ." She paused, and Kathy saw the sorrow in her eyes. "Paul would look at me with such a funny expression when I'd finally come out. It hurt him a great deal."

"And then?"

"And then one day, in one of my more rational moments, I realized what the end of the line might be, and I decided it wasn't worth it. If I needed companionship, I could do more with Paul. If I needed someone to share my interests with, I could take a class. I decided that loneliness wasn't the worst thing in the world."

"You felt lonely, too?"

"Yes. I went through a time when I was very bitter. That was when I realized Paul couldn't fill all my needs; but it was unfair of me to expect him to. He can't, anymore than I can fill all his needs."

"I wish we had talked about this before."

"But Kathy, don't you remember? The day we had lunch at Zilkies?"

A scene flashed across Kathy's mind. She turned away, biting her lip. So Myra had seen the blind spot, too.

"It seems so clear now, but so help me, I couldn't hear what you were saying."

"Doublethink," said Myra shortly.

"What?"

"Doublethink. Convincing yourself that you don't understand something you really do understand. You knew what I was talking about in some corner of your brain. But you had already made a choice to go ahead in spite of it."

Kathy flushed with anger. She turned away and grasped the edge of the bench with shaking hands.

"You see, my dear friend, it was only an out. By saying that you didn't know what was happening, you take away your guilt."

Kathy was shaking her head, murmuring, "No. No. It isn't true."

Then Myra asked the question that spun Kathy's world around.

"Tell me. What did you say to yourself the day you left home without your temple garments on?"

Kathy gasped. The question rumbled around in her head, louder and louder, demanding an answer, forcing her to face her guilt in a way she had avoided till now.

She had made a choice, and she knew it. At the time, she had been playing a deadly game with herself, a game of cloak and dagger: cloak the truth and do what you want to do, without letting yourself know you'd made a conscious decision. And pretend there is no dagger.

There was no pretense now. The dagger pierced and turned within her. She sprang from the bench, leaving a startled Myra behind, and began to run, threading through the mixed traffic of the park path. She ran until she could run no further, and when she stopped, choking and gasping for breath, she found herself on a footbridge arching across the White River. She leaned against the rail, breathing heavily, and looked down at the river as she caught her breath. Brown water ran swiftly below, flowing smoothly under the bridge, parting in ripples with little back waves where the river came around the bridge supports.

"Ol' man river," she said, mesmerized. "He don' do nuthin'. He jus' keep rollin' along." Lucky old man. To be without consciousness, doing what natural law required. Kathy watched the river and, watching, felt herself slip a notch. She wasn't sure why she was there; she was only sure of the river.

And of her guilt. She was guilty, guilty, guilty. She had planned to sleep with Jay; she had looked forward to it. She had arranged to leave home without wearing her temple garments.

To get a dress altered! she thought hysterically. *The orange dress, and I don't even like orange!* She felt herself slipping again and grabbed the rail more tightly.

"Guilty, guilty, guilty," intoned the jury. "Hopeless," said the judge. "Put her away forever," said the prosecuting attorney.

Kathy shook her head desperately to rid herself of the voices, then leaned on her hands to look down into the river again. The water flowed smoothly to the bridge, disappeared under it, and slipped away. Flowed and flowed. Unthinking and unknowing. Easily it flowed and beckoned her to flow with it too. Kathy felt herself drawn down into a great yawning blackness that had opened up within—she couldn't hear anymore, couldn't think anymore, could only see the river flowing under the bridge and herself floating with it. It took her a long time to recognize the humming in her ear as a human voice, Myra's voice calling and calling, to feel Myra's hand tugging on her sleeve.

"Kathy, Kathy what are you doing?"

From far away, Kathy said, "Look at the river. It looks so nice and soft and warm . . ." And she leaned far over the railing.

"Kathy!" Myra pulled her away from the railing and dragged her off the bridge. "If only I hadn't played psychiatrist!" she muttered savagely. She got Kathy down the path to the parking lot and into the car, upbraiding herself all the way.

Kathy came without resistance. It was easier to follow in a world that had suddenly gone dark. Everything had a nightmarish quality about it. Though the park was still full of sunshine, she herself had reached a different and more dreadful place.

"Before rehearsal I was going to the alteration shop on 4th street to have a fitting on that orange dress," she said in a frighteningly flat voice.

"That orange dress you've never liked?"

Kathy nodded dumbly.

"Kathy, I'm sorry for what I said. I had no right to ask a question like that. I was feeling smug and superior, I guess."

"But you were right."

"That may be so, but I had no idea how it would affect you. Oh, hon, you look so awful!"

The park, the shops, the highway full of traffic, the gates marking her subdivision, Kathy saw none of these as they flashed by the car windows. Her attention was turned entirely inward. After weeks of tumultuous emotions, of painful denial and wavering hope, she finally felt nothing at all, nothing but a numbing cold, colder than she had ever felt before, creeping up her limbs; a black, vaporous cold extinguishing all that was left of hope and light. Now only the judge and the jury were left, looking at her accusingly.

If I were dead, they couldn't stare at me so, she thought. *If I were dead, I wouldn't be so cold. It would be over, blessed oblivion, forever and ever, hallelujah, hallelujah.*

"Kathy, we're home."

Kathy turned as if in slow motion. She looked out the window. Yes, that was the place she called home, but it wasn't her home anymore. She wasn't mother, wife, inspiring teacher. She wasn't ironer-of-the-shirts, kisser-of-hurts. She wasn't reader-of-scriptures, giver-of-testimonies. She was only Kathy-with-an-A. She climbed heavily from the car, and Myra helped her as she walked lethargically into the house that was no longer her home and up the stairs past her staring daughter to the room that was no longer her room. She knew that if she didn't lie down, she would fall, so she lay down on the bed and closed her eyes. She didn't respond to Myra's reluctant leave-taking or to her daughter's concerned inquiries. All she wanted to do was to sleep—to sleep and have that be the end.

Robert negotiated the rush-hour traffic without giving thought to it, too caught up in awareness of the force impelling his family forward to some crisis; he could feel it as surely as he could feel the pain in his chest reaching critical level. The crisis would come soon, if Kathy was as bad off as Jay thought she was.

She must have looked a wreck today. Jay had been obviously shaken by his chance encounter with her; otherwise, he would never have come to the office and certainly would never have made the threat of going to the bishop. That was rather serious and put a different light on everything.

Robert could see Kathy now in his mind's eye, hovering uncertainly like a pale blimp without a navigator on board. She was in trouble, and he knew it. The notion that he was too close to see the devastating culmination of months of gradual change was neat but not true. He had seen what was happening and had watched it with an odd mixture of anger and enjoyment. Now he realized he had let it go on too long. He increased his speed, weaving in and out among the slower cars, his shame causing him to drive recklessly. That Jay should be the one who had finally awakened him to her plight! He barrelled up the driveway and braked abruptly.

"How's your mother?" he asked Sue as he rushed into the family room.

Her answer confirmed his premonition of trouble. "I don't know, Dad. She went to White River Park with Myra. I thought it would be good for her to spend the afternoon there, but when she got home, she looked . . . I don't know . . . queer, I guess. She just went straight up the stairs to bed. I had Grant check on her," she added with a frustrated wave at her crutches. "He said she was asleep."

"You don't know what happened?"

"No. Maybe nothing happened, Dad. But I have a funny feeling about it."

"Well, don't worry. I'll take care of it. First I'm going to call Myra and see what she has to say."

Robert made the call from his home office, impatiently tapping on the desk top while he waited for an answer. Then Myra was on the line.

"Myra, did something go wrong when you and Kathy were at White River Park today?" he asked abruptly.

"Oh, Robert! I'm so glad you called. I had in mind to call you, but I didn't think you'd be home yet."

"So something did happen."

"I'm so upset! I just wanted to get Kathy out of the house, you know. I thought it would do her good. And . . . oh, darn it, Robert! I blew it, that's all, and I thought I was being so helpful."

"What did you do?"

"I pushed her too far. I asked her something I had no business asking her, and she . . . well, she flipped out! That's the only way I can explain it! She took off running, and by the time I caught up with her, she was standing on the bridge, just staring down into the water! She looked so strange—I was scared to death! I didn't know what to do, so I brought her home. She is all right, isn't she?" Robert could hear the fear in her voice.

"I don't know. She's sleeping," Robert said, wondering whether it were normal for a person to sleep so much. "What did you ask her, Myra?"

"It was a dumb question. I over-stepped the bounds of friendship."

"What was the question?"

"Robert, I'll tell you later, if it's still important and if Kathy doesn't mind your knowing, but not now. Now the most important thing is to take care of her—" She began to cry, a muffled sound that came through to Robert even though she had covered the mouthpiece.

"Come on, Myra," he said sternly. "It's probably not as serious as you think. Stop crying now!"

"Oh, but it is! If you had seen her, you'd know! I'm such a dumbbell—I didn't even stop to think. Good old Myra, charging ahead as usual!"

That the ever-confident Myra would say something like that impressed Robert even more with the seriousness of Kathy's reaction.

"Myra, listen. I'll go to work a little later tomorrow. That way, I can make sure everything's all right before I leave. How does that sound?"

"I'll feel a lot better, knowing you'll be there in the morning. You'll call me if . . . ?"

"If there's anything to tell."

"Thank you," said Myra, subdued.

Robert hung up the phone and took the stairs quickly to the master bedroom. The room was fuzzy-edged in the gathering dusk, and Kathy was only a hump of covers in the middle of the bed. Not even her head was visible from where he stood in the doorway. He walked up to her, pulled the spread back enough to see her slack, pallid face, and tried to awaken her. She didn't respond, though he shook her quite roughly. Finally he turned and descended the stairs. He answered Sue's questions as best he could, made sure the family was fed and the dishes were done, then sat in the wingback chair to wait. He was like a careless fisherman who goes out heedless of warnings, then suddenly looks up to see a wall of water moving with monstrous speed toward him and knows he can do nothing but let it crash down around him.

Nineteen

Kathy awoke to the grey light of a rainy June day. The sound of heavy drops and the dampness in the air was oppressive. She lay still, listening, heavy and dull herself. She stepped inward, timidly, as when a guest enters a closed room, not knowing if the owner is there, but she found no one: no voice, no echo, no pain. She thought absently that she should get breakfast for Grant, yet she didn't move. She could hear Robert's voice from far off and wondered why he was still home, but she didn't get up to ask him. She just lay, eyes open, looking at the ceiling. There was a large cobweb on the light fixture.

There shouldn't be a cobweb there, thought Kathy. *There shouldn't be any cobwebs in my house.* At that, she remembered what had happened the day before. *Oh,* she said to herself, *it's all right. It's not my house anymore.*

Physical necessity moved her finally. Then, because Grant came in and took her by the hand, insisting she make his breakfast, she came down the stairs. Grant took his usual seat at the table and watched his mother as she began the routine. She moved as if time had slowed—it was fascinating yet awful, and the suspense brought Grant to the edge of his chair. She pulled a pan from the cupboard ever so slowly and now . . . now . . . now! she put it on the stove. She shuffled to the refrigerator, and her hand snaked, wavering, toward the egg carton. Now she had it in her hand, and now—

Suddenly she dropped the carton, and eggs splattered

over the floor and onto the cupboards and the refrigerator door.

"Mom!" Grant cried, startled, but she just stood there. "Dad!" he screamed, running out into the yard where his father was picking up toys and twigs off the lawn. "Dad, come quick! Something's the matter with Mom!"

Robert, hearing his cry, thought *so now it's come,* then began to move.

They both ran back into the kitchen where Kathy was still standing, staring blankly at the mess of broken yolks and scattered shells. Robert drew her away from the spreading mass on the floor and asked "What happened? What's the matter?"

She looked at him without recognition, unable to respond. Fear rose in his throat like gall. "Kathy, Kathy! Say something!" But she only looked at him, eyes unblinking.

"Mom! Dad! What's going on?" cried Susan, balancing on her crutches in the doorway.

"Grant, Sue, see what you can do about that mess. Your mother's not feeling well, and I'm taking her back upstairs."

He led her like a child, helping her into bed and pulling the sheet up. All the time he was murmuring to himself and to God, "Oh, Father, I wanted her to suffer. I was glad she was suffering—she had to suffer as much as I was! But this . . ."

He sat down beside her and tried again. "Kathy, please tell me what's wrong! Tell me what I can do!"

It took her a long time to realize he was speaking to her, and then it didn't seem important enough for her to muster strength to answer. She closed her eyes instead. Robert sat for a long time looking at the face with skin stretched over bones, devoid of expression. It suddenly reminded him of a death mask, and the words he had allowed in his thoughts came rushing back. "No," he whispered to himself. "I don't wish you were dead. I want you to live. I want us to be happy again." He could hear Jay's anguished voice, "How could you sit back and watch her die a slow death when a little compassion would change everything?"

How close to the truth was Jay's accusation? Surely it was only a figure of speech. Yet he himself had watched Kathy withdraw bit by bit from everyone and everything that had been important to her. He had watched her eat and eat and sit blankly in front of the television for hours, blocking out a reality that had become too painful. Had she been cutting all the ties? And when the last was severed, what then? *Maybe compassion could save her yet,* he thought desperately. Certainly his forgiveness could. Still there was this pain, that Kathy had been with another man. He couldn't bear the thought! During nineteen years of marriage, he had treasured their intimacy, and the picture of Kathy and Jay, alone in the dark, tormented him.

Now it was before him again, and it drove him to his feet. He began pacing uneasily, to the closet, turn; to the window, turn; to the bedroom door. He paused to call down an answer to Susan's worried query, then continued pacing, hands clenched, jaws tight. The faster he strode, the more emotion was released. Tiny tears squeezed out from the corners of his eyes, and he felt an enormous roaring in his ears. He ran into the sitting room beyond their bedroom, smashing his fist in rage against the doorframe as he passed.

He loved her and he hated her; but his anger was the stronger of the two emotions now. He felt it as a red-hot moving liquid, rising from within, threatening to consume him and everything and everyone around him. He picked up a cushion and threw it across the room, then another and another. He rammed his clenched fist into the back of a chair and then found himself on his knees, pummeling the seat of the chair with all the strength of his bitterness and anger.

This inner reservoir of rage seemed to have no end, but finally the fury of his flailing arms weakened, and something else moved within, equally frightening. He dropped his head on his arms and cried, the jerky, painful sobs of a man who hadn't cried in years. He could see himself as an uncertain, awkward boy again, crying "Oh, Aunt Emmie, what should I do?" And somehow it was as if he could hear her gentle voice saying, "Actually, there's only one thing that matters: love."

He raised his head and took a deep, shuddering breath. He knew what he had to do. Or more precisely put, he accepted what he had always known, deep inside, would be his ultimate task. If they were to have any chance of happiness again, together or apart, he had to be willing to forgive. More than that, he had to forgive! And with the grace of God, forget. He had to lay his hurt pride and anger on the altar and ask the Lord to accept them as an offering.

"I'll be honest, Father," he said aloud. "There's part of me that doesn't want to forgive. I've felt justified in my anger. I've wanted revenge. But Father, more than that . . . more than that . . ." His voice cracked again, and again bitter, unaccustomed tears fell. "I want my wife back again. I want my family to be whole . . ."

He stayed on his knees for a long time. Finally he arose, different from the man who had bruised his knuckles on the doorframe. The lines of the face had softened; there was a childlike, uncertain eagerness in his eyes. He walked over to Kathy and called her name. He sat down on the edge of the bed and took one of her cold hands in his.

Kathy felt a warm touch intrude into her dark shell. With effort she rose through the layers separating her from awareness and opened her eyes. What was Robert doing? Why was he here? She became aware that he was speaking, but his words moved like unread ticker tape through her head. She struggled to understand what the movements of his mouth meant.

"I'm ashamed of the way I've been behaving, Kathy. I don't know if you even want to hear this right now, but I want to say it. The family means more to me than anything." He paused, then struggled to continue. "You mean more to me than anything. If there's a way for us to be happy again, I'm going to find it. The only question is, will you forgive me?"

She looked at him, her eyes suddenly quickened. "That's not the question," she said in an awful whisper. "'To be or not to be, that is the question.'"

Robert's face blanched. He stared at her eyes, which were glittering horribly in her colorless face. A new and more dreadful fear rose over him like a dragon. If he had been a man less dedicated to self-reliance, a man less distrustful of doctors and psychiatrists, he would have followed his first impulse to run for help. Instead, he sat rooted, watching her lips move as she quoted Hamlet's monologue, drawing from long untapped memory stores. "'To sleep, perchance to dream . . . ah . . . there's the rub!'" Her voice came out in a thready whisper, then stopped.

He was in an agony of anticipation, watching the change that crept over her features. "'But, oh, what dreams . . .'" she began. "'What dreams . . .'" He wasn't sure if her memory had failed or if the thought itself had struck some barrier. Bright waves of color suffused her cheeks, and she looked at him with feverish eyes.

"There's no way out, is there?"

"No way out? I'm not sure what you mean."

"There isn't any sweet sleep, is there? No warm, dark oblivion, no final rest!"

Suddenly his mind made the leap from where he was to where she was. If she had been tottering precariously on a ledge of stone, he could have wrenched her back to safety, but he didn't know how to deal with this chasm of the mind. He reached out to her instinctively, but she jerked away from him.

"I want out! Permanently out! But there's no place to go, you hear me!" She was screaming now, her hands pounding the bedspread in rage. "No place to go, no place to go!"

"Kathy, please!" He grabbed at her swinging arms, caught her and held her. She stopped screaming but the vibrant emotion in her voice chilled him.

"I'm stuck, aren't I? Even if I were dead, I'd still have this hanging around my neck! I'd still be me, right? Right?" Her voice was rising again.

"Yes," he said, knowing that it was not the answer she wanted to hear. He prayed a desperate prayer.

"Just what's so wonderful about eternal life, tell me

that? You're the scriptorian. You're the returned missionary. Who wants to be with their family forever? That just means forever problems, forever worries, forever sorrows. Not me! Not me! Are you listening, God! I don't want your pretty plans. I want out, do you hear! I WANT OUT!"

Their bedroom door opened, and a white-faced Susan looked through the crack. Robert rushed to her. "Go back downstairs, Sue," he said urgently. "You can't do anything here." Then he added, "Neither can I. Please go now!" But Sue couldn't drag her eyes away from the sight of her mother screaming, arms flailing and legs thrashing.

As Robert turned back to the bed, a wave of helplessness broke over him. He reached for the phone on the night stand, then swore as he realized that the list of therapists his doctor had given him was on his desk at work. *I'll have to call my secretary and have her read off some names,* he thought. Then the obvious occurred to him: Randy Green. He paused again as the image of the man he was about to call came up before him. He didn't like Randy Green, but he knew that Green was a solid man, whatever his quirks. He found the number and dialed.

Kathy's voice was hoarse and failing her now, but carrying on a conversation in the bedroom would still be difficult, so Robert moved to the sitting room.

Randy was not at home, as Robert had expected. He wrote down the office number Maggie Green gave him and dialed it. The phone rang only twice before Green answered.

"Yes."

Robert felt his neck stiffen. The very sound of that voice and the arrogance of his monosyllabic answer irritated him. *That's not important, remember what's important!* Robert reminded himself.

"Randy, Robert Montgomery calling. My wife is in a very bad state, and I don't know what to do for her. Can you possibly come to us?"

"Ah." It was a response that made no sense to Robert. But Green had been thinking a lot about Kathy and her situation ever since he had received the phone call from their bishop. From all that Bishop Mangus had told him, he had expected a crisis in the near future, but the bishop had asked him to make no move on his own, to wait until called. He had expected the call to come from the bishop himself, however, not from Robert. He knew he irritated Robert, and the fact that Robert was now on the line convinced him of the seriousness of the situation.

"It's close to ten now. I can clear the rest of my morning and be there by eleven, but no sooner than that. And there is a possibility of delay. Do you think she might harm herself?" he asked abruptly.

Robert felt his knees give way, and he sank onto the nearest chair. "I don't know," he answered dully. "If I weren't with her . . ."

"Can you stay with her until I come?"

"Yes. My daughter is at home. I'll tell her to expect you, but she's on crutches at the moment, so just give the bell a ring and come on in. We're at the end of the hall, upstairs."

"Right."

Robert hung up, then looked in at Kathy. She was exhausted, dry-eyed and voiceless, but her lips were still moving, and she was gripping at the covers with clawlike hands. He sighed; he was himself exhausted by the strain of the morning hours. Closing his eyes, he rested for a moment before dialing his office. He told his surprised secretary that he wouldn't be in at all that day and that he wasn't sure about the next day, that he'd call her tomorrow. Then he called Kathy's mother.

"Oh, Robert, it's you! How's Kathy?"

"She's . . . not doing too well right now," he said, his voice unreliable. "Do you think you could come up for a while?"

"Are you sure I should? My last visit wasn't so successful."

"It's a totally different situation now. We need you. All of us."

"Send Brad to pick me up at the bus station," said Clarice. "I'll make the arrangements and call you back with the arrival time. It'll probably be quite late."

Robert came back into the bedroom and sat down by Kathy again. She was still now. He took her hand in his and pressed it to his lips. He had wondered again and again how he could ever touch her after what had happened, but it was so easy. When there was no choice left but to love or to hate, to live or to die, it was so easy. He uncurled her fingers gently, then touched the deep marks left by her nails. He counted her fingers one by one, as one counts a child's fingers, and twisted her rings back so that the diamond he had given her would be centered.

How her eyes had glowed that evening! She had flung her arms around him and covered his face with eager kisses. "I'll be the perfect wife, just wait and see!" she had promised, her face shining with confidence.

And I told her not to make a spectacle of herself. I was worried about what other people would think! He wished with all his heart that he could have that Kathy back again and the chance to start over. But he knew there could be no new start. They would have to carry the flotsam and jetsam accumulated over the years along with them into the sunset.

It was noon when Robert heard the doorbell ring and Green's deep voice calling, "Brother Montgomery?"

Robert rose stiffly and went to meet him. In the time since he had made the telephone call to Brother Green, Kathy had not spoken. He had been frightened to leave her side, but he had, long enough to talk to Susan, who was terrified. Now he moved down the hall, grateful that Green was here at last.

"I got here as quickly as I could," said Randy Green, coming up the stairs quickly. Robert's irrational dislike for him surfaced again as he watched the young bearded man. The beard was part of his dislike—not the beard per se, but the reason Green wore the beard: "I wear a beard to give the Saints practice in tolerance." Robert had to admit, however, that he at least was one who needed the practice.

"How is Sister Montgomery now?" Green questioned.

"She completely wore herself out in screaming and then went to sleep shortly after I talked to you. She's awake again now, but all she does is lie there. She won't talk to me."

"Can you tell me what precipitated this situation?"

Robert's life-long habit of denying weakness brought a lump to his throat. He cleared it painfully. "You know . . . you know Kathy was excommunicated?"

"Yes, I know. The bishop recently asked me to help if I could."

Robert nodded, hardly surprised now. "The time since then has been very difficult for all of us, but worse for Kathy than I had realized. That was made clear to me yesterday. I came home intending to do all I could to help her, but something a friend asked her sent her off the deep end."

"Do you know what it was?"

"No. But I know who said it. Myra Fuller. If you need to know she may tell you—she wouldn't tell me."

"Kathy's awake now?"

"If you can call it that. The bedroom's this way."

"Wait," said Green, laying a hand on Robert's shoulder. "I'm not concerned only about Kathy. I'm concerned about you as well. How are you holding up against the pain?"

"Pain?"

"The pain you've been having the last few weeks. Is it an ulcer?"

Robert couldn't resist the certainty and depth of caring in Green's face. He almost wept with relief to have his burden shared.

"I'm holding on. Just. And it's not an ulcer. It's angina."

"You've seen your doctor?"

"Yes. He's referred me to a specialist. I'm to see him tomorrow . . ."

"Don't worry, you'll probably be able to keep your appointment," Randy assured him. "Now take me to Kathy."

If Kathy's eyes registered anything as the slim, bearded figure came into the room after Robert, it was a very faint wash of surprise.

"Hello," he greeted her, his melodious deep voice sounding so calm, so sane. For both Robert and Kathy the very sound seemed to lighten the nightmarish atmosphere ever so slightly.

"May I sit here?" Green indicated the chair Robert had pulled up to the bedside. A barely perceptible nod of her head gave him permission.

"You look tired," Green said pleasantly to Robert. "Why don't you relax downstairs—have a bite to eat and then speak to your daughter. She looked quite worried. You might even lie down. I'll let you know when we're finished."

It was a dismissal, and Robert knew it, however pleasant Green's tone had been. He stood uncertainly a moment longer, then left with a sigh.

Green looked at Kathy now, his gaze understanding and accepting. "Had a pretty bad time of it?"

She nodded.

"Would you like to tell me how you're feeling right now?"

"Stuck." The word was barely voiced, but clear. Then she asked the question again, but this time quietly, with resignation. "There's no way out, is there?"

"Depends on what you want out of."

"Everything. I want to take the ultimate powder. I want to go away and never come back."

"You can. You can go anywhere you want to, in this world or out of it, but you'll have to take yourself with you."

Her whole body seemed to come alive with emotion. "You see! That's what I meant! There's no way out!"

"Perhaps not in the sense you mean. But there is another option."

She looked at him questioningly. "What do you mean?"

"Well, there's always the option of facing one's problems and solving them as far as they're capable of solution. Of course, that means growing up."

She looked at him, startled, then she laughed, a distorted sound.

"What's funny?"

"I think I've just had an enormous temper tantrum!"

He relaxed back into his chair. He had been very worried about what he might find here, but whatever crisis Kathy had suffered, she was in no immediate danger, not if she could joke about what had happened.

"Did you enjoy it?"

Again his words startled her, but she smiled faintly. "Yes. I think I did. My throat is awfully sore from all the screaming I did, though." She touched her neck as she spoke.

Green rose. "I'll get you a glass of water. There are cups in your bathroom?"

"Yes."

He brought her the water, and, after she had taken several sips, Green asked her, "Who were you screaming at?"

Her eyes sought the cup. "I think I was screaming at . . . God." Her voice had dropped to a whisper.

"What did you want to tell God?"

Her voice rose again indignantly. "That it was unfair to set things up so that there's no escape!"

"What would you like to escape from, Kathy? It's all right if I call you Kathy, isn't it?"

She nodded, then answered his question. "From pain, from sorrow. From . . . guilt."

"Those feelings can be pretty hard to live with—"

"I can't live with them any longer!" she cut in.

"But you yourself said there's no escape."

She groaned.

"And that's true, absolutely true," continued Randy, "as far as pain and sorrow are concerned. There's even those verses in the *Pearl of Great Price* that talk about God himself weeping. But I thought he took care of the problem of guilt very nicely."

"You mean repentance, I suppose," she said despairingly.

He smiled. "The Celestial Cleaning Service is excellent. It has a reputation of getting rid of every last fleck."

"But you don't know what awful thing I did!"

"Do you want to tell me?"

"I committed adultery." She paused, then added the

phrase she had heard her father use often: "With malice aforethought."

"I see," said Randy. His greenish-brown eyes didn't waver, his eyebrows remained steady, his voice was still soothing and warm, but Kathy's face registered surprise.

"Aren't you going to tell me how awful I am, how you can't stand to look at me?"

"Is that what you expect me to say? Sorry to disappoint you, but that's not the way I feel at all."

"You don't?"

"No. Should I?"

"Everybody else does!"

"Who's everybody?"

"Robert. Brad and Susan too, though Sue is talking to me again."

"Doesn't sound like everybody to me."

"It feels like everybody!" Kathy said earnestly.

"Everybody important, at least," Randy clarified.

She nodded.

"Why is it so important to you how they feel?"

"That ought to be obvious. They're my family, I love them! I want them to love me too!"

"And if they don't?"

"I couldn't stand it! I'd die!"

"But then we're right back where we started, aren't we. You yourself just said there was no way out, that being on the other side doesn't solve any problems."

Kathy was crying now, her despair total.

"It's a hard thing to accept, I know. But you can't count on your family, your husband, your parents, to always be loving; they're fallible, the same as you. There is, however, one person whom you can depend on, always and forever."

The tears kept falling, and Green's heart ached as he watched her.

"Kathy, don't you know that God loves you? That he has always loved you and loves you now and will never stop loving you?"

She didn't stop crying, but Green sensed a change;

something had happened. "He does love me, doesn't he?" she said with wonder. And Green understood the nature of the change he had witnessed. The affirmation she had longed for had finally come in a warm rush; the 'hug' she had wanted had come in overwhelming measure. She was silent for a long time, and Green did not interrupt the silence.

Finally she said, "But I still want my family to love me."

"Yes, of course. And I believe they do, even if they can't express it right now."

"Do you think so? I'm afraid they'll never get over feeling disappointed and angry."

"They'll get over it, when they get around to repenting themselves."

"What?" Her eyes and mouth were round.

"We're all in the same spot, Kathy. Dependent on the mercy and grace of our Savior. When a person really repents of his own sins, he is much less quick to condemn other sinners. It's very humbling, repentance is."

"And hard," added Kathy. "Sometimes I think it's impossible, especially when the sin is the result of some congenital weakness in character or of faulty education or poor example."

"I'm not sure what you mean."

"I've looked back into my life, and I can see certain things . . . certain ways of looking at things . . . building up to just this point."

"Hmmm. Well, we all have weaknesses fostered by our personalities and our family systems, that's true. But one can always say no."

"You make it sound so simple, like Robert does. 'Just do what you're supposed to do, and everything will be wonderful!'"

"You feel angry when he says that, don't you?"

"You're darn right I do. It isn't true, no matter how many times he says it!"

"You're right."

"No guarantee and no cancellations," she said with a sigh.

"Not the kind of cancellation you were wanting, no."

"But forever seems like such a long time! Always having to make choices, to suffer . . ."

"To love . . ." he added softly. "The old 'one day at a time' trick works because of God's love and Christ's sacrifice for us. Using the gifts of repentance and forgiveness is an integral part of it."

"I think maybe I'm ready to start the process of repentance, finally," said Kathy thoughtfully. "I guess it isn't possible to repent until you can admit what you've done. I did make a choice, I know that now. Maybe I couldn't feel close to my Father in heaven because I was fooling myself, pretending I was innocent."

"And now?"

She smiled slightly. "Since there is no oblivion, I have to face up to who and what I am. And since I don't want to go trailing my sins into eternity like some negative exposure of Wordsworth's clouds of glory, I'd better give myself time to get to the 'cleaners'! I don't want to go back to my Father looking a mess."

He patted the hand that lay on the woven spread and said, "That's right. Give yourself a chance, and your husband too."

He paused a moment, wondering if he should take the risk of telling her about Robert's condition. Her eyes were clear and steady, her posture firm. He decided that now was as good a time as any. "You know, Robert's got a problem of his own to deal with, Kathy. He's going to need your support as much as you'll be needing his."

"Problem? You mean dealing with my excommunication?"

"No. That's not what I mean, Kathy. You've been too caught up in your own problems to notice that he hasn't been feeling well for a long time. Robert's ill, Kathy."

"But what . . . I didn't notice . . . what's the matter with him? Is it serious?"

"It could be. But if he takes good care of himself and makes some adjustments in the way he lives, he should be okay."

"Please, what is it?"

"It's called angina, Kathy. Essentially it's the pain that signals the possibility of a heart attack."

"Oh, no!"

"Kathy, I said *possibility!* He's all right now," Green assured her. "And if he makes the changes his doctor is sure to suggest, he won't have any problem. Do you understand?"

"I . . . I think so."

"Now, do you want me to call him? He's probably worried about what we've been doing in here so long."

"Yes," she whispered.

Green gave her hand an encouraging squeeze, then went to the door and called. Robert came out of Grant's room, where he had been trying to rest, but his eyes were red and his features were drawn.

"How is she?" he asked fearfully.

"The worst is past, although there is a lot of work yet to be done," Green replied cautiously. Then he added, "I told her about your condition. I thought she ought to know."

Under normal circumstances, Robert would have considered Green to be terribly presumptuous. Now he just nodded, and when Green put his arm around him as they walked to the bedroom door, Robert didn't object. If anything, he had stopped struggling against the outpouring of concern from the thin, bearded man. He entered the room somewhat timidly, afraid of what he might see, and drew a surprised breath when he saw Kathy sitting up against the headboard, looking real and warm, though totally worn out.

"Robert," she said, holding out her hand. "Robert, I'm so sorry, I didn't know . . ."

What happened next would have been comical were it not for the depth of emotion that accompanied their words, for Robert and Kathy were each trying to comfort the other, each trying to take the blame. "It's my fault." "No, it's my fault." "I should have been more considerate." "No, I'm the one who was unfeeling." Like two people trying to get through a doorway at the same time, the protestations finally ended in a standoff.

"The important thing now," Green said, "is that you both realize you each have a share in the blame and you each have a responsibility in the healing process."

"What should we do?" asked Robert.

"Well, it's up to you, of course, but I would recommend some counseling. Something this serious is not easy to deal with alone."

Robert's head dropped. "I know. We tried it on our own and this is where we ended up. We need . . . help."

Kathy could hardly believe what he had said. Was this actually Robert sitting beside her? She searched his grey, fallen face and his eyes, pale behind the lenses. How had she missed what was written there? Her heart went out to him, and she brought his hand to her cheek.

"Do you have any time to take us on?" she asked Green a bit later.

"We could find a time. If you both want me to work with you." He stressed the word *both* and Robert looked up, recognizing that his feelings were being taken into consideration. Neither had any illusions about the difficulty of the project facing them. Though there had been a moment of true intimacy and caring in the hall, in many ways they were still opposites. Robert had no doubt that there would be times of open antipathy, but he would never be able to call into question the genuine concern that Green had for them both.

"Set the time and day," Robert said finally, looking away. "We'll be there."

They settled on Thursday evenings. Then Green shook Kathy's hand (it was more of a squeeze than a shake), and Robert walked down to the door with him.

"Well, Robert," Green said as they stood in the doorway.

Robert's chin began to quiver. He shifted uneasily, surprised and embarrassed by the unbidden emotion. "I don't know how to thank you," he said at last.

"No thanks necessary," said Randy. "Consider it the favor of a friend."

Robert nodded, shaking Green's hand once more before he left. Then he went back up to Kathy. He stood in the doorway, and they looked uncertainly at each other from across the room. Then Kathy raised her arms and Robert went into them.

PART SIX

Twenty

The moment of quiet they had in each other's arms following Green's departure was the last quiet moment of the day. Myra, subdued and penitent, appeared at the doorstep, and Susan invited her in. She entered the bedroom hesitantly and asked the question she had been rehearsing for hours. "Kathy, will you ever forgive me for being so presumptuous? I had no business asking you that."

"I'm not sure there's anything to forgive," Kathy replied gently. "It was a question that had to be asked, and a question I had to answer."

Later on in the day the bishop, who had learned of the crisis from Green, arrived with one of the Montgomerys' home teachers to give Kathy and Robert each a blessing. Beth Hubbard came later with a casserole, a salad, and dessert, staying just long enough to put the casserole in the oven and promise Susan that she'd drop in the next day. Then late in the evening Brad picked up his grandmother. As soon as she got off the bus, Clarice asked what was going on. Brad didn't know much since he had been at work most of the day, and as soon as they reached the house, he retreated to his room, so he didn't hear his father's reply to Clarice's repeated query.

Living through the upheaval had been bad enough; retelling it over and over again was worse—it threatened to rob the experience of its immediacy and significance. Finally Robert said, "Simply put, everything that's been building up all these months exploded today. Luckily, nobody was fatally injured, but there's a lot of healing that needs to take place, and there's more chance of that happening if we all go to bed."

Both Robert and Kathy were painfully shy as they retired that night, but they found themselves turning to each other, reaching out. Robert put his arm around Kathy, and Kathy rested her head on his shoulder.

"When is your appointment?" she asked as they lay in the darkness.

"9:30," he replied.

"Do you want company?"

"Thanks, but you'd only have to wait in the office. Do what your mother suggested: stay in bed. She'll take care of breakfast for the kids. There's no reason for you to get up early."

"Well, if you say so. But I will go with you if you want me to."

"I appreciate that," he said, tightening his arm around her. "But don't worry. I'll give you all the details when I come home."

Although Robert fell asleep almost immediately after their short conversation, Kathy couldn't, in spite of her exhaustion. "Don't worry," Robert had said; that was a laugh. However, after weeks of feeling nothing besides empty coldness, Kathy was grateful that she now had the capacity to worry. Finally, she fell into a deep sleep, and as she slept, she dreamed that Change had appeared as a little girl to play a game of Mother, May I? with her.

"How many steps may I take?" Change asked.

Kathy replied, "Mother says, 'Three baby steps.'"

"Mother, may I?" Change then asked.

"Yes, you may," she replied.

And so it went. Kathy always said, "Five baby steps," or two, or one, as if not trusting that change should come any faster. But even as she slept, the healing work had begun. Thus, she woke in the morning without a grimace or sense of dread—she simply opened her eyes to a new and different day.

It took her a moment, however, to discover what made

the day so different. At first she thought the silence was responsible—the house was unusually quiet. She rolled over and looked at the clock radio; it was already nine. No wonder the house was quiet; Robert would have already left for his appointment—*Oh, please, let him be all right,* she prayed—and Brad for work. Grant would have long since gulped his cornflakes and gone out to play.

But she wasn't experiencing an external stillness only; she felt an internal quietness as well. She lay still, giving herself up to the strange feeling of expanse and inner openness that was like a field after a carnival has packed up and left: finally quiet, finally at peace, grass beginning to stand up again where booths and rides had been.

She got out of bed, went to the window, and looked out on the jungle-green yard. Everything seemed to have grown gangly and unruly overnight, and Kathy found herself impatient for the sun to come out so that she could clip and pull and mow—an impulse she hadn't felt in months.

Maybe that's it, maybe that's why I feel so wonderful, so aware. I've made the decision to live!

She showered, dressed in a brightly colored caftan, thinking at the same time that it was too bad her fat couldn't have disappeared overnight as well, and went down the stairs to the kitchen. She still moved slowly and carefully, but for a reason different than she had before: in spite of the wonderful sense of release, she felt fragile, as if her heart were tender to the touch and must be guarded.

As she came into the kitchen, she saw her mother sitting at the table making out a grocery list. Clarice looked up, and their eyes met; she rose, and they held each other tightly for a long moment. Kathy felt her mother's tears through the cloth of her caftan.

"Why Mom, what is it?" Kathy cried. "Everything's all right!"

But Clarice kept on crying, the tears finding the furrows in her cheeks. "I was so frightened!" she finally managed.

"So was I. But believe me, I'm going to be fine now. I only hope Robert will be okay too."

"Oh, I hope so too. So much happening, and all at once! It doesn't seem fair!" But then she straightened and said firmly, "And since when is life fair? The world isn't going to end, no matter what comes of this. So what do you want for breakfast?"

Kathy burst out laughing. "You remind me of a story I heard once in church about a sister whose home was burned to the ground by the mobs in Independence. When morning came, she looked around at what was left of her home, and then she did what she had always done: she fixed breakfast for her hungry children, cooking on the coals of their burned-out cabin! You could have been that woman, you know."

"Maybe so," agreed Clarice. "I figure you must be famished after yesterday's ordeal. What'll it be?"

"Oh, just juice and maybe an egg." She looked around. "Where're Sue and Grant?"

"Oh, that boy!" Clarice laughed. "He was here long enough to eat breakfast and get a good-morning kiss, then he was off to the park to play with the neighborhood kids. That child's always on the move, isn't he?"

"He sure is. And Sue?"

"Well, she's been stuck here for some time, so I felt she needed to get out of the house. I drove her over to Jamie's."

"Mother! I thought you didn't drive anymore!"

Clarice looked pleased with herself. "Sue assured me I wouldn't have to go on any busy streets, so I thought I'd try."

"Good for you!" Kathy then sat down as Clarice set a soft-boiled egg and glass of orange juice in front of her. She picked up the glass and sipped some of the juice before broaching the subject that had been bothering her. "Uh, Mom, have you talked with Brad much since you came?"

"No. He really needs to talk, but he doesn't want to; he's holding it all in. I'm more concerned about him than anyone else right now."

"So am I. When Susan started talking to me again, I'd hoped that Brad would too. I guess it's not going to be so easy for him," Kathy said sadly.

"No," agreed Clarice. "But Susan's been a real Trojan, hasn't she? You ought to come outside. Even with her ankle like it is, she's tried to keep some of your flower beds in order. And she's done quite a bit around the house as well."

"Yes, I know. If it hadn't been for you and Myra and Sue, the place would be a pig sty."

"How did you ever let it get so awful? You're always so particular about how your house looks."

"I guess I didn't really notice what was happening, and I couldn't bring myself to care anymore."

"That should have been a sign you were seriously ill. You should have had help long ago!"

"Don't talk to me about signs, Mother. Robert was giving off a few of his own, and I didn't see a one of them. I can't cast any stones."

"I have a confession to make, Kathy," said Clarice slowly. "I've been so angry at Robert! Every time I called and he said that things were 'going as well as could be expected,' I wanted to shake him! But I realize now that he had a lot to worry about."

Kathy nodded wordlessly.

"And something else. I overheard a conversation that was very private. I shouldn't have listened, but . . ."

"What?" asked Kathy, her curiosity piqued.

"I'll apologize to Robert when he gets back."

"Mother, what on earth are you talking about?"

"I heard Robert talking to Jay!"

"What? When?"

"This morning. I was walking by the door to the den, and I . . . well, I couldn't help overhearing."

"Oh, Mother! For heaven's sake, what did he say?"

"I didn't listen to all of it, you understand?"

"Mother, please!"

"I heard Robert telling Jay he would see to it that you got the help you need."

Kathy gasped and then pressed her hands against her eyes to stop the stinging.

* * * * *

As Robert waited for the specialist to review the tests he had been given, he distinctly felt that he was headed into a confrontation with himself. The lines were clearly drawn. One of the California companies he had been sounding out had contacted him several days previously, issuing an invitation to fly out for interviews sometime in the next month. He had told them he would be delighted to; they would be discussing the sort of position he had been working toward all his life. He had, however, accepted the invitation without fully considering what such a move would entail. A new job, a new ward, and a new home to adjust to all at once would surely add up to an overload of stress, which was exactly what the specialist, Dr. Parkinson, advised against when he looked up from the charts.

"Get out from under," he ordered. "Get more rest. Take time off. Quit a little earlier in the day. Learn to relax." He handed Robert a list of classes designed to help angina patients deal with their illness, including biofeedback, stress management, relaxation techniques, yoga, and hypnotism. Robert was appalled at what he read.

"This is nothing but quackery!" he said as he threw the list down on the doctor's desk.

"Listen carefully, Robert," said Dr. Parkinson brusquely. "You can fight your illness only one way: change your life. You would be amazed at the number of patients I have, only slightly different versions of yourself, who lie in ICU and wonder why they ever thought their work was worth it. Every person has to find some meaning in his life sooner or later; and the ones who make work into the most meaningful part of their lives regret it. *If* they live to regret it."

"But it's not just work," said Robert defensively. "I have Church obligations as well, and I just can't ignore my obligations to my family."

"I've heard all of that before. At the risk of offending you, I can guess how you run your family—the same as you run your job: control is everything."

At that, Robert turned livid, but Dr. Parkinson continued before he could be interrupted. "Let life come to you, Robert," he said a little more kindly. "You don't need to manage everything. Think of this: life isn't all vertical; there's a wonderful horizontal spread of experience that you're missing."

Robert drove home with those words sounding in his ears. Any other time he would have dismissed such a statement, but the turmoil and uncertainty of the last hours had rendered him vulnerable. He was unable to ignore the fact that the very premise upon which he had built his whole life was being challenged. The California offer and what he would do about it occupied a pivotal point in his thinking; his response to it would measure the success or failure of the challenge. He wanted that job! To give it up was asking too much!

He suddenly recalled Aunt Emma's words: "The thing you think is the hardest is often the easiest and most beneficial in the long run."

Why do I keep thinking about Aunt Emma? he asked himself. He hadn't talked to her in years beyond the impersonal exchanges at family reunions that centered on weather and what his children were doing. Yet twice in the past two days he had found her ready to comfort and guide him.

These thoughts slowed Robert's steps as he left the car and walked through the front door into the family room where Kathy waited.

"What did he say?" she asked anxiously.

In answer, he tossed the list of classes onto the couch where she sat. "Look at that! Can you believe I'm supposed to take this seriously? 'Lifesaving Skills for the Type-A Personality!' What garbage!"

"Oh, that sounds interesting," Kathy said, picking up the paper. "I think we ought to take that one together."

"What?" He hadn't expected that response from her.

"Well, you are a perfectionist, you know. I'm not, but I've been acting like one; maybe I could get some benefit from a class like this too."

He laughed humorlessly. "Counseling, yoga, biofeedback—I'm going to be quite up-to-date if I do all of that. Why does this have to happen right now? What am I going to do? Kathy, I want this job!"

"Did you mention it to Dr. Parkinson?"

"Yes."

"What did he say?"

"He said if I could come to grips with the fact that I'm a sick man and treat myself as such, I could probably handle the change."

"What did he mean by that, for heaven's sake?"

"Well, if I go to work at eight and come home at five and forget that I'd ever worked an eighteen-hour day, I'll most likely be all right."

"He said that to a workaholic?" Kathy's voice portrayed her astonishment.

He moved away from her in protest. "I don't think I'm a workaholic."

"Alcoholics don't like to admit their addiction, either."

He turned back toward her abruptly, jaw clenched. "I resent that comparison!"

Kathy caught his hand and drew him down beside her. "Oh, Robert, don't get mad. We're both compulsive in one way or another. With me, it's food. With you, it's work."

"I think I could work an eight-to-five day," he said as he sat down.

"I don't. I don't even think you could cut back your hours to a seven-to-six schedule," she replied.

"And why not?"

"What would you do after you came home, answer me that. You don't have any hobbies; you don't read unless it has to do with your work or the news; except for an occasional sports program, you rarely watch TV; you don't belong to any clubs. Most likely you'd accept a call to be bishop and fill up your hours with something else stressful!"

Her words suddenly became animated for him. Robert could see himself clearly, and understood what the doctor had meant by horizontal and vertical. He was taut and narrow, strung out from reaching continuously upward. "I don't know what I would do," he admitted soberly. "I'd have to learn to enjoy other things."

"You know what?" she asked quietly, "I think you're as doubtful about whether you can actually do it as I am."

He didn't answer.

A thought occurred to Kathy. "Have you told these California people about your health problems?"

He looked away. "Not yet."

"You know, you really ought to. I'm sure they're expecting you to commit yourself totally to this job—they might not be too happy if you arrive with the news that you're going to keep the same hours as your secretary."

He sighed, resigned. "You're right, of course. They may withdraw their offer. That's one positive aspect for you. It would save me the necessity of making the decision, wouldn't it?"

"No," she said softly. "Whether or not you decide to go to California, you have to make a decision about how you're going to spend the rest of your life." She paused. "Like I did."

Twenty-One

Making the decision was the easy part, Kathy realized as she began picking up the threads of her life. She was so determined that she tried to do too much too soon. She forced herself out of bed the next day far earlier than she needed to rise on a summer's morning, then showered and, for the first time in months, performed the culturally prescribed ritual of shaving. It gave her a feeling of being clean and fresh until she looked in the mirror and saw her unruly bush of hair. *I'm going to get this mop cut today! If I can't find someone else to do it, I'll cut it myself!* she thought vehemently.

The old maternity pants and oversized shirts she had been wearing were also repugnant. *All right, so I'm fat,* she told herself. *But that doesn't mean I have to look sloppy. I'll buy some decent things to wear until I get back in shape.* By noon, she had located the nearest Weight Watchers meetings, had been to the beauty shop for a new, sleek cut, and had purchased several inexpensive slacks and matching tops in flattering colors; but she was so tired that she spent the rest of the day in bed.

"Slow down, dear," Clarice told her daughter. "You've been ill as surely as if you had had pneumonia; you need time to recuperate. Nobody's asking you to be Wonder Woman."

Kathy knew her mother was right. Inside she felt as if there was a new, little Kathy who needed to be nurtured and strengthened, who needed time to develop. The discrepancy made Kathy think of the largest and smallest dolls in a set of Ukranian nesting dolls, intricately painted figurines that come in a set from very small to quite large, each fitting perfectly into the next largest.

So she set a more leisurely pace. She "worked" in her flower beds, sitting with face upturned to the sun as often as she delved into the rich, loamy soil. She walked when she felt like it, not berating herself if she didn't want to, nor putting herself down when she had a momentary lapse from her new diet. She enjoyed her afternoon naps, grateful that she no longer dreaded the moment of awakening.

"I'm even looking forward to our first session with Randy," she told Robert.

"I'm not," he replied honestly.

But on Thursday he went anyway.

"You're not happy about being here, are you?" Randy questioned Robert after he and Kathy had sat down.

"No," said Robert.

"What don't you like about it?"

Robert, wanting to avoid a discussion of his need to be in control and to be self-sufficient in all things, picked on something seemingly innocuous. "Well, for one thing, I don't like the way we're sitting," he said.

"Oh? Tell me why."

Robert shifted uncomfortably on the couch he and Kathy occupied. If he responded frankly, his answer would lead precisely where he did not want to go. "It emphasizes your position too much," he said finally, and with great reluctance. "It gives you all the power."

"And you don't like being in a situation you don't control?"

"Who does?"

"I'm asking about your feelings, not anybody else's."

"Okay, I don't like it."

"If you were in control tonight, where would you be sitting?" asked Randy.

"Behind the desk," blurted out Kathy triumphantly.

"I was talking to Robert," Randy chided her, but Kathy's outburst precipitated a lengthy discussion of Robert's fondness for dealing with life from the far side of his desk. With

Randy's help, Robert was able to understand the way he used it both to establish his position as the person in charge and to ensure a certain distance between himself and others.

"I understand what you're saying, but I'm not entirely convinced it's true," Robert said to Randy.

"Then look at how you're sitting."

Robert turned to Kathy and realized that the space between himself and his wife was about the width of a desk.

"You can close up that distance between you, you know," Randy commented.

Kathy moved toward Robert, and he put his arm around her.

"Why don't you try sitting like that whenever you have a problem to discuss," suggested Green. "And be sure to pick a neutral place; avoid Robert's office." He suddenly grinned. "Then again, you might even decide there's room enough for both of you behind that desk!"

Kathy laughed. "Two heads are supposed to be better than one."

"What about it?" Randy asked Robert.

"It sounds kind of nice," he admitted.

"You can tell me how it works when you come next week."

Robert was aware that both Kathy and Randy were waiting for him to say something, but he didn't speak immediately. Although the stated purpose of the sessions with Randy Green was to help both of them discover the destructive behavior that had contributed to their marital problems, he had had the idea that they were primarily for Kathy's benefit. This session, however, left him with no doubt that he was also fair game. He had had the feeling lately that all things were pushing him toward change, and while in his head he wanted to resist, he knew that he couldn't avoid it. *I suppose it's what is called an "out reaction,"* he thought.

"Sure, okay," he said finally. Then he answered the real question: "We'll be here next week."

* * * * *

Clarice was relieved when the first session had come and gone. She had resolved to stay in Lemburg until Kathy and Robert had it behind them—she wanted to make sure that they were moving in a positive direction before she went home. Friday morning she said to Kathy, "I think I'd like to take the bus home tomorrow, dear. I need to take care of my plants and get back to my Sunday school class."

"Do you have to?"

Clarice smiled. "I think it's time, don't you?"

Kathy nodded slowly. "Yes, but you know I don't want you to go."

"I'm not going that far. We can call each other, and you can visit anytime. I'd better get a ticket today, if I want to have a seat on that bus."

"Forget about the bus. One of us can surely find time to drive you home," said Kathy, taking her mother's hand in her own.

"I'll get a ticket anyway, then I'll be sure to have a seat if it doesn't work out. Now, how about fixing up a nice supper and eating out on the patio tonight? We can have a going-away party."

"Why not?" said Kathy delightedly. "We've got some short-ribs in the freezer. Let's have a barbeque."

When Robert got home that evening—he actually arrived early at 4:30—Kathy asked him to start the coals.

"What're we celebrating?"

"Mom's going home tomorrow."

"Oh."

"For someone who never complains when his mother-in-law leaves, you don't sound very enthused."

"It's just a feeling. When something critical happens at work, everybody rallies around to make sure the problem is solved. But the initial crisis always gives way to a day-by-day working out of the solutions that have been adopted. Your mother's leaving signals that we've entered that stage."

"Does that worry you?"

"Yes. That's when we find out if our new measures are really working, and make adjustments if they're not. It's the longest and hardest part of the process."

"Then I don't think you need to worry; if we need to make adjustments, we will."

Touched by her faith, he leaned down to kiss her forehead, then went out to start the coals.

He nursed them to an even glow before putting on the ribs. Then he played badminton against Sue, who balanced gamely on one crutch, and Grant. As they played, he could hear the rise and fall of women's voices coming from the patio where Clarice and Kathy minded the grill. The sound of their voices was pleasant, as was the pungent odor of barbeque sauce and browning meat. Robert felt a deep contentment as he enjoyed this afternoon with his family. Only one person was missing, and he would be home soon.

He heard Brad's car pull up into the driveway a while later, but he kept on playing with the other kids, expecting to see Brad come out of the house momentarily. Minutes passed, but Brad didn't come, then Kathy called to say the ribs were done. "I'll go see what's keeping Brad," he said and went into the house. He found Brad in the kitchen making a tuna fish sandwich.

"Hey, Son! You put all that stuff away. We've got a feast out on the patio—ribs, potato salad, seven-layer salad, and chocolate cake!"

Brad went on making his sandwich, and Robert's smile faded.

"Okay," he said brusquely. "I've been trying to avoid this conversation, hoping that you'd come around. But now I see there's no other choice. We've got to talk about your mother and how you've been treating her."

"I don't want to talk about her."

"We've got to. Your mother's in the middle of a crisis—a very dangerous crisis."

"She's been having one crisis after another for months. What's so different about that?"

"You remember the day I sent you to pick up your grandmother?"

"Yeah. What about it?"

"You don't know much about what happened that day, do you?"

"No. And I don't want to know."

"Things were touchy that day, Son. It was a matter of life and death."

"You're exaggerating," said Brad coldly, all the while searching his father's face.

"No, I'm not. I had to do some hard thinking that day. I had to do something very, very difficult that I didn't want to do."

"Oh yeah? What was that?"

"I had to lay down my anger toward your mother. I've forgiven her, Brad. Or at least I feel like I have, and I pray to heaven that I have."

Brad's face reddened. "That can't be true! How could you forgive her? I'll never be able to, and I didn't think you would either!"

The hot glint in Brad's eyes shook Robert. *I hope I never looked at Kathy that way,* he thought. To his son he said, "I didn't think I ever would myself, but I had to, if I wanted to live like a human being again. Brad, hatred was eating me up—the way it's eating you up!"

"My anger's making me strong!"

"That's not true. It took more strength to get on my knees and ask the Lord to forgive me for hating Kathy than it took to hate."

"No, that's not the way it's supposed to be! You're not the one who should get on his knees, she's the one! She should come crawling, begging!" Brad's voice splintered, and he was close to tears.

"And then what? Would you say you forgive her, then hold it over her head the rest of her life? Brad, I look at you and I see myself. I encouraged you to condemn your mother; it was a way of hurting her more, I guess. But I was wrong!"

"No! She deserves to suffer!"

Robert cringed as his own words, complete to the minutest inflection, came from Brad's mouth.

"Look at her! She's got everybody worried about her. Even Grandma came on the bus, and she hates riding the bus! She's like the prodigal son—she gets the feast!"

"Oh, Brad. You don't think she's enjoying this, do you?"

"Why not? She's got Myra in an uproar, calling all the time. Her visiting teachers are always sending notes, the home teachers drop by on their way home from work, and now she's got you where she wants you! She's got everybody busy taking care of her! It's not fair!"

"I know it seems that way, but—"

"It's the same all over," Brad interrupted. "The bishop and the quorum presidents are all worried about the guys who are messing around with girls and drugs. Same thing in school. The guys who are flunking get the special classes, and the dopers get the rap sessions. What about the ones who are doing okay? What about us? Nobody's busting a gut to find out how we feel and what we want out of life. Everybody just expects us to go along like good little boys and not make any waves!"

"That's not too much to expect . . ." murmured Robert under his breath.

"What?"

"Nothing. Just something I used to say to myself a long time ago."

Robert looked at his son, who was tall and fierce in his anger. *He's eighteen years old,* thought Robert. *In no time he'll pack his bags and leave for the 'Y' with his mitt slung over his shoulder.* "We haven't told you very often how proud we are of you, have we? You're a fine young man, Brad. And you're right. We have just expected that you'd keep on doing everything you were supposed to do without a word of encouragement or praise. I'm sorry about that."

"It's a little late," said Brad scornfully, but he was startled to see his father's eyes fill.

"No, don't say that, Son. It can't be too late; we've all got another chance ahead of us!"

"Well, it'll be a long time before I give her"—his lips curled on the pronoun— "another chance!"

"Brad, please. She's human; she makes mistakes. We all do."

"Then why do you keep feeding us all of that 'Be-ye-therefore-perfect' junk? You know, until now, I actually thought you and Mom were pretty close to being perfect? I've been trying all my life to live up to you and the things you've told me about Grandma and Grandpa Montgomery. I'm glad, you know! I'm glad Mother had her little fling! Now I don't have to worry about disappointing you!" Tears were rolling down the side of his nose, and his jaw muscles tightened. "Now I know it was a farce, all of it!"

In a flash, Robert saw in his son the same striving after an unreachable goal that had made him feel so pressured as a boy. "I'm so sorry, Brad. I should have told you there was another side to the story. I should have made it clear that we all have problems and doubts."

"You? Problems and doubts? Don't put me on. You're the great purveyor of all wisdom, the encyclopedia of the one right and true way to do everything from riding a bike to choosing a career. It's all so easy for you."

Again Robert winced. "I do have doubts. And problems and fears. If I thought I didn't, I know better now. That day with your mother, when I thought I might lose her . . ." His voice failed him.

"No! Don't you cry! Don't you dare cry! You're supposed to be the strong one! If you cry, who is going to hold us together?" He was shaking Robert's arm in anger and fear.

Robert caught Brad's hand and held it tightly. For a moment it was almost as if they were testing each other's strength. "We'll just have to hang onto each other, I guess," Robert said.

Then Brad jerked his hand free. He walked slowly to the door, eyeing his father warily. "You almost got me then, didn't you? I almost gave in, but I won't, not that easily! It'll be a hot day before I give in the way you have!" He turned and fled from the room, slamming the door behind him.

Robert took off his glasses and rubbed his eyes. Wearily he put them back on and went out to the patio where the others were eating.

"Brad's not coming out, is he?" asked Kathy.

"No. He's already had something to eat. Boy, this looks good!" he said brightly and began filling his plate.

But Kathy set hers down on the flagstone. "He'll never forgive me," she said.

"He will, he will," said Robert encouragingly.

"I've forgiven you," said Grant through the potato chips in his mouth. "I know all about it."

Kathy started, then questioned Robert with her eyes.

"I had to explain what was happening, you can understand that. It didn't make much sense if he didn't know it all."

"All!"

"Yup, you did something you shouldn't have," Grant said importantly, "and you can't be part of the Church for a long time. That's why you've been acting so weird and crying and stuff. But Daddy says you're feeling better and that if we all help, you'll get to be baptized again next year. Hey! I'll be eight next year—maybe we can get baptized together!" He beamed at her, pleased with himself and his magnanimity, entranced by the idea of a family baptismal service with himself and his mother as stars.

"Bless the simple sweetness of children," said Kathy, caressing his tousled hair.

Twenty-Two

Brad drove his grandmother home that Sunday, returning late in the evening of the same day. He was somewhat less belligerent in the following days; Kathy was sure Clarice had taken advantage of time alone with her grandson to talk to him seriously about the family situation. While Brad still didn't initiate conversation with his mother, he responded in a reasonable tone when she spoke to him. It wasn't much, but it was something, and Kathy was grateful for it.

She was learning to be grateful for little things: for a day or even an hour entirely free from despair, for times when reading scriptures or praying was a joy, not a struggle; for moments when she truly believed she and Robert could make a new life together.

"It's a long road, Kathy," Bishop Mangus had said during one interview. "You've made it through an extremely critical time, but there's more to come. I know it seems almost too much to bear, but I want to warn you about some of the things you'll experience so that you can recognize them for what they are."

Kathy had listened with eyes downcast; she hadn't wanted to accept the fact that there was still more to wade through. She had wanted so much to believe in a magic moment, in a once and forever cure, that she had not given equal weight to all that Jesus had told the adultress: "Go, *and sin no more.*" Jesus had given the adultress a lifetime task. So Kathy had listened, but with resentment even though she learned soon enough that Bishop Mangus was right.

She found herself subject to recurring depression that descended without warning, like a thick fog, immobilizing her. At such times she cried out to God in fear, and often she felt buoyed up as she struggled against the depression. "How can I get it to stop?" she begged Randy Green during one session. "I can't stand it anymore."

"I can't teach you how to stop it completely," he replied, "but I can give you some ideas. For instance, most of the time a negative thought precedes the feeling. Whenever you feel the beginning of depression, ask yourself what you were just thinking. Nine times out of ten, you'll find that a thought of discouragement or of worthlessness and hopelessness has crossed your mind. Give it a red flag, Kathy, and fight back. Say loud and clear, 'That's not true!'"

"That sounds too simple!"

"But doing it over and over again will rob those negative thoughts of their power."

Kathy learned the value of his suggestion. She came to believe that Satan himself didn't need to tempt her into failure, that her own mind was quite capable of doing that without any outside aid. In her effort to fully repent, she endeavored to understand fully the seriousness of what she had done and of her own complicity, but as her understanding grew, she found it difficult to resist being overcome by feelings of worthlessness, shame, and guilt.

Sundays, too, were still painful. Although she was strong in her love of the Lord, she felt isolated from the community of Saints. She especially longed to partake of the sacrament and express her testimony. She asked Randy Green what she could do, and he suggested that she write in her journal while her thoughts were fresh and that she set aside some time on Sundays to tell Robert what she was thinking and feeling about the gospel. The latter was especially difficult, but she tried, and Robert, touched by her efforts, learned to listen as he had never listened before.

To her sorrow, daily observances of personal prayer

and scripture reading were still a stumbling block. She had to consciously struggle against her rationalizations—*I don't have time; I don't really want to; what good does it do anyway?* by repeating the phrase, "It's not true," again and again. She found that the more she repudiated the lies, the less often they appeared.

But there were moments of saving grace and humor too. One such moment occurred the day she had asked Robert to come to her office. He had looked at her quizzically but had followed her, down to the laundry room! How funny he had looked, perched on a stool as he folded towels. The ridiculousness of the situation had broken down barriers, and they had talked with rare ease about many things.

Then there was one counseling session that more than any other, helped strengthen her, though at first she balked at the idea. One evening in late July Randy Green had picked out a speech pattern she constantly used. She was describing her reaction to something Robert habitually did by saying, "It really makes me mad!"

"You know, I've heard you say that a lot, Kathy," Randy commented. "It concerns me because it reflects a belief in something that just isn't true. Nothing can make you mad."

"Well, this sure does. It makes me furious!"

"Nothing can make you furious."

She pursed her lips in exasperation. "You know what I mean."

"Yes, and that's what I'm challenging. Robert's actions can't make you furious; you choose to be."

Kathy shrugged. "What's the difference?"

"There's quite a big difference. Many people accept the idea that emotions are like fate: they happen to you. But that's not quite the case. You feel the way you do because you interpret things in certain ways. You may be teased or provoked, but even then you can determine how angry you get, or if you get angry at all. Robert can't make you mad anymore then he can make you happy. That's your job."

"But I thought that was why a person got married . . ."

"So their husband or wife could make them happy? That's fairy-tale mentality, Kathy. You have to make the magic happen in your own life."

Randy could see she was struggling against this new idea; he gave her a moment, then said, "When you put the burden of your own happiness on another person, you're asking too much. Robert can tell you that."

Robert was silent.

"Go on, tell her how you would feel if you didn't have to worry about making her happy."

Robert sighed. "It'd be a relief," he admitted.

"Try being your own fairy godmother this week, Kathy," suggested Randy. "Let Robert off the hook. Be responsible for your own emotions."

That night, unlike most times when Kathy left the sessions, she walked to the car exhausted and with a headache. She discovered during the next few weeks, however, that taking responsibility for her own happiness left her more stable, confident, and unselfish.

There was one other problem, though, that bothered her, a problem she was wary of discussing with Robert, Randy, or the bishop, fearful that she might be misunderstood, for it had to do with Jay.

She felt she had effectively cut all ties with him, which was a major task in her repentance. She had given up singing with Parker-Jeffry Chorale and had, in fact, joined another group that sang just for fun. She had arrived at a point where, thank God, he no longer occupied her mind. If he did cross it, she no longer felt the instant fluttering of her heart or the heat of flushed cheeks.

But Jay still lived in Lemburg. The town was not that large; and his apartment was on the same side of town as her home. Sooner or later, she knew, there would be a chance encounter as there had been that day at the gas station. She did not fear a reawakening of the feelings that had so devastated her, but she did fear the awkward first moment when she might not know what to say. There were times when she wished it would happen and be done with, so that she could be completely free.

For Robert, the counseling sessions challenged his most cherished assumptions, and logical man that he was, Robert admitted that much of what Randy Green had suggested was true. For instance, when Randy questioned him about how he perceived his role as head of the household, Robert replied that, according to his personal interpretation, the role of a father was to make sure everyone in the family did what they were supposed to do.

"And if they don't?" Randy had asked.

"Then I've failed."

"You mean if someone in your family makes a mistake or doesn't toe the line, you're not successful? By that criterion, how successful was God with his spirit children?"

Robert's shoulders slumped.

"I'm not surprised you're tired," Randy had said gently. "You've been carrying an unnecessarily heavy load. You aren't entirely responsible for the choices your children make, especially as they become teens, and you aren't responsible at all for your wife's choices. You've been trying to force them into certain modes of behavior, and that's not your task as husband and father."

"But what would happen if I don't? They might not do it on their own."

"That's true, but fatherhood is always a risky business. Our Heavenly Father chose to take just that risk, and I think you'll find that you would have a lot more influence on your family by letting go than by controlling."

Robert had thought about that a lot; he had had to consider it seriously, even though it went against the grain, because what Randy had said sounded a lot like what was in the last thirteen verses of the 121st section of the Doctrine and Covenants. Realizing that had done much to increase his confidence and trust in Randy Green; in subsequent sessions, he had slowly begun opening up, even though each time he had felt as if he were betraying an unwritten tenet of his upbringing. One time, while he and Kathy were discussing the role of the Church in their lives, he had found himself talking about something he had never even revealed to Kathy. "My parents were always on top of things;

they never had a moment's doubt about anything," Robert had said.

"They never had any doubts at all?" questioned Randy.

"Well, it seemed that way to me. I always wanted to be as sure as they were."

"And you're not?"

"No."

Kathy looked up, startled.

"Well, that puts you in good company," Randy observed. "Most people have doubts, whether they admit them or not. It's not such an awful condition; in fact it's the only condition in which faith can operate."

"That may be so," said Robert soberly, "but doubt wasn't allowed in my family. Believing without question isn't too much to ask for someone whose ancestors crossed the plains."

"Come again?" said Randy, clearly astonished.

Robert found himself explaining the phrase that had governed so much of his life. It was difficult; the place from which it had risen was extremely sensitive. "It means that we don't have any choice about what we do; there are certain assumptions by which we live our lives."

"You mean you never stop to ask yourself why you're doing what you're doing?"

"No. It's a waste of time. I do what I have to do."

"How do you feel about that?"

The words came out hotly, "I'm sick of it!" But almost immediately, Robert got himself under control. "Sorry, I don't know why I said that."

"Don't shut off your emotions, Robert. They're important!"

But Robert had retreated. "That was just a childish outburst. I take pride in doing what must be done."

"Is that why you came tonight?"

"Yes. I'll do what I have to do in order to keep my family together."

He had no idea where Randy was going; Randy's next statement shook both Kathy and him deeply.

"You're assuming you and Kathy will stay together."

"But isn't that what this is all about?" he asked sharply, taking Kathy's hand in his.

"Only partly. From what you've said in our sessions, I get the idea that both of you have spent a good deal of your lives acting as if you have no choices. But you do. The best outcome of these sessions would be to choose to stay together because you really want to, not because you think you must for the sake of temple covenants. They certainly wouldn't be valid if you didn't love each other."

Robert and Kathy looked at each other fearfully, and afterwards left that session feeling more uncertain than they had felt for many weeks.

Twenty-Three

Thus the summer weeks went by, strung like line from Thursday to Thursday until the week Robert flew to California to meet his prospective employer. He went into his interviews, however, with restraint. Everything about the company looked good, very good in fact, but Robert felt an inner detachment, as if all of the meetings he was attending were for the benefit of someone else. Because of that, he viewed the proceedings with an eye unclouded by his usual prejudice. It was during his next-to-last interview that he had a singular experience. Being who he was, he would never call what happened to him then a revelation, but a vision suddenly rose before him of an endless line of pinstriped executives, all polished, all blow-dried, moving to a measured cadence as each in turn slipped into a slot: replaceable parts to keep the machinery of business running.

Had being one of them brought him happiness? He had a real sense of accomplishment in his present work; he liked the excitement and even the tension he experienced when making important decisions. In fact, boring maintenance tasks and occasional personality difficulties aside, he liked everything about his job. He was lucky in that—his career had offered him immense satisfaction. But happiness? Joy?

When he cast back into his memory, he could identify a few times he had felt something akin to joy. Each incident, whether it had to do with his family, his job, or his Church work, was essentially a matter of relationships. He had felt joy when he had been personally involved and loving.

If that's what I want more of in my life, no job is going to provide it for me, he thought. He realized then that the decision to stay in Lemburg had already been made.

This in mind, he explained his medical problems to the company officials when they met the next morning. With grim amusement, he noticed the immediate change in their approach; suddenly they became far less certain about him and their offer. In spite of their protestations, Robert knew how relieved they were when he thanked them for but regretfully declined their flattering proposal. As he spoke, the Spirit confirmed his decision, and he went back to his hotel smiling.

Later, he called and told Kathy what had happened.

"Well, that was fast," she said. "Just think, now you can come home early and take a minivacation."

"Uh, I think I'll get my flight changed so I can have a stopover in Salt Lake City. As long as I have the time, I think I'll drive down to the ranch."

"Any special reason?"

"No. I just want to, that's all."

Kathy chuckled. "Did you hear what you just said?"

"I didn't say anything odd."

"It's just unusual for you to do something simply because you want to."

"Oh. Well, I'm making progress then, aren't I?"

"Umhum. Listen, have a good time. I'm glad you have a chance to do this."

"You don't mind?"

"As a matter of fact, a bunch of us were thinking about leaving early Friday morning for Minneapolis and spending Friday and part of Saturday there."

"Who is 'a bunch of us'?"

"Myra, Beth, Ronnie, and me."

"What are you planning on doing?"

"We thought we'd get some theater tickets or symphony tickets, depending on what's available. We'll do some shopping too and visit the Art Institute and anything else that looks like fun."

"Well, why not?" said Robert. "Is Sue going to babysit Grant?"

"Yes, for a fee! But I told her she could ask Jamie to stay those two days with her. I'll probably be back late Saturday afternoon."

"Sounds good. We'll both get back about the same time." Robert could imagine her smiling.

"That's all you're going to say?" she asked.

"That's all," he replied. In times past, he would have given her a list of things to do before going, and then he would have reminded her not to spend too much money.

"You know what," she said, "I think we're making progress."

After he hung up, Robert thought a long time about the telephone conversation. He appreciated the irony of their situation: two middle-aged adults finally learning to take care of themselves, to be responsible for their own feelings. He felt that a great burden had been lifted from him, yet he realized its absence would leave a large empty space in his life that he would have to fill with something else. He thus went to bed with the queasy anticipation that accompanies the beginning of a great journey.

The next day after he had flown to the Salt Lake airport, he drove to Beaver in a rented car. It was a strange drive, for the landscape was obscured by an overlay of remembered faces, scenes, and emotions. Most of the scenes were pleasant to remember, but sadness tinged many of them. He knew he had missed a lot in his youth.

The evening was far advanced by the time he pulled into the yard of the weathered ranchhouse. His younger brother Abe, who had turned out to be the rancher among them, greeted him warmly.

"This is certainly unexpected," he said, shaking Robert's hand. "I didn't believe it when Helen told me you were coming. I think this is the first time you've come here since Mother died, except for reunions."

"That's probably right."

"It's a real pleasure to have you here, big brother! Let's get your things and go on in. By the way, is there anything particular you'd like to do while you're here?"

"Not really."

"Well, I've got business in town tomorrow morning, so you'll be on your own for a while."

"That's fine. Maybe I'll go for an early morning ride. It'd be nice to get out in the hills by myself—when everybody's here, I don't get a chance to do that." He chuckled as he remembered something. "Kathy says going for a ride with the Montgomerys is like moving the Saints from Winter Quarters to Salt Lake!"

"She's right," Abe said, grinning. "Let one person head for the tack shed, and the whole bunch is ready to go. If you want to go by yourself, you'd better leave before the kids have their chores done, or you'll be sure to have company. Take Blue; she's the Appaloosa over by the watering trough. She's got a smooth gait and a lot of spirit. But not too much."

"That's good; I haven't been on a horse for a long time," said Robert as they went into the house together.

The next morning before the sun breached the mountains, Robert rode out of the yard, wearing a cotton flannel shirt topped by a heavy wool shirt, a Stetson, and some leather gloves. He and Abe had dug deep into the utility closet until they'd found among the old boots a pair that had once belonged to Robert. "You know how it's like on a ranch—you don't throw away anything," Abe had said, somewhat embarrassed. The boots had been stiff, but a good application of saddle soap had softened them up a bit, and they didn't feel too uncomfortable as Robert leaned down from his saddle to open the gate.

The valley he rode in still rested in blue shadows, but the mountain ridges were sharp against the golden sheen marking the advent of the sun. It was eerily quiet. Robert, whose ears were used to the constant hum of city noise, found it disconcerting to hear only the sounds of the Appaloosa's shod hooves and the squeak of the saddle as they moved up the road. He reached down to pat Blue now and again and found himself saying again the crooning words he had once said to his own horse, Nuggets.

He and Nuggets had been inseparable from the time Robert's father had taken Robert to the barn to see the wobbly-legged sorrel foal. He had spent part of every day with her: he had helped break her; and on days when he didn't go riding, he had brought an apple or a carrot out to her in the evening, then spent a few minutes talking to her as he brushed her down. That changed when James Montgomery died and Robert took over the ranch. He had become a man responsible not only for himself but the welfare of his family. After he began his studies, he had had even less time for the horse. Once, as Robert and Kathy were getting ready to leave after a visit to the ranch, Kathy said, "Look! Nuggets is lonesome. She wants you to scratch behind her ears." But he had been too busy loading the car to do anything more than call to her. As he drove down the lane, he could see her in the side mirror, her neck stretched over the fence, watching him drive away. It was the last time he had seen her. He and Kathy moved to Lemburg, and the horse died before they returned to the ranch for a visit.

"I never said good-bye," said Robert aloud, wishing he were riding her instead of Blue; he missed her, and to his surprise, it still hurt after all these years.

Blue sidestepped as a small animal scurried into the brush by the side of the dirt road. Robert soothed her, then turned in the saddle just in time to see the sun surface over the eastern mountains, flooding the valley with light and almost instant warmth. He unbuttoned the wool shirt and took some field glasses from the saddlebag. Starting at the northern edge, he scanned the valley from north to south; but when his sweep brought his Uncle John's place into view, he paused for a long moment, then lowered the glasses. With a clarity that matched the sharpness of dry mountain air and the view it gave, he understood why he had come home. Someone was here who had been important to him during his growing-up years, someone who had loved him and loved him still: Aunt Emma. He had come home to see Aunt Emma.

He replaced the binoculars in the saddlebag and urged the horse forward. It seemed only minutes before Marion was greeting him at the door, her curiously youthful face aglow. "I'm glad you came to see Mama," she said. She led him into the living room and then returned to the kitchen, where she was busily making a cake.

He had steeled himself for what he might see, but he couldn't help smiling broadly when he saw his shrunken aunt coming out of the family room to greet him, her silver hair done up as always, with a bright green ribbon around it.

"You always were flamboyant," he said as he took her hands in his.

"Old habits die hard," she said, giving him a kiss.

He lifted her hands so that he could look at them more closely. "They did a wonderful job, didn't they?" he asked, touching her knuckles gently.

She flexed her now-straight fingers, which were graced by brilliant red nails.

"They're good as new, aren't they? Whenever I see someone with hands as bad as mine were, I tell them to get some plastic knuckles. I'm a walking commercial! 'Course, now that I've got them fixed, my eyes are so bad I can't do much with them anyway." She shrugged eloquently. "That's how the old body goes: one part after another!"

She sat down on the couch in the parlor and patted the cushion next to her. "Enough of that! You sit down beside me; I want to hear all about you. But first, tell me why it's taken you so long to come and visit me."

Robert grinned, embarrassed. "You know how it is."

Emma nodded, but the look in her eyes told him it wasn't good enough.

"Actually, I've always had the feeling that you were disappointed in me," he said.

"Why should I be disappointed in you?"

He shrugged.

"Tell me," she demanded. "And don't act like you don't know what I'm talking about. We used to spend a lot of time together. I haven't forgotten how to read your face—looking at you now, I see a lot of a young man I used to know. In fact, I see more of that young man than I've seen in many years. What's happened? Everything's all right with my Kathy, isn't it?"

"Now it is. But we've had some troubles. We're both going through a rough time."

"So you came to see your Aunt Emma. What can I help you with, dear?"

"Nothing, really. We're getting plenty of help."

"Maybe you just need a hug from your old auntie; you used to come for hugs when you were little, remember?"

She reached out her arms, and as he leaned over to embrace her, he noticed she smelled old and fragile, like dried leaves. His eyes were wet as he said, "You can still give the best hugs!"

"How come you're not getting enough of them at home?"

"I guess we're just not huggers."

"Oh, posh. You hug people, and they'll just naturally want to hug you back. You give my Kathy a bushel of hugs when you get back, you hear?"

"I will," he promised. "You know, I do feel a lot like that kid you were talking about—so . . . so unprotected."

She smiled gently. "Only because you're not used to it. You boarded yourself up and nailed a 'No trespassing' sign right out front, you know. I wasn't a bit surprised when you started studying accounting!"

"Why not?"

"Numbers are pretty predictable and safe, aren't they? They provided an escape from the things you feared the most."

"Only it didn't work," he said, turning away from her.

"You go ahead and cry if you need to," she said, stroking his bent head. "The world's a pretty scary place when you discover that it's unpredictable and unsafe; it's less scary when you discover you can rely on God's love."

The words had a familiar ring. "Have we had this conversation before?" he asked his aunt, wiping his glasses with the embroidered handkerchief she offered him.

"Probably," she replied.

"I have the strangest feeling that I'm back at 'Go.' It's as if I have a chance to remake a decision I made years ago about how to live my life. I know it can't change the past, but I have the feeling it's going to change the future."

"With the grace of God."

"With the grace of God," he repeated.

Her timing exquisite, Marion entered the room with a tray in her hands. "Anybody hungry?" she asked. "My chocolate cake's done. I like to bake. I like to show people what good cakes I can make. I made a gooey chocolate cake for you. You like chocolate, don't you?"

"I sure do. It looks delicious," said Robert.

And it was.

The next day Robert spent with Abe and his family. They filled the hours with simple but satisfying activities and for the first time in many years, Robert experienced again the enjoyment he had felt when working on the ranch with his father. Early in the morning, Abe drove him out to see the stock. As they leaned against the side of the old red pickup, chewing on salt sage, he explained what he was doing and what he had planned for the future of the ranch. Before them, the herd was quietly grazing, the mountains forming an expansive backdrop. When they got back to the ranch, Abe brought out the books in an unexpected show of trust. The two brothers discussed them, sitting at the desk that had first been James's, then Robert's, and now Abe's.

Robert was moved by his brother's openness and impressed by his sound understanding of the operation. The ranch was in good shape and showed little signs of the recession. When he complimented Abe on it, Abe flushed and suddenly turned shy. *He wants me to approve of him; more than that, he wants me to like him,* Robert thought in surprise. He did like Abe; he liked all his brothers and sisters. But until now he had not felt it necessary to keep in touch with them, and he had justified that neglect by faithfully attending the yearly reunion.

In the late afternoon they all took their horses and went out for a ride. When they returned, Abe's children scattered to do chores: the boys fed and watered the stock, the younger children gathered eggs and fed the chickens, and the older girls helped in the kitchen. Robert's sense of the past coming into the present increased as he watched them, especially as they sat down around the table for supper. Helen had not changed the house much beyond adding bright, decorative touches. Except for some new upholstered pieces, the furniture was the same as it had always been. Even the meal was right out of Robert's childhood: fried potatoes, fresh cottage cheese, sliced tomatoes, and homemade bread. But in spite of all these similarities, something was very different.

He puzzled over it until he realized that the difference was Abe's family itself. They didn't differ much in looks—they resembled to a surprising degree the aunts and uncles who had grown up around this very table. But there the similiarity ended. Abe's children were handsome and bright, but they were also boisterous, rather undisciplined children. Robert felt a constant urge to shape them up, but he followed Randy Green's advice to breathe deeply and observe passively whenever he felt like controlling. As he observed them, he realized they were good children. They were loving and willing to help each other; and they responded well to their father's humor, warmth, and easy approach. Robert was amazed.

Those qualities carried over as well to the relationship between Abe and Helen. They smiled at one another, cooperated with respect and caring as they worked together, and solved their problems in a laid-back fashion. *Where did they learn to do that?* Robert wondered. Then it occurred to him that they might not have had to learn it the same way he had had to learn. Because he didn't have any close friends, Robert had never had the opportunity to find out how other families operated; he had only his own interpretation of his parent's family as a guide. *I must have missed something somewhere,* he thought. *Abe seems to know a lot about relationships I'm still struggling to learn.* What moved him most of all, however, was that they extended that same caring and respect to him as well.

"This has been a great visit," said Abe as he carried Robert's suitcase to the car the next morning.

"It sure has," said Robert.

"I hope you don't wait so long before you come again."

"I won't," said Robert warmly.

The two brothers shook hands and hugged each other in an unusual display of emotion. Then Robert climbed into the car and drove down the lane. He headed north when he reached the highway, driving by instinct because his mind was preoccupied. After a while he noticed that he was speeding—he was in a hurry to get home to his family.

Twenty-Four

It was still dark when Kathy climbed into the back seat of Myra's van Friday morning; the women had decided to leave early so that they would arrive in Minneapolis before noon.

"This is going to be so much fun," said Kathy as she stowed her suitcase and tote bag. "I don't think I've done anything like this since I got married! Hey, where's Ronnie? I thought you were going to pick me up last."

"Ronnie decided not to come," said Beth.

"Why? I know she wanted to. Are her kids sick?"

"No," said Myra. "She really could come, but Ronnie has this idea that she can't justify going anywhere if her wash isn't caught up, her house spotless, and her freezer full of precooked, labeled meals. Oh, and then there're the little love notes that have to go in pockets and lunch sacks."

"There's nothing wrong with doing any of that!" protested Kathy, who, before packing, had cleaned her house, done the wash, and left out frozen spaghetti sauce and stew to thaw.

"The thing is, Ronnie wants to go," continued Myra, "but she doesn't think she can allow herself any fun unless she's perfect."

"Now I know you're exaggerating," said Kathy, laughing.

"Only a little."

"I understand perfectly," said Beth. "I was like that myself the first couple of years after my baptism." Her laugh was warm and rich. "Do you know, I was a member for a year before I discovered baking bread wasn't a commandment!"

"Not really!" exclaimed Kathy as she slid forward and leaned her elbows on the back of the driver's seat.

"Well, not quite, but I thought I had to do it all. In homemaking meeting I made glass grapes for my living room table; I made nightshirts for my girls from Ed's old dress shirts; I gardened; I canned. I even made a compost heap, but I never could get it to 'cook.'"

"I remember those grapes," said Myra as she pulled out onto the freeway. "At the time four or five of us lived in the same neighborhood; a nonmember neighbor who knew us asked me in all seriousness if glass grapes had some significance in our religion!"

"I'm not surprised that she was confused," laughed Beth. "It took me awhile to figure out the difference between values that are central to the gospel and those that are not."

"Give me an example," said Kathy, unconsciously using Green's phrasing.

"Faith is a core value of the gospel; breadmaking isn't."

Myra picked up on it. "Keeping the Word of Wisdom is; being a vegetarian isn't."

"Wait a minute," said Kathy, "I'm thinking. Oh, here's one for Paul: obeying the law of the land is; being a Republican isn't."

Myra laughed heartily. "Better not let him hear you say that!" Then she began relating her husband's latest conservative cause.

They still hadn't run out of things to talk about when they pulled into the parking lot of their motel on the I-494 strip. In fact, it seemed to Kathy that they spent the whole trip talking. They talked while they shopped—Kathy splurged on a wonderfully flattering basic dress at Dayton's; they talked over lunch in the art deco atmosphere of Scottie's; and they were still talking, though with lowered voices, as they strolled through the Art Institute. The only real break came when they went to Orchestra Hall for a performance of the Minnesota Symphony.

Only later, as they were sitting on the motel beds in their nightgowns, sipping diet pop and eating corn chips dipped in picante sauce, did they speak of things more personal.

"How are you doing, Kathy?" asked Beth Hubbard.

Without warning, Kathy burst into tears.

Myra quickly put her arm around her friend, and Beth got some tissue from the bathroom. Then both women waited patiently until Kathy finally blew her nose and raised her head. "I'm sorry, I didn't know I was going to do that!"

"Don't worry about it," said Myra. "You must've needed to cry."

"I don't know why; we're doing pretty well, I think. It's just that repenting is a lot harder than I ever realized."

"It's a difficult process, for sure," Beth said.

"Feeling remorse for what happened that one night was only the beginning. I've had to examine my whole life and make wholesale changes."

She hesitated before continuing. "I was so angry at the Lord when I was excommunicated. I blamed him for what had happened because I didn't want to admit I had brought all that suffering on myself and my family. When I finally admitted that I had chosen my actions, I felt that I had to punish myself to make up for the suffering I had caused. But that's not repentance."

"No," said Beth, and Myra nodded. "You're making real progress if you understand that."

"There's still a lot I have to work out. Randy Green says Robert and I have to make a conscious decision about whether we stay together. He says we have to be sure we love each other." She bit her lip and drew a long breath. "That scares me. Right now we're just getting to really know each other for the first time—what if we find out we don't like each other after all!"

"Do you really think that's a possibility?" asked Myra.

"No, I guess not. But we're still apart . . . in so many ways."

* * * * *

When Kathy got home late the next afternoon, the first thing she did was check to see if Robert's briefcase was in its usual place. It was. Suitcase in hand, she went swiftly up the stairs.

Through the doorway of their room, she could see him unpacking. Her step slowed; she felt flushed and uncertain. She watched him for a moment without speaking, then said, "Hi."

"Well, there you are," he said, turning to face her. "How was your trip?"

"Fine, great," she answered.

"Here, let me help you with that." He took her suitcase and put it on the bed.

"Did you have a nice visit at the ranch?"

"Yes. I saw Aunt Emma; she asked about you."

"How is she doing?" Kathy inquired as she opened her case.

"Surprisingly well; she's so proud of how her hands now look that she's grown her fingernails out and paints them an outrageous shade of red."

Kathy laughed. "That's Aunt Emma." She paused to gain courage, then said, "You must have had a good trip; you look different somehow."

"Really? How?"

"Oh, I don't know," she said, embarrassed. What she was thinking she didn't have the courage to say, that he looked gentler, more approachable, more lovable. She said instead, "You look rested, and that sunburn you've got puts some color into your face."

"You look good too," he said, and their eyes met.

To cover her confusion, Kathy pointed to something in his suitcase. "What in the world is that?" she asked him.

He held up the object for Kathy to see. "It's a boot. I brought home an old pair of mine; they must've been in the bottom of the utility closet for twenty years."

"Whatever for?"

"Oh, I thought maybe I'd take up riding. I have to have something to do when I'm not working. You still like horses, don't you?"

"Yes, but I haven't been riding for years."

"So it's time we went. There're supposed to be nice riding trails in the bluffs along the river. What about it?"

"Sounds fun," she said. Then she looked at her hands so she wouldn't have to see his face when she asked the question that was really on her mind. "Robert, we're not staying together just because we think we have to, are we?"

There was an excruciating pause before he replied. "I don't think so. We've got more going for us than that."

The relief she felt was so great, she almost sobbed.

"By the way," Robert said, clearing his throat, "tops on my list of things to do is to call the office and arrange to have some personal time off. We've got the cabin on Split Hand Lake for a week starting next Wednesday."

She should have known that he was serious when he mentioned the list; still she laughed when she found it a few days later in the pocket of a shirt she was about to put in the washing machine. Then after reading it, she wept. It was the blue notebook all over again. The goal: Build a Good Relationship with Kathy. Underneath it, points A, B, and C in logical order, and underneath them, 1, 2, and 3. *It's true,* she thought, *the more things change, the more they stay the same.*

The day they left for Split Hand Lake was hot and muggy. Although it was only eight-thirty, Kathy already felt sweaty and sticky as she walked through the house to check windows and lights, and then went downstairs to make sure that the iron wasn't plugged in. Satisfied, she went out to the car. Susan and Grant were already in the back seat, anxious to get on the road. Brad was waiting by the car, and Robert was getting some last-minute equipment. But Kathy was not that anxious to leave—she didn't like the idea of leaving Brad.

"Are you sure you don't mind being home alone?" she asked him.

The expression on his face matched the disgusted tone in his voice. "Do I have to say it a hundred times? No, I don't mind. I'm past the age of being afraid of the dark, Mother. Besides, I'm looking forward to being alone."

The brutal frankness of youth, thought Kathy, *but at least I always know where I stand with them—that's something.*

Brad had kept himself purposefully ignorant of what had happened to her during the crisis, but he was troubled by it, nonetheless. He was also troubled by his father's condition. He could sense the changes that were coming, and he was frightened by them. He wanted his life to go on as planned. Parents had no right to mess up things.

"Well, everything is in good shape," said Robert, coming out of the garage, his new fishing gear in hand. "You really don't have to do much except maybe mow the lawn. That is, if it rains. If it doesn't, forget mowing and water instead."

"Yup," said Brad.

"And keep the paper picked up and the mail brought in."

"Really, Dad."

"Just reminding you. We'll be going up I-35 to Minneapolis and then by U.S. Highway 169 to Split Hand Lake. I wrote it all down, and the telephone number of the cabin as well, in case you need to get in touch with us."

"I won't, but thanks anyway."

"There's plenty of stuff in the freezer, Brad," said Kathy. "You can invite some of your friends over for supper now and then if you want to."

"Thanks."

Robert had finished packing the last of the gear, and now he stood by the open door of the station wagon. He held out his hand to Brad. "I wish you were coming with us," he said as they shook hands.

"You know why I'm staying. I need the money for school."

Robert knew that wasn't the real reason—he had offered to add the amount of missed wages to Brad's account. They all knew what the real reason was, for that matter.

"Take care of yourself, Son," said Kathy, hesitating at the door. But he made no move toward her, so she waved half-heartedly, then got in. She kept her eyes on Brad as the car moved down the drive, and at the bottom, she waved one more time. But Brad had already begun to walk back toward the house. By the time the car turned the corner, blocking the view, the door had shut behind him. She closed her eyes and leaned her head against the back of the seat.

"Don't take it too hard," said Robert, patting her knee. "Don't let it spoil our vacation, okay?"

"Okay," she said, smiling weakly.

"Tell us what the cabin's like, Dad," Sue said, trying to liven things up.

"I can't tell you much," he replied. "I've only seen pictures of it, you know."

"Yes, we know," teased Kathy.

"Hey, I never could take off enough time to make it worth the drive up and back," he began, but he caught himself and shook his head ruefully. "I'm doing it again, aren't I?" He sighed. "Well, I know it's very nice. It has all the conveniences, and the area is supposed to be really pretty. Everyone who's used it says it's great."

"Can't wait!" said Sue.

"You'll have to wait; we've got quite a way to go," Robert said, smiling at Sue in the rearview mirror.

As they had so often done on trips out to Utah, they passed the first few hours singing, talking, and playing word games. Then they wound down; Grant and Kathy went to sleep, and Sue started reading a book. Robert turned on the radio for company, adjusted his seat, and got down to serious driving. On either side of them, fields of green and darker green flowed by, silos, barns, and rows of windbreak trees standing out against them. Above the fields and farm buildings, heavy grey clouds held in the heat. Robert had plenty of opportunity to enjoy the landscape—the road was straight and flat, like a conveyor belt moving them north.

When Kathy awoke several hours later, they were winding through the hardwood forest of northeastern Minnesota. Not too long after, they reached the edge of the small lake. The minute they pulled into the drive leading to the cabin, Kathy knew she was going to love it. The building was picturesque and cozy; and thirty feet from the porch was the lake, whose wooded shore snaked in and out of view, forming coves and points.

"I just hope it doesn't rain," said Robert, looking up at the rows of puffy clouds. "I'd hate to spend a week cooped up inside."

"Don't be a pessimist!" Kathy retorted. "Besides, you'll suffer more if you have to try out that new fishing equipment you bought, so don't count on being saved by rain!"

He grinned. "And don't you get sassy!" But he knew she was right. He had bought the equipment, not knowing how he would fill his days if he didn't have something to do. He hadn't fished for thirty years, but he supposed it was rather like riding a bike: one never forgot. Still, fishing seemed a pretty pitiful weapon against ennui. He looked around him. There was the cabin. There was the lake. There was his family, already barefoot and wading along the shore. And all around them was the forest, growing gloomy in the late evening slant of sun. He drew a deep, shuddering breath, then joined the rest of them.

Of course, he hadn't forgotten how to fish. He took Grant out evenings or mornings, and sometimes even in the afternoon, depending on the fishing reports.

"That's cheating!" protested Sue. "The poor fish haven't got a chance."

Grant didn't care; he was in seventh heaven. Robert was in agony. After getting out on the lake, there really wasn't much to do between strikes but worm the hooks and check the line of fish already caught. Robert envied Grant's ability to enjoy the lapping of water against the sides of the boat, the fields of water lilies, and the loons, which, in an instinctively choreographed ballet, always dipped their heads below the water in perfect synchronization. He did enjoy Grant's enthusiasm, however, and they all enjoyed eating the fish, which Kathy cooked in a variety of ways.

He also envied Grant's ability to let a day unfold before him without worrying about what was going to happen next. An entirely open schedule seemed vaguely hedonistic to Robert, who usually planned vacation days down to the last minute. Montgomery family get-togethers too were always well orchestrated, from amusement park excursions to temple excursions, from family picnics to family prayers. This was entirely different and unsettling, for while he didn't have to do anything he didn't want to do, he found that he didn't really want to do anything that he didn't have to do. *Management by obligation,* he thought with a sigh.

Still, he had chosen to do this. He had wanted more than anything to be with his family in a different setting. And the vacation was working out the way he had hoped. While Grant and Sue were happily engaged in their own activities—it was amazing what they could think of to do—Kathy and Robert had time to themselves, sitting side by side on the porch in the warm quiet or walking down the forest paths, talking and holding hands. Almost every evening, they spent the last sunlit moments in a canoe on the lake, listening to the strange, melancholy calls of loons as the woods darkened and the glassy water blazed with sunset. For them, these moments were to be the frail beginnings of renewed love.

They were, after all, still Robert and Kathy Montgomery, with three children and a Tudor-style house in Lemburg, Iowa. Robert still had a difficult time talking about his feelings and accepting limitations; Kathy still had a deep longing for openness, for emotional exchanges, for romance. Robert still preferred reading newspapers and trade journals; Kathy still needed music and the excitement of drama. Robert still felt the need to be in control; Kathy still wanted to be taken seriously but, at the same time, to be protected and cared for. Trying to change their way of relating to each other was like trying to change a room by rearranging the old furniture while everything else in it remains the same.

But Robert and Kathy found themselves enjoying their time together more and more. The harmony and peace of their surroundings permeated their lives, and acceptance, tolerance, and the ministrations of the Spirit hastened the rebuilding process. Kathy keenly sensed the changes as they walked down the green-tunneled road the day before they were to leave. It made her aware of Robert in an intense, totally different way. It made his gaunt frame desirable, his stern, rather homely face dear. She looked at him shyly and ventured, "I don't know if I've ever thanked you properly for what you did when you called Randy. I know that wasn't an easy thing to do."

"No. But it was the only thing I could do. I've never felt so helpless before."

"I'm sorry I caused you so much worry, but that's all in the past. Nothing like that will ever happen again."

"Thank heaven!" The words were propelled by an explosion of relief as the memory of that terrible day rolled up within him. "I thought . . . I was actually afraid you would do something drastic."

"So was I," she said, looking at the dirt road before them. "I think I might have, if it hadn't been for my belief in the Savior. The thought of having to stand face to face with him and my Heavenly Father made me think twice; then I realized that if I believe in Christ, I must also believe he died to give me the opportunity to repent. And that's what kept me going: if repentance is possible, there's always hope!"

Robert was moved by her words. Still unused to expressing his feelings, he found it easier to draw her to him. After resting a moment in his arm, she asked, "Robert, have you forgiven me?"

Forgiven her? With a start he realized that the inward gnawing that had tortured him for months was no longer there. He couldn't say when it had left, but he knew it had disappeared through no effort of his own: it was the work of the Spirit. His lips against her hair, he whispered, "Yes."

"Thank you," she said simply. "Now I can put it all behind me. Except for Brad. I wish . . ."

"So do I," he said. "Looking at him is like looking into my own face. I'm ashamed to think you've seen me with that same expression."

Kathy looked up at him. "It's not there now," she said softly.

He was amazed at the warmth and hope that glowed in

her face. Could it be the same face that had frightened him not so long ago? Did his own face look as different as hers did today? It felt different. He knew the tension around his eyes and jaws had lessened. Smiling, he took her hand, and they turned back toward the cabin.

It was difficult for Kathy to keep from looking at him as they walked, but her sideward glances were veiled, for she was afraid he would be able to read her thoughts. They had grown close in the past weeks, closer than they had been in years; but physically there was still a distance between them that distressed her. She wondered if they would ever enjoy a moment of physical intimacy again.

Caught up in her thoughts, Kathy was surprised to notice that Robert had stopped walking. "What is it?" she asked, noting with a flutter of anxiety how brilliantly blue his eyes were. Then she realized that it was not anger but a different emotion altogether that brought such color into them. He pulled her to him and began kissing her, and Kathy relaxed into his embrace, knowing that the time for complete forgiveness had come at last.

Twenty-Five

The fall of the year that Kathy Montgomery turned thirty-eight was a time of double-edged beauty: a time of endings, yet also a time of beginnings. "Back to School" signs had appeared in store windows, and children were buying boxes of crayons and yellow number-two pencils for the first day of school. The growing season was winding down, and harvests of wheat and corn had begun, leaving some fields stripped bare. Trees had just begun their color changes, and the leaves were tinged with pale gold or light burgundy.

The Montgomery household was seeing new beginnings, too, as Robert adopted a modified work schedule, signed up for a class in stress management, and bought a pair of Nikes and a 35mm camera. Kathy organized her fall series of classes and registered as a part-time student at the university, setting up a family job schedule in consultation with Grant and Sue so she wouldn't have to do so much of the daily maintenance. Her two youngest started planning for the school year, and Brad began packing for his first year at Brigham Young University.

Of the changes that were taking place, Brad's impending departure was the most disquieting of all. It was a marker in their lives; as a family, they were entering into a new stage. Brad himself felt it keenly, beginning with the day the rest of his family had arrived home from the cabin in Minnesota.

He knew something was different from the moment

they walked into the house. He could see it in the way his father kept touching his mother, in the way they looked at each other and smiled. *They're together again,* he thought.

Sue and Grant were all smiles too. Grant eagerly sought out his big brother, stumbling over the tackle box in his excitement.

"Guess what I did at the lake? I went fishing with Dad, and I caught six fish in one day!"

"Big deal," said Brad sourly.

"It is a big deal," said Sue. "He's never caught a fish before."

"Fishing's stupid," said Brad, shrugging, resentful that his father, who had never taken him fishing, should have taken his little brother.

"Like baseball?" asked Kathy. Robert had spent hours teaching Brad to throw and catch and had supported him by going to as many of his games as possible.

"Yeah, like baseball. Like just about everything!" he retorted.

"Don't mind him, he's just ticked off because he couldn't come with us," said Sue to Grant.

"Don't kid yourself; I could have come if I had wanted to!"

"You mean you didn't want to? Really?" asked Grant.

"Really!" But Brad felt keenly that he was not a part of the group that had returned. He could sense that they had gone on without him, leaving him stuck in a quagmire of resentment and hurt.

As the days following their return went by, the other Montgomerys settled into their normal routine, a routine he was no longer part of. His mother took Sue and Grant shopping for school clothes—Brad declined the offer for help with his shopping—and they started school the last week of August. Because Brad wasn't working anymore by then, he was home to see them go.

First Sue, dressed in her new Esprit pants and blouse, flashed through the kitchen in a blur of excitement: it was the first day of her last year at Washington Senior High School. Later on, Grant put his new school box in his backpack, took his lunch in hand and walked, all slicked-down seriousness, to the bus stop. From the window, Brad watched the knot of kids straighten out into a line as the yellow bus came to a stop at the corner. The line disappeared into it, then the bus drove on. Brad leaned against the window frame and watched it go; he felt it pull his childhood out and away from him forever.

He walked back into the kitchen, wondering what he was going to do with the time between his last work day and the departure date circled on the calendar. Kathy was at the table, a pile of cookbooks in front of her, planning her fall series of classes. As he came in, she looked up and said, "There's buttered toast in the oven if you want another piece."

Brad got a still-warm piece of toast, put some jam on it, and wandered out onto the patio. He sat in a lounge chair and looked around the yard as he ate. Everything was familiar yet somehow strange. It was as if the knowledge that he would soon be leaving had sharpened his vision. It wasn't a final goodby; he would be coming back for summer and vacation, but he couldn't escape the fact that, from this point on, his parent's home would only be a layover on his way to or from the business of living his own life. All of his high school years had been spent planning and working for this change, but at the moment he was afraid.

He had been afraid ever since he'd heard his father and mother talking about the job offer in California. In a flash, he'd seen his empty room, the hall full of boxes, the moving van outside, and even a new house, where his things, still in boxes ("We didn't know what you'd be wanting"), were stacked in the corner of an extra bedroom. He had been swamped with a horrible feeling of homelessness. Then he realized that even if they didn't move, it wouldn't make much of a difference: home wasn't the house, after all; home was the family. And he was afraid that in his heart he had already left home.

Kathy, too, felt some of Brad's unease. Although Brad had told her not to shop for him, she could think of nothing else to ease the pain of his imminent departure but to do so anyway. Shopping was something she had done for him or with him every fall since he had started kindergarten. *I'm only getting things I know he needs,* she told herself as she bought him socks, underwear, a new belt, and a couple of pairs of jeans. However, when she saw a colorful nylon sports bag, she didn't even think twice about buying it.

But all her shopping couldn't rid her of the queasy, anxious feeling she had. Not only was her oldest child leaving home, but next year at this time, Sue would be getting ready to depart as well. She herself had finally decided to get her undergraduate degree, and she was taking two general education classes and one nutrition class fall quarter. She was excited about them, but she was also worried. Could she manage her cooking series and the college classes at the same time? Could she find time to study and read her scriptures? Could she do all those new things and still be a good mother and wife as well? She thought she could; and she had in her favor the fact that she had embarked on this course with Robert's agreement and the Spirit's approbation.

She was so preoccupied with balancing her thoughts and her packages, that she didn't see Jay until she nearly collided with him.

"Careful, there!" he said, helping her rearrange her purchases. But every time he balanced one, another threatened to fall. For Kathy it was a welcome diversion—by the time the packages were secured, the dreaded first moment was past.

"Thanks," she said and then smiled, first tenuously and then more broadly as she found she could look at him directly without embarrassment. "I was about ready to drop them all."

"No problem," he said. "It's been a long time, hasn't it?" He paused, then asked intently, "How've you been?"

"Fine, and you?" she answered, trying to avoid an involved conversation.

"I'm all right," he said, but Kathy noticed his face was too thin, and his eyes reflected an inner smoldering she hadn't remembered seeing before. "You look great," he added. "You look happy."

"I am happy."

"Things have really improved since I saw you that day at the station, haven't they?"

Kathy had hoped they could avoid mention of their past involvement, but it was obviously not possible. She kept her answer brief. "I'm not the same person," she said.

"I can see that," he replied thoughtfully.

Nor was she the Kathy who had sat across from him for hours after rehearsals. He sensed a maturity and strength in her he had not known before, a deep contentment and peace. He had loved many Kathys, each of them to an extent his own invention, but this woman standing before him resembled to a disconcerting degree the Kathy he had finally enshrined in his heart. She was managing the formidable task of ordering her life, he realized. A sense of pride in her accomplishment pervaded him, but he also felt keenly the sense of loss and finality.

"Well," he began somewhat abruptly, "I mustn't keep you."

He began to turn away, but Kathy stopped him. There was some unfinished business here, and she felt compelled to take care of it. She extended one hand as far as her packages would allow. "Jay, thank you for what you did."

He shrugged disparagingly, then said, "No thanks necessary." Touching her extended hand in salute and farewell, he turned away. But he was troubled that while she had made clear and compelling strides toward her goals, he was still not even sure what his were.

Kathy watched him go with a prayer in her heart that he might one day find some measure of peace and joy in his life. Then she turned away with a sigh, relieved that the chance meeting was behind her. One by one, the problems in her life were lessening. The one big obstacle left was Brad.

Once she got home with her packages, Kathy doubted the wisdom of her decision to buy clothes for her son. "I bought all these things, and now I don't know how to give them to Brad," she complained to Robert.

"Probably the best thing is to not make a big deal out of it," he said, putting his arm around her. "Just act like nothing's happened, and do what you would normally do."

"Think it'll work?"

"Brad's softening; he's not as belligerent as he was. Go ahead and give it a try."

"Okay," she said. "Kiss me for good luck."

She went to the bottom of the stairs to call Brad, but he was already on his way down.

"Uh, Brad, I picked up a few things for you when I was shopping today. Would you like to look at them?" she asked him with an uncertain smile.

He would always remember what he saw in that smile; it was a revelation of what being a parent means. He saw tenderness, hope, longing, and the pain of letting go, and he couldn't resist it.

"Sure," he said thickly, clearing his throat and following her into the kitchen where the packages lay on the table.

Item by item, she took out her purchases and held them up for him to see; he tried to murmur something nice about each one. Kathy was taking the sports bag from its sack when she felt his hand on hers.

"Mom."

The tone of his voice brought her eyes to his. "Oh, Brad!" she said, and held out her arms; he came into them like a child.

The interview Kathy had with her bishop a little more than six months after her excommunication did not signal the end of the process she was going through; it was, however, a marker indicating the direction she was heading. She went to it gladly, for though she had at first been extremely bitter about her excommunication, she had come to regard it as the catalyst that had brought about necessary and beneficial change. She looked forward to the day when Bishop Mangus would consider her application for rebaptism; and this meeting was a step toward that time.

He met her at his office door and invited her in. They took their seats, then looked at each other, smiling simultaneously.

"Oh, this is a pleasure, a great pleasure," said Bishop Mangus.

"Yes," she agreed.

"You feel very good about things, don't you."

She nodded.

As they talked, they covered many things, among them the continuing sessions with Randy Green, her feelings for Robert and her relationship with the children. She told him about her reconciliation with Brad. "I'm so glad he didn't leave feeling the way he did before," she said. "The only thing that worries me is that he studiously avoided any mention of Jay and what happened. I think we'll have to talk about it sooner or later."

"Perhaps," said the bishop. "Leave the timing up to Brad."

Having mentioned Jay's name, Kathy felt constrained to tell Bishop Mangus that she had seen him briefly.

"Do you have any feelings for this man, Kathy?"

"Yes," she said, then hastened to explain herself. "I feel concern for him—he's still suffering. But in the sense you mean, no. I don't love him. There's nothing between us that could be the cause of worry."

"I'm glad to hear that," said Bishop Mangus, clearly relieved. "And what are your feelings about the Church?"

She had known he would ask that question, and she had given it much thought in preparation for their meeting. Now she smiled wryly and said, "Do you mind a two-part answer?"

"Fire away."

"I believe in the gospel with all my heart. I love sacrament meeting; I feel more a part of it than I ever have, even though I'm not allowed to participate, because I've truly learned to love my Savior and worship Him. I've been reading the scriptures, and I'm getting a lot of comfort and strength from them."

She paused.

"Are we coming to part two?" asked the Bishop, eyeing her carefully. He could tell it was difficult for her to begin by the way she straightened her skirt and then clasped her hands before speaking.

"The problem is, I believe in the gospel, but I'm not sure how I feel about the organization of the Church right now."

"Oh?" He shifted forward on his seat.

"To me the organization of the Church represents all the things I've been having trouble with, all the shoulds and oughts and lists . . . Bishop Mangus, I just can't do it all anymore. I've done my 'duty' ever since I married Robert, and look where it got me. I'm not saying there's nothing to be gained by having a sense of duty," she added, "but right now, I'm doing only the things I want to do. I suppose that sounds awful, but I hope the time will come when I'll want to do some of the things on my lists again, only this time because of love."

"Love has some fine imperatives of its own," the bishop reminded her.

"Yes, but that's just the point—love's imperatives are internal. The Spirit is teaching me what those imperatives are, Bishop, so you don't need to worry about me, really. I'm not off on a tangent. I feel like I'm on the right track at last."

Bishop Mangus smiled. "So do I. I'm confident that there will be a baptism held in this building another six months or so from now."

Her smile was radiant. "Oh, I hope so, with all my heart!"

When the interview was over, Bishop Mangus walked out to the parking lot with her. The night was clear, the stars were high and bright, and the smell of dried leaves and wood smoke was in the air.

"I do believe it might freeze tonight," said Kathy.

"I'd better cover the tomatoes when I get home," agreed the bishop.

Then there was one last shaking of hands, and she got into her car and headed home. She was smiling as she drove, smiling and drawing in deep, delicious breaths. She felt whole and strong; she was glad to be who she was, in spite of all that had happened. Or was it because of all that had happened? Would she have ever reached this pinnacle of hope and peace without having had to struggle up from the depths?

She sighed. She knew that all she had learned had to be learned one way or another, sometime or another, but she also knew that there were easier but equally valid, less painful ways to learn. Her actions had brought them all perilously close to the edge, but she felt grateful that the gospel had afforded her a second chance. She was smiling as she drove into her subdivision and up Ridgeview Road to the Tudor house with the front light on. She parked the car in the garage and opened the door to the family room.

"Hello," she called.

"I'm in here," Robert answered from the kitchen.

And she moved toward the sound of his voice.